"A book that weds a compelling and gritty narrative to characters that are real and full-blooded merits a special place on anyone's bookshelf. Michael Miller's *The Hip Shot* is that exceedingly rare book that captures the spirit of the place he writes about while weaving a dynamic tale that draws the reader fully inside. Miller is a storyteller *par excellence,* a fresh voice whose work demands attention."

—Greg Fields
Author of *Arc of the Comet* and *Through the Waters and the Wild*

"*The Hip Shot* starts with a nice, slow, easy roll and moves at a strong pace, drawing the reader along, and building a mystery with an intensity that doesn't disappoint. It's an exciting story, full of earthy Southern color and charisma, unabashedly revealing a side of Southern culture often hidden by polite Southern charm. The story stays true in its realism, building a diversity of characters, while never letting the entertainment value fade.

"I was born in South Carolina, grew up in Florida and North Carolina, and have lived in Virginia for most of my adult life. *The Hip Shot* feels like the South, and Michael's characters seem to be friends and relatives of mine. They're easy to get to know and identify with; some you love, some you love to hate, and some just need sympathy. Then there's the ever-present evil, even in the places we trust the most. Michael masterfully gives characters their own flavor and diversity while weaving his web with action and suspense.

"It's a wonderful read, and I have to admit I've missed a day of work to finish it. I highly recommend *The Hip Shot!*"

—Brandon Currence
Author of *Looking for the Seams*

The Hip Shot

by Michael L. Miller

ISBN 978-1-64663-528-3

This is a work of fiction. The characters are both actual and fictitious. With the exception of verified historical events and persons, all incidents, descriptions, dialogue and opinions expressed are the products of the author's imagination and are not to be construed as real.

Published by

◣ köehlerbooks™

3705 Shore Drive
Virginia Beach, Va 23455
800–435–4811
www.koehlerbooks.com

THE
HIP SHOT

MICHAEL L. MILLER

VIRGINIA BEACH
CAPE CHARLES

For Marcia

"I like the way the Southerner figures things out."

—Pat Conroy

CHAPTER ONE

IT WAS COLD INSIDE THE SHACK. A kerosene heater in the middle of the room was the only source of heat, but it couldn't compete with the air seeping through the cracks of the old tumbledown dwelling.

House. Hovel. Shack. Luther Peacock didn't know what to call it. The ramshackle structure with its two rooms, tin roof, and creaky front porch might once have been a sharecropper's home.

It had taken Luther forever to find it, and he took pride in knowing his way around the back roads and hunting trails in this part of the county. But this place was in the middle of nowhere, on a dirt road deep in the woods off Grayson Road. *Reedy Creek must be nearby.* Luther could smell its muddy scent.

He had gotten directions from the man who owned the shack, or maybe he was just using it. Luther wasn't sure. He'd only met him a few weeks ago and liked him right away. The man said his name was Harold, but people called him Deacon. He'd added with a laugh that folks at a church he used to attend called him that but offered nothing more of an explanation for the nickname.

Funny, Luther thought. The man didn't resemble any deacon he'd ever known, and Luther's daddy had been the chairman of the board of deacons at the Free Gospel Baptist Church where Luther had snuck out of services as a kid. Those deacons were a bunch of solemn old men who wore polyester suits, paisley neckties and Old Spice. This guy's sun-weathered skin, wiry features, and tightly wound countenance didn't suggest he'd been passing the collection plate on Sunday.

He did have some strange religious notions, however, but he didn't talk about them very often and was never heavy-handed with it. It was Deacon's steely stare and quiet confidence that impressed Luther. They were traits he wished he possessed.

Two folding stadium seats faced the heater like easy chairs in front of a fireplace. A couch sat along one wall underneath one of those big, yellow *Don't Tread on Me* flags. A queen-size mattress was on the floor in the back, sheets and a blanket tossed loosely on top. That's where the woman was, her wrists and ankles bound with duct tape.

At least she's stopped with the moaning and groaning, Luther thought. He hadn't been keen on this idea, but Deacon said it would be all right. They were just trying to make a point, he'd said, and after all, they were helping a friend.

"Luther," the woman whimpered from the bed. "Why are you doing this? I ain't never done nothing to you."

"Shut up. Start up with that crying again and I'll tape your mouth shut."

"Luther, why? Please help me . . . please."

Luther rose from his seat in front of the heater, walked over to the woman, and picked up a roll of silver duct tape from on the floor by the mattress. He began to peel off a strip.

"Luther, please don't."

"Just be quiet, okay?"

"Okay."

Luther stood there a moment. "I don't know what Ronnie ever saw in you anyway."

The woman closed her eyes and sobbed quietly. Luther looked at his watch. *Almost 3 a.m.* He'd been cooped up in this shack since late afternoon. He was tired, cold, and wanted this to be over. He'd done what he was told to do and that was an end to it as far as he was concerned.

God dang, he thought, *how do I keep getting myself mixed up in stuff like this?*

Luther's life had been one foul up after another. He'd been a pretty good baseball player in high school and was hoping for a minor-league contract after graduation, but that never happened. So he ended up bouncing from one job to another, hampered by the occasional run-in with the law over things such as drunkenness and bar fighting.

Before he could sit back down, Luther heard the powerful growl of a big, black Dodge truck idling in front of the house. He crept over and peeked out a front window. It was Deacon.

"Thank goodness," Luther muttered. "Maybe I can go home now."

CHAPTER TWO

MERVIN TURNED TO HIS TWO FRIENDS.

"Weren't we at the clay pit?"

"Yeah, I think so," Perch said. "I had my granddaddy's .22 and we were shooting pumpkins."

"Where'd we get the pumpkins?" Boot wondered.

"I don't know," Mervin said, "but I remember that rabbit came scooting through there and Perch shot at it."

"Yeah!" said Perch. "It was a hip shot."

"The hip shot!" Boot chortled.

The three men sitting at the bar in Bill's Corner laughed at the story again just like they'd done off and on for fifty years or so. They'd been teenagers at the time, ages fifteen and sixteen, and the clay pit was an abandoned highway department dig on the edge of town. It was tucked just far enough away from inhabited streets, so most people didn't know it existed.

Perch had seen the rabbit and turned with his rifle at waist level. The bullet soared nowhere near its target, but the crack of the .22 on that autumn afternoon in 1969 had gone down in history as "the hip shot."

Mervin and Boot were laughing so hard, tears were brimming, but Perch, the shot's author, merely grinned and sipped his shot of Jim Beam.

"You thought you were the Rifleman," Boot said. "What was his name? Chuck Connors!"

"Yeah, that was him," said Mervin. "Where's Skeeter? He was there that day. It was him who brought those Miller Ponies and took your rifle away when you shot at the rabbit."

"I ain't seen him," Perch said. "I don't know where he is."

Skeeter was the fourth member of the group. Regular drinking buddies. Pals since high school who had come and gone and come back to town, kept in touch, been married and divorced, stayed single, and for some reason or another, found themselves all together again in Preston, South Carolina. Now in their mid-sixties, they kept whatever regrets they had tucked deep inside and took refuge in the warmth of Bill's Corner, where beer, shots, and tales of bygone days helped deal with rapidly advancing old age.

Mervin, Boot, Perch, and Skeeter. Graying, going bald, and a tad too thick around the middle. Except for Boot who was somehow just as rail thin as senior year. In a place where almost everyone loved the Lord, flag, and their guns, not necessarily in that order, these four were certainly outliers. Not to say they didn't care about those things, just not to the stifling degree of most of their neighbors.

Mervin Hayes went to USC in Columbia to study business. He hated it and got a degree in history instead. During his senior year, he took a part-time job selling cars and was exceptionally good at it. He'd made a bundle over the years by shrewdly investing the money he'd made from buying and selling car dealerships in Georgia and South Carolina.

Henry "Perch" Gordon also went to Carolina, stuck with business school, and became a banker in Columbia. Years later he came home to Preston to take over his family's insurance business. His nickname was the result of catching a large Warmouth perch in the lake at the state park and claiming over and over that it was a record for that species in South Carolina. "Perch" Gordon was born, although his record catch was never verified.

James Boudreau "Boot" Pearson went to Clemson for a year, got homesick, and came back to work the family farm, which covered hundreds of acres, featured an impressive two-story, turn-of-the-century farmhouse, and several barns and storage sheds that lined a road behind the house.

Boot never identified Cajuns in his lineage, but he always insisted that *Boudreau* was French for farmer. He eventually inherited the farm but gradually moved away from growing grains and soybeans to concentrate on a more lucrative cash crop.

August "Skeeter" Ellington was a year older. He graduated from Preston High in 1971, went to Davidson and the UNC Law School in Chapel Hill, then came home to Preston and joined a small firm. He never married, went fishing every now and then, and played a lot of golf. For a few years in the 1990s, he'd coached the Preston High golf team. It wasn't like him to miss a Friday happy hour.

"Yeah, where is Skeeter?" Boot asked before taking a small sip of Jack. "I haven't seen him since Tuesday."

"Maybe he had to go out of town," said Mervin.

"Nah, he'd a told one of us," said Perch. "Let me call his landline."

This brought more laughter. They knew Skeeter hardly ever used his cell phone. He had one, and he'd learned to text a couple years ago, but a text from Skeeter was about as rare as an albino alligator.

"His machine picked up," Perch said. "Hey, Skeeter, where you at?" The other three lifted beers and listened as Perch left a message. "We're at Bill's and was wondering if you're coming in. Call me back, or if you can manage it, send me a text."

More laughter as Perch ended the call, but there was also a hint of worry in the chuckles.

"I'll ride out there tomorrow and check on him," Mervin said. "He's probably just in one of his moods."

"I'll go with you," Boot said. "We could stop by the clay pit, see if it's still there."

"It's still there," Perch said, "but it's all overgrown with scraggly old bushes and pine trees. You can make out where it was, but it ain't the same clay pit from back in the day."

"It was a strange place back then," Mervin said. "Spooky at night."

"You remember those stories Skeeter used to tell us about the things his daddy saw there?" asked Perch.

"Those things didn't happen at the clay pit," Mervin said. "Skeeter might have told us about 'em when we were at the clay pit, but that stuff happened somewhere else, a lot further out of town."

"If they happened at all," Boot muttered.

"Skeeter didn't make that stuff up," Perch said. "His uncle was a deputy sheriff. Times were different. There weren't no Black lives matter back then."

"Whoa, whoa, we're not talking about the 1920s," Mervin said. "That was the late sixties."

"So?" Perch said, as he and Boot looked at Mervin to see if he'd make a case for things being better now than in the 1960s.

Bill walked up before Mervin could say anything and asked if they wanted another round.

"Shots, too?" Bill asked. "Who's shout?"

"Put 'em on mine," Perch said reluctantly.

Bill was around six-feet-tall, stocky but not overweight. His hairline had long receded and laugh lines had become etched around his eyes. At age fifty-six, he was considered a youngster by Mervin and his pals. Bill had overseen the conversion of the abandoned department store on the corner of Main and Fourth Street into this watering hole twenty years ago, and he attributed his longevity behind the bar to multi-vitamins, Dr. Scholl's massaging-gel inserts, and a nice measure of single-malt Scotch every night at closing time.

He set the beers and shots on the bar in front of Mervin, Perch, and Boot, then moved down to wait on a young couple who'd just walked in.

Mervin lifted his shot of Jameson and said, "To the clay pit!"

Boot grinned and added, "To the hip shot!"

The glasses clinked, contents thrown back and then placed reverently back on the bar. The three friends sat with arms crossed, staring up at the silent TV behind the bar where two sportscasters were talking and waving their arms about, sports news scrolling across the bottom of the screen.

"I'll go check on Skeeter tomorrow," Mervin said.

"I'll go with you," said Boot.

CHAPTER THREE

AROUND TEN THOUSAND PEOPLE lived in Preston, and that was down from a population of fifteen thousand forty years earlier. Most kids graduated from high school, went off to college or the military, and hardly ever set foot in Preston again unless it was to visit the folks for a few days.

Good jobs were scarce in Preston. Check that; jobs in general were scarce in Preston. Agriculture, fast-food joints, whatever was available at the bigbox stores out near the interstate. That was about it. Many of the kids who couldn't get into college or weren't drawn to the armed forces migrated to Myrtle Beach to work in hotels, restaurants, and outlet parks.

Preston itself was a pleasant enough town. Its broad main street had four lanes and angled parking. Tree-lined streets wandered through neighborhoods whose architecture changed by decade the further you ventured from the center of town. Old antebellum homes gave way to smaller 1950s bungalows, which gave way to ranch-style houses from the 1960s and '70s.

Mervin and his wife Becca lived in one of those ranch-style houses on a quiet, leafy side of town. Three bedrooms, bath-and-a-half, and a nice double carport. A big magnolia stood in front of the house and tall pine trees lined the lot out back.

Saturday morning dawned clear and bright, and after breakfast, Mervin told Becca he had some errands to run. Said he wouldn't be gone long. He backed his dark green Chevy Silverado out of his side of the carport, careful not to nick Becca's polished little Acura TSX. He'd circle around town to Boot's place, which was across the interstate, then take a more direct route back through Preston to get to Skeeter's house.

Boot had told Mervin that he would come to his house, but Mervin said he'd go out and pick him up. For some reason, he didn't want Becca asking questions about where he and Boot were off to so early on a Saturday morning.

Mervin turned off the two-lane state highway onto a road lined with ancient pecan trees that led to Boot's house. Boot was standing on the front porch waiting for Mervin.

"Yo, big daddy!" Boot bellowed as he climbed into the truck's passenger seat. "What'd you tell Becca you were doing this morning?"

"Told her I had a few errands to run."

"You ol' dawg. And she was okay with that?"

Boot Pearson got married when he was nineteen to his high school sweetheart Kathy Lee, and that union survived almost twenty-five years out on the farm. But Kathy finally had enough of Boot's drinking and laziness, and after their son James Jr. left for Parris Island to join the Marines, she said goodbye to Boot and moved to Charlotte where she got a job as a bank teller.

Boot didn't seem all that bothered by it at the time, although he regretted his shortcomings as a dad for James Jr. Nevertheless, he remained unperturbed by his failure at marital bliss and was always curious about how other people made it work.

"She didn't care," Mervin said. "She didn't even look up from her crossword."

Boot nodded thoughtfully, and they settled into the trip through town. It was a sunny morning but kind of cold by Carolina standards. The temperature was hovering around forty and would only get up to the mid-fifties by afternoon. Mervin was wearing Carhartt khakis and a polo shirt under a fleece jacket. Boot had on his camo pants and a heavy sweatshirt over a T-shirt. Both were wearing beat-up ball caps. Boot's was emblazoned with a big Clemson tiger paw, and Mervin's said *TaylorMade* in reference to the golf clubs he played.

It would take about twenty minutes to get out to Skeeter's place on the river. Straight down Main Street to the beach highway, across the Little Pee Dee, then a left on Redbud Trace, a state road that had finally been paved. Skeeter's house was one of several on the narrow lane that circled down to a boat landing.

Mervin pulled into the driveway behind Skeeter's Toyota Tundra. "His truck's here so he must be home," Boot said.

They climbed out, crossed the front yard and went up some steps to Skeeter's broad, front porch. Mervin banged on the door. He and Boot stood there for half a minute. Mervin banged again, still no answer, so he tried the door. *Locked.*

"Let's go around back," Boot said.

As they circled the house, Boot walked over and put his hand on the Toyota's hood. It was cold. Dried mud on the tires indicated the truck hadn't moved in a while.

A covered jon boat sat on a trailer in the backyard, and a large utility house at the back of the lot. Mervin led the way up some steps and across a deck to the backdoor. He knocked, waited a couple seconds, and when he reached for the doorknob, the door pushed open easily.

Mervin looked back at Boot, who just shrugged. "I guess we ought to go in."

By now they were expecting the worse, like finding Skeeter sprawled out on the living room floor dead from a heart attack.

Mervin stepped inside and yelled, "Skeeter! It's me and Boot. You here?"

The house was silent. Mervin and Boot entered a big kitchen that also doubled as a dining room with an antique wooden table and high-back chairs. Mervin saw a coffee mug and an empty dirty plate on the table. Next to the mug was a pair of reading glasses and a copy of *The New Yorker* magazine. A dirty skillet sat in the sink, and the coffeemaker on the kitchen counter was off but still half filled with cold coffee.

Mervin yelled again. "Skeeter!" Boot was still hanging back by the door, and Mervin nodded that they should take a look around. They quietly made their way through the house.

Skeeter had a nice place. It reminded Mervin of an old hunting lodge with its exposed beams and hardwood floors. Skeeter had filled it with large, comfortable leather chairs and sofas. A variety of Indian and Persian rugs were scattered on the floors. The fellows had been out here many times over the years, watching ball games, drinking, and hitting golf balls into the woods from the back deck.

Mervin and Boot didn't find anything in the two large downstairs rooms. The living room had a huge stone fireplace at one end and an almost equally large flat-screen TV on the wall at the other. Ashes from an old fire gave the house a faint smoky fragrance, oaky and pleasant.

The second room was Skeeter's study. It was lined with bookcases and featured an old mahogany desk and a lovingly worn sitting chair with a lamp and a pile of magazines on the floor. A long, leather couch with a knitted Afghan stretched out on the cushions was along one wall.

"Ol' Skeeter must have made a packet lawyering," Boot said, looking around the sumptuous study.

It was the same story in the three empty upstairs bedrooms. The bed was unmade in the largest room, the one Skeeter used. His watch, wallet, and keys were on the dresser. Worry settled deep in Mervin's spine.

The house had two full-sized bathrooms, one upstairs, one down, and Mervin and Boot dutifully checked those, too.

"What do you think?" Mervin asked when he and Boot stepped back into the kitchen.

"Man, I don't know," Boot said. "This ain't like Skeeter at all. His truck's here. His wallet and keys are upstairs. There ain't nowhere he could have gone on foot, unless he walked down to the boat landing or back out to the highway. But why would he do that?"

"I don't know. I don't see him doing either of those things."

"Me neither," said Boot.

They stood in the kitchen for a few seconds, pondering the situation. Then Mervin said they should go. He pulled the backdoor closed behind him, thought for a second about locking it but didn't.

"Let's just walk around a little bit," Mervin said. "Maybe we'll see something."

"I think there's a trail back there that goes down to the river," Boot said, nodding at the far corner of Skeeter's lot.

After making their way through about fifty feet of thigh-high broom straw, they found a well-worn path that led through the woods. It was narrow, so they set off single file with Boot in the lead. They walked for fifteen minutes or so, and then started to smell the distinctive swampy aroma of the Little Pee Dee.

When they reached the black-water river, they found a stretch of sandy shoreline where you could beach a kayak or a canoe. There was a large area where the undergrowth had been hacked away to make room for a fishing spot or picnic space. *Not a bad place to hang out and drink a few beers*, Mervin thought.

He and Boot looked up and down the river and poked around in the bushes for a few minutes but didn't find anything.

"I don't know what else to do," Mervin said. "Let's head back."

They'd barely retreated up the trail a hundred yards when Boot said, "What's that?"

He was looking off to his right, under a pawpaw tree, where he thought he saw something glimmer like a piece of glass. Mervin pushed by him and crunched through the leaves to the tree.

"Damn!" he said.

Mervin reached down and picked up a cell phone, perfectly intact, one of those basic models old folks used.

"That's Skeeter's phone," Boot said.

"You think so?"

"I know so," said Boot, not bothering to hide his excitement.

Mervin pushed the power button, and the phone pinged to life. A menu came up, and he tapped on *messages* and almost dropped the phone. His name was at the top of a list of messages sent, and when he opened the file, he saw an unsent draft from two days ago.

Mervin call me, it read. *Hurry.*

Mervin showed the message to Boot.

"We gotta get back to town," Boot said.

Mervin and Boot raced up the trail as fast as their sixty-five-year-old legs would carry them, burst into Skeeter's backyard, and started to dash around the house.

"Hold up a minute," Mervin shouted as he puffed hard and bent over to catch his breath.

"What's up?" Boot asked.

"You go on to the truck. I gotta get something."

Mervin bounded up the steps to the deck and went in the backdoor of Skeeter's house. He hurried through the kitchen and living room and took the stairs two at a time up to Skeeter's room.

He walked over to the dresser and picked up the keys to the Tundra. Mervin had watched enough cop shows on TV to know that what he was doing wasn't cool. He stuffed the keys in his pocket and turned to leave, but instead picked up Skeeter's wallet and opened it. Credit cards, Medicare card, and seventy-seven in cash. Mervin looked at Skeeter's driver's license.

"Millard Augustus Ellington," he said quietly. "No wonder you didn't mind being called Skeeter."

Born Dec. 11, 1953. He would be sixty-seven in a few weeks.

"Where the hell are you, Skeeter?" Mervin called.

CHAPTER FOUR

HAZEL OWENS REACHED OVER and punched on the studio mic.

"That was a great track, fellows," she said from the control room. "Y'all happy with it?"

The eighteen-year-old lead singer flipped his hair out of his eyes and said, "I guess so. What y'all think?"

His band mates, a guitarist of similar age and a bass player who looked even younger, nodded and agreed that maybe it was okay. The drummer, who was noticeably older, didn't offer an opinion.

"Cool," Hazel said. "Let's take a break and then try the next song."

The quartet, an indie-rock band from Lumberton who called themselves WeirdoCat, looked relieved and began taking off their guitars and turning off amps. They had booked the studio for the entire Saturday afternoon in hopes of recording four songs. They'd be lucky to finish three.

Hazel looked at the control board, saved the settings for the take, and headed outside to catch a smoke. She didn't mind working with younger bands because she had been there once herself.

Clarke Studio was in a decrepit strip mall on Highway 301 that bisected the north end of Preston. Its four busy lanes were lined with fast-food joints, tattoo parlors, check-cashing places, and auto-parts stores. Hazel could smell the cheap laundry detergent from the Fluff-N-Fold three doors down. Besides the Mexican restaurant two doors past the laundromat, all other storefronts in the strip mall were vacant and filled with the dusty remains of long-gone businesses.

What a pitiful place, Hazel thought as she lit up.

Hazel graduated from Preston High in 1980, smack in the middle of punk rock's heyday. Her spiky hair, piercings, and leather jacket set her apart from the other school kids who either mocked or ignored her. She did have a few close friends who shared her rebellious, rock-chick attitude. They might not have been punks themselves, but they were into music more than sports and knew they didn't fit into Preston's cozy conservative confines.

Hazel's friends were straight, and she did her best to put up a genial, acceptable front. It was a struggle. She went on some dates with nice guys but knew all the time she wasn't into them. When it looked like she wouldn't be able to keep up the charade much longer, one of her best friends came to the rescue.

Douglas Jonathan Clarke, better known as DJ, was a short, skinny kid who was more into Springsteen than Black Flag, but Hazel forgave him for that because he owned a Fender Stratocaster and an Ampeg amp. More importantly, he knew right away that Hazel was gay, and he let her know he thought it was cool and she should just do her thing. It was like a cool wave washed over her and she could get on with life. As a bonus, Hazel knew DJ was just as anxious to get out of Preston as she.

After graduation, DJ moved to Atlanta and Hazel went to Charlotte. She fronted a punk band there with three guys, but after a while, the bass player's rude comments about Hazel's purple hair and plumpness were too much to bear, so she hightailed it to New York.

The scene there had been much more vibrant and tolerant, and Hazel flourished. After a couple band misfires, she found her groove with three other women who also liked to play loud and fast. They clicked from the very first rehearsal, playing songs by The Clash, Dead Kennedys, even turned Bob Seger's "Night Moves" into a two-minute burner.

Afterward, they laughed and hugged and went out to get drunk and talk about the future. They decided to call themselves Purple Hazel in homage to Hazel's hair, and for the next two years went about building a fan base that grew at every show.

Purple Hazel became a staple on the New York punk scene, and Hazel became a trimmed-down, beautifully buff rock presence. The band had a manager, sound guy, and a stoner roadie who happily lugged their equipment from gig to gig.

Articles were written about them in fanzines. Their reworked version of ZZ Top's "Sharp Dressed Man," a searing punk tune called "Sharp Dressed Bitch," was a crowd favorite. The sky was the limit, yet Hazel was struggling.

Her income from the band barely covered the cost of living in New York. Her partner, a classically trained musician named Lisa, turned out to be bipolar, loving and kind one minute, angry and abusive the next. Hazel loved being onstage with the band, but when the show was over and the adrenaline faded, she felt like she was suffocating.

Then one day, a letter arrived via the band's manager from her old friend DJ. He'd seen a story about Purple Hazel in *Spin* magazine and decided to write. He was still in Atlanta and working two jobs, the early shift in reception at a big downtown hotel, and evenings as a production assistant at one of Atlanta's most popular recording studios. He told Hazel he was extremely proud of her success in Purple Hazel and included his number in case she ever felt like giving him a call.

Hazel felt like it and dialed the number. DJ was delighted to hear from her, and they talked for an hour.

They kept in touch over the next few months, and then one day a letter from DJ arrived with an unexpected offer. Apparently one of DJ's uncles, who'd always had a soft spot for the boy, had died and left him a truckload of money. DJ was thinking about moving back to Preston. His newfound wealth would go a lot further in the small town, and he would be there for his parents who were getting up in years.

But the most intriguing part followed. DJ was planning to open a recording studio in Preston. He'd researched the region, crunched the numbers, and concluded that it just might work, providing he could advertise widely and attract clients from other towns in the area.

DJ was wondering if Hazel might consider moving home and becoming his business partner. Her experience in the music biz from a performer's perspective would be invaluable. She could handle the administrative end of things, such as promoting the studio and dealing with the clients. He would handle all the technical stuff, fitting out the studio and overseeing all the recording, mixing, and mastering.

Moving back to Preston was a last resort for Hazel, or so she thought at first. But the more complicated her life became in New York, the more attractive DJ's offer began to sound. After a particularly bad day of big-city madness and her girlfriend shouting at her, Hazel had an epiphany. *Even Preston's better than this.*

She was going home. Back to the South. Back to Preston. And it was like a tremendous weight had been lifted.

Telling her band mates was the hardest part. There was much crying and hugging, but they took it surprisingly well. As it turned out, they all knew they'd taken Purple Hazel as far as they could, and they were ready for a new start. Hazel left a note at the apartment for her partner that said something like, "We've had our moments, but I hope I never lay eyes on you again," grabbed her bags, and headed for Grand Central and the train to South Carolina.

That was thirty-one years ago. Now here she stood on a chilly Saturday in November, fifty years old and not a trace of purple in her hair. She kept it dyed jet black, and she loved it.

The transition from New York City to Preston had been hard at first, but she and DJ were so consumed by creating a top-notch studio that she hardly had time to dwell on it. DJ was still short and skinny and looked like a long-haired stoner. Well, he was a long-haired stoner, but this older version was smart, talented, and ambitious. Hazel caught the recording bug and began to absorb all of DJ's knowledge about how to turn a rough idea into a polished piece of recorded music.

The studio struggled at first, but word eventually spread about its reasonable hourly rates and impressive results, and before long, DJ and Hazel were recording everything from bluegrass groups and gospel choirs to folksingers and rappers.

For the next fourteen years, Hazel and DJ had a ball. Clarke Studio was their kingdom, and they relished the refuge they'd created. Hazel managed to buy a small house in a hardscrabble part of Preston, slapped some paint on it, and even planted a vegetable garden in the back. She never thought she'd find this kind of contentment in her hometown.

Sadly, good things don't last forever, and in 2003, DJ was killed in a horrific, multi-vehicle pile-up on the interstate. He was coming home from a trade show in Nashville. Hazel was at the studio when the phone rang. She was asked to identify the body. She put the phone down and wept like she'd never before. She knew she loved DJ, but she never knew how much until that moment. It was not a romantic love or even the brother-sister kind. It was deeper, more meaningful. They had always been there for each other, and that was enough.

When DJ's will was opened in a downtown law firm, Hazel was stunned to learn that he'd left not only the studio to her, but also the entire strip mall. She never knew he owned it, but now it made sense why there were no other businesses. DJ always said they were lucky that they didn't have to worry about noise bleeding into their recording sessions from next door. Hazel decided to maintain the tradition. Besides, she didn't want the headache of having to collect rents from lowlifes anyway.

Hazel was elated, numb with grief, and not sure what to do. It was hard, but she carried on. A few years later, she met a new friend who gave her good advice, counseled her, and eventually became her lover. A physician at the Doc-in-a-Box on Main Street named Carol Baxley had treated Hazel for a sinus infection, and they both felt the spark of recognition that queer women felt during such encounters.

Carol wasn't as tall as Hazel nor was she as physically buff. But she took care of herself and was a devoted runner. At forty-eight, ten years younger than Hazel, Carol had sparkling blue eyes and short hair that had gone completely gray, silver, actually. Many nights she listened to Hazel talk about DJ and how cool he was. How they'd managed to turn a dream into a reality in such an unsuspecting locale. Years might have passed, but nevertheless, Carol helped Hazel deal with grief that had been festering for a long time.

Hazel took a slow, gentle drag on her cigarette and marveled again at how two people like she and Carol would meet in a town like this. Just then, WeirdoCat's drummer pushed through the door, stepped outside, and lit up, too. He was a muscular, long-haired dude named Daniel Sims who looked like he'd been around the block a few times.

"You okay with how it's going?" Hazel asked.

"It's all right," he said. "Not the greatest material to work with."

Hazel silently agreed but knew better than to say so.

"It just needs a little more energy," she said. "We'll work on it."

The door to the Fluff-N-Fold flew open and an old Black man emerged with a big plastic trash bag filled with clean clothes. He waddled over to a beat-up Giant mountain bike and straddled it for the ride home.

"Yo, Jerome!" Hazel called. The old man turned to look at her. "When you gonna let me record you singing some of your songs?"

"Sister, you don't need to waste no time on me," he said. "I just sing 'em to be singing," he added with a grin.

"That's what I'm saying," Hazel said. "You gotta let me hook you up."

"Go on now," he said and pedaled off.

Hazel turned to the WeirdoCat drummer and said, "You should team up with old Jerome. That man sings some of the scariest blues you ever heard."

"Anytime," Daniel said. "Please, anytime."

He dropped his cigarette and crushed it out on the sidewalk and went back inside. Hazel took out her phone to see if Carol had responded to her texts. Carol had been acting strange lately. When Hazel asked, Carol had said it was nothing, just a difficult project at work. But it was getting better, Carol said, because a retired attorney had been helping her, and he was very connected in the community. She didn't elaborate and said there was nothing to worry about. Everything would be fine.

Hazel had no idea why Carol would need the help of a retired attorney. *What kind of difficult project is she talking about?* Hazel hoped it wasn't a malpractice suit. She scrolled through her texts. Still no response from Carol.

CHAPTER FIVE

BARBARA LOWRIE DIDN'T MIND working weekends. The office was quiet during the day, and at night the good ol' boys blowing off steam after a work week were always entertaining. It mostly amounted to a lot of drunkenness, fights, and maybe a fender-bender or two. Sure, things got serious on occasion, but stabbings and shootings were rare.

And since she was a sergeant, Barbara was usually the highest-ranking officer on weekends in the Preston police station. It was a status she enjoyed and one she'd worked hard to earn. In fact, she felt lucky to be a police officer in her hometown at all.

Barbara studied criminal justice at Pembroke State before it became the University of North Carolina at Pembroke. Her grades were stellar, and she graduated with honors, but she still knew it was a long shot when she applied to the Preston force. Barbara was a Lumbee Indian, and while she wasn't Black, she was still considered a person of color to some serving officers at the time, and also to a fair amount of the Preston public.

Thankfully she applied during the tenure of a kind, open-minded police chief named Wendell Moody who hired her on the spot and guided her through the trials and tribulations of small-town policing.

That was twenty-two years ago. She was now on the verge of turning forty-five, and she commanded the respect of all thirty members of the Preston force, even that of the current chief, a more hardnosed commander named Lawrence Holt. No one called him Larry. It was always Chief Holt.

Barbara was proud of her rank and service record, and of her Native American heritage. A tall, solidly built woman with broad shoulders, she wore her jet-black hair in a long ponytail, and her uniform was always immaculately crisp, with the three sergeant's stripes on her sleeves gleaming like polished bayonets.

She traced her family lineage back to the *Lowrie Gang,* a group of cousins and brothers who in the 1860s took offense at being conscripted by the North Carolina Confederate Home Guard to help build forts, roads, and bridges. Legend has it that the Lowrie boys took to hiding in the swamps, only to come out occasionally to stage a robbery and knock off two or three Confederate soldiers who got in their way.

After the war, the Lowrie Gang continued its criminal ways, and over time became mythologized as a sort of Lumbee Indian version of Robin Hood and his Merry Men.

Barbara knew her kin had been nothing but crooks and murderers, but she did appreciate the fact that they stood up to those Confederate soldiers. Most of the Lowrie Gang was eventually hunted down and either captured or killed, but there was a story about how the gang's leader, Henry Berry Lowrie, disappeared into the swamp and was never found.

Barbara knew it was just a fable, but sometimes when she was shoving some loudmouthed redneck into a cell, she'd think of old Henry and smile. He would have been proud of the Lumbee warrior exerting power over the White man oppressor.

Just more romantic fantasy, Barbara thought as she sat at her desk and scanned news reports on her laptop. She had earned respect despite the color of her skin, but that didn't mean the old prejudices and hatred had vanished. On the contrary, they were making a frighteningly rapid comeback, especially in the Deep South.

Barbara had been following recent events in Charleston, Charlottesville, Pittsburgh, and El Paso, and she'd tracked FBI reports of increased growth of White supremacy groups in the Carolinas. She was, in fact, reading new evidence in a study from the Southern Poverty Law Center when Patrolman Jimmy Glover came into the squad room.

"Sarge, two guys out front want to file a missing-person report," he said.

"Then take the report," Barbara said, not looking up from the computer screen.

"They say they want to speak to the officer in charge," Glover said. "They're kind of agitated."

Barbara sighed and got up from behind her desk, went out to the lobby, and found Mervin Hayes and Boot Pearson leaning on the counter.

"What's got you two out and about on a Saturday morning?" she said and extended her hand to shake with the men.

"It's Skeeter," Mervin said. "Nobody's seen him since Tuesday, and he didn't show up at happy hour yesterday. I know that doesn't sound all that bad, but he's always at Friday happy hour."

"Yeah, I know all about you fellows and how tight you are," Barbara said. "Who's the other one? Henry Gordon?"

"Yeah," Mervin said. "But me and Boot just went out to Skeeter's house and there's no sign of him."

"And his truck's sittin' in the driveway," Boot said. "We went all through the house and he ain't there."

"You went in his house?" Barbara asked in an unapproving tone.

"We tried the backdoor and it just pushed open," Mervin said. "Look, we're worried. We know Skeeter, and while he'll mosey off sometimes, this don't feel right. Plus, there's this."

Mervin placed Skeeter's phone on the counter and tapped the messages file.

"We found it in the woods behind Skeeter's house next to a trail that goes down to the river. Look at his last text."

Barbara turned the phone around on the counter and read Skeeter's text to Mervin. They stood there quietly for a minute then Barbara looked at Mervin and Boot, sizing them up.

"He's a lawyer, right?" she said. "His name is August Ellington?"

"He was a lawyer," Mervin said. "He had a practice with another fellow who was a good bit older. Herman Spencer was his name, but he died, oh, ten or twelve years ago. Skeeter kept the firm going by himself until he retired three years ago."

Barbara thought for a few seconds. "Okay, I'll ride out there and take a look. He's on Redbug Trace, right? Near the river?"

"Red*bud* Trace," Boot said. "But you won't find nothing. We went all through there."

The look Barbara gave Boot said that she was Sergeant Lowrie, and he best let her do her job.

"But we really appreciate it," Boot said.

"Yes, we do," added Mervin. "Please let us know if you find anything or if there's anything we can do."

"I will," Barbara said.

CHAPTER SIX

IT WAS NOTICEABLY WARMER when Mervin and Boot walked out of the police station and climbed into the Silverado. Mervin took off his fleece jacket and tossed it into the back of the king cab.

Preston's Main Street on Saturday morning wasn't nearly as bustling as it had been forty or fifty years ago. But it had made a bit of a comeback in the past few years. There were a few boutiques and specialty shops, a diner, and a pizza place. Several cheap fashion joints had filled abandoned store fronts, and an Asian buffet called The China Palace was where the old S&S Cafeteria used to be. There was even a boutique hotel a block off Main, with a nice, semi-formal dining room that was a favorite among Preston's more well-to-do citizens.

Mervin and Boot rolled down Main Street from red light to red light, waiting at each one amidst cars and trucks filled with folks who'd come to town for some Saturday shopping. They didn't say much to each other, both lost in their thoughts about what could have happened to Skeeter.

Boot called Perch and told him about their trip to Skeeter's and visit to the police station. They agreed to meet at Bill's around five.

Mervin pressed the gas pedal when they were clear of town, and ten minutes later he was circling in front of the two-story farmhouse Boot's family had called home for generations.

Boot climbed out of the truck and saw his two coonhounds, Jack and Joe, moseying around a corner of the house, ears flopping and tails wagging.

"Where y'all been?" he hollered at the dogs. Mervin got out of the truck and got down on his knees to be at Jack and Joe's level. The dogs were happy to see Mervin and went straight to him, slobbering on him for a minute or two while he scratched their bellies. They were good dogs, brothers, each deep orange and white. Mervin could tell them apart thanks to a strip of white fur that ran between Joe's eyes down to his nose. Satisfied, they turned and trotted back toward the house.

"Man, those dogs got it made," Boot said. "All they do is eat, sleep, and come and go as they please."

"Kind of like their owner," Mervin said with a grin.

Boot ignored this. "Man, I'm worried about Skeeter. This doesn't feel good. What should we do?"

"I don't know," Mervin said. "Wait and see what the police say, I suppose."

Boot stood there for a few seconds, the truck idling with a low growl. "Okay," he said. "I'll see you in a bit."

He shut the door to Mervin's truck, careful not to slam it, turned and walked up the steps to his front porch, following Joe and Jack. Mervin watched Boot's shoulders sag as he unlocked the front door and went inside. He took out his phone and called Becca.

"Hey, you got any plans for lunch?"

"No, I was just waiting to hear from you," she said.

"What if I was to stop at Jessie Mae's and get us a couple of takeouts?"

"That's sounds great," Becca said. "You know what vegetables I like. I don't want chicken. Meatloaf if she has it. Otherwise, anything but chicken."

"I'll see you in about half an hour," Mervin said. "I've got something to tell you."

"That doesn't sound good," Becca said.

Mervin climbed back into his truck, pulled out onto the highway, and pointed the pickup toward town. He punched on the stereo, and there was a CD already in the player. A song called "A World of Hurt" by the Drive-By Truckers filled the cab. Mervin liked the Truckers, especially the songs written by Patterson Hood whose raspy voice and power-chord approach really hit home.

Hood wrote some of the most courageously honest songs about the South Mervin had ever heard. He'd worn out the band's 2012 record, "Southern Rock Opera," which attempted to explain, as Hood put it, "the duality of the Southern thing."

Mervin knew exactly what Hood was talking about—the yin and yang, the evil and goodness in America's most misunderstood region. The Deep South was filled with immense natural beauty, historical intrigue, and an omnipresent vibe of easygoing charm. There really was something to that old Southern hospitality claim.

But percolating beneath all this virtue was a sense of anger, paranoia, and hatred that sometimes bubbled to the surface and resulted in confrontation, violence, even bloodshed.

Mervin listened to the Truckers, marveled at the full-blown fall colors in the trees along the highway, and thought about Skeeter, remembering how he was the one who always encouraged others to be more tolerant and less judgmental. Skeeter, Mervin, Boot, Perch, and a few others floated through school in the 1960s and early '70s during a time of great social upheaval that never really reached Preston.

The civil rights movement and school desegregation were things that were just happening, just changing times, something they hadn't given much thought. They were just trying to pass chemistry or calculus and pick up girls on the weekend.

Of course, this couldn't be said of all their classmates. Many kids came from homes where fathers viciously opposed integration, and they passed their racism down to their sons and daughters.

And it keeps getting passed down, Mervin thought as he approached the outskirts of town. *Maybe it always will be.* Despite such misgivings, he appreciated the duality of the South, the fact that many Southerners held much more open-minded views for which they were seldom given credit. Were these free-thinking Southerners the majority? *Probably not*, Mervin thought, *definitely not in Preston.*

But then again, take a closer look at the town of Preston and there it was, the old Deep South yin and the yang. Neighborhoods were segregated, churches were segregated, and the schools had been successfully resegregated with the creation of *independent* and *Christian* schools that operated outside the purview of government-run public education. No doubt that some of those stories Skeeter told them years ago of clandestine police brutality were true, and it was evident that a yearning for those old ways remained in some.

But there was a ubiquitous sense of community in Preston. When you broke it down to feet-on-the-ground, interpersonal interactions between people of different ages, races, sexual orientations, or ethnic backgrounds, you found that folks cared for one another and would go out of their way to help you if they could. Mervin hadn't been surprised at all when the ladies auxiliary from the First Baptist Church took boxes filled with socks, underwear, toothpaste, toothbrushes, and other necessities to the camps of Hispanic farm workers out in the country. It was the right thing to do, no matter if your neighbor or boss or colleagues at work were grumbling about illegals taking their jobs, filling up the emergency room, and not speaking English. The Southern thing, it was complex, like Patterson Hood said.

Mervin's thoughts were interrupted by one of those new, hot Mustangs that roared up behind him, pulled out and passed on the double yellow. "Go ahead on, son," Mervin muttered, but he couldn't help but smile. He'd been there, behind the wheel of a muscle car, and that warm memory carried him through town and into the dirt parking lot in front of Jessie Mae's house of home cooking.

Jessie Mae's was a popular meat-and-three restaurant in a neighborhood known as The Hill, although there wasn't any discernible rise in altitude there compared to other parts of town. Not that long ago, The Hill would have been referred to as a colored town, and Mervin was sure some townsfolk still called it that.

He'd gotten to know Jessie Mae and thought the world of her. She reminded him of his granny except that Jessie Mae was Black and about four times the size of his late, pint-sized grandmother. Granny would pile your plate with vegetables, rice and gravy, biscuits, fried chicken or roast beef, and then after you were stuffed to the gills and pushing away from the table, she'd ask what else could she get you.

Mervin weaved his way through tables of lunchtime diners in the big front room, nodding a hello here and there to folks he recognized. He spotted a plate filled with chicken bog and knew right away what he was having.

At the far side of the room was a counter with a register, and Jessie Mae's sixteen-year-old granddaughter, Helen, was standing behind it taking an order over the phone. Mervin caught her eye and smiled, and she grinned back as she asked the customer if that would be all and told them it would be ready in about fifteen minutes.

"Hey, Mr. Mervin," Helen said. "What can I get you today?"

"Y'all are busy on Saturday," Mervin said, "as usual, right?"

"We are busy, a little busier than usual, I'd say. Christmas is coming, so I guess more people are coming to town to do some shopping."

"Maybe so," Mervin said, "or they just wanted to get out of the house." He looked up at the big chalkboard menu behind the counter. "I see y'all got chicken bog today. That's what I want, with butter beans and sweet potatoes. Let's get Becca the meatloaf, with rice and gravy, butter beans, and fried okra. Cornbread for both of us."

Mervin knew he'd be poaching a few pieces of fried okra from Becca's plate. Jessie Mae's fried okra also reminded him of his granny. It was just like she used to make it, perfectly crisp on the outside and soft in the middle.

Mervin paid Helen and took a seat in one of the chairs near the counter for takeout customers. He sat two chairs down from a big Black man in work boots, a bright plaid flannel shirt, and flecks of gray in his hair.

"How you doing?" Mervin said.

"Good, good," the man answered. "You all right?"

"Doing fine," Mervin said. There was a hint of recognition between the two men.

"Haven't I seen you in Bill's every now and then, drinking with your friends?" the Black man said.

"Yeah, you probably have," Mervin said. "Now I know you. You come in the bar a lot, too, but you're not usually wearing a flannel shirt like that."

"No, no," the man said with a laugh. "I work for the highway department, and I'm usually wearing that getup they give us. Me and a friend like to have a drink in Bill's sometimes after work. Cedric Goins," he said, and extended a big, calloused hand.

"Mervin Hayes." They shook. "Nice to meet you."

Before they could say anything more, Jessie Mae appeared around the end of the counter with a plastic bag filled with a couple Styrofoam containers and hollered, "Cedric Goins!"

"That's me," Goins said, and he hopped up to fetch his lunch. "You take care."

"You, too," Mervin said.

Jessie Mae spotted Mervin and said, "Mr. Mervin, yours will be out in a few minutes."

Mervin just smiled and waved. He knew Jessie Mae wouldn't be into small talk when the restaurant was this busy, but a few minutes later when she reappeared and held up a plastic bag for Mervin, she said, "How's Becca doing? I ain't seen her in a while."

"She's good," Mervin said. "Still teaching third grade but ready to retire and put her feet up."

"Well, they better get somebody good to take her place 'cause she really did good by my grandkids. Y'all come in sometime and let me fix you something special, some flounder or something."

"Some of those salmon patties?"

"Just let me know when," Jessie Mae said. "And I put a little extra okra in there for Becca 'cause I know you gone be stealing some."

Mervin laughed. "I'll tell Becca you said hey."

He made his way back through the restaurant, stood aside, and held the door for more lunchtime diners who were coming inside, anxious for Jessie Mae's home cooking.

CHAPTER SEVEN

PERCH GORDON FINISHED his Subway sandwich, balled up the wrapper, and tossed it toward the garbage can by the kitchen counter. He tried to bank it off the back wall, but it clipped the rim and landed on the floor.

Perch sighed, pushed his glasses up on his nose, and rose with a grunt to fetch the wrapper and deposit it in the trash. He took his Miller Lite into the den where an early college game was on the sixty-inch flat-screen, the sound muted. He flopped into a big La-Z-Boy recliner and levered up the footstool.

"East Carolina versus South Florida," he grumbled. "Now there's a game of real national interest."

Perch had thought about going for a walk earlier just to get some exercise, but he didn't get around to it. He didn't like feeling so flabby, but what was he supposed to do? At this age, almost every joint ached, and his metabolism had slowed to a crawl; he was sure of it. Besides, he was starting to make peace with the extra pounds.

Perch had gone to Carolina in 1972, earned a business degree, and stayed in Columbia for a couple decades, working for one of the larger regional banks. He fell madly in love with one of his colleagues, a loan officer named Janice Adams, and to his surprise she liked him, too. They were married in 1982.

Five years later, Perch's dad died, and he and Janice moved to Preston so Perch could take charge of his old man's insurance business. Janice had grown up in a small town, too, so she embraced the move to Preston as a means of slowing things down and simplifying life. She was certainly hoping children would be in the equation but that never happened.

Regardless, she and Perch loved each other mightily. They laughed all the time. Boot used to say that sitting on the deck with Perch and Janice for an evening would make you feel better about the whole wide world.

Then Janice got sick. They did everything they could. Skeeter made calls and found the best oncologist in Charleston. Mervin and Becca brought food over and sat with Janice for hours on end. Boot would get Perch out of the house, take him fishing or to the golf course, anything to get his mind off what was happening back home.

When Janice died four years ago, it almost ripped the will to live right out of Perch's breastbone. It was a dark time, but his friends didn't desert him. They became even more determined to give him the strength to go on.

Perch got through it, and as a result, the bond of friendship he had with his three fellow retirees became that much stronger.

And now Skeeter had gone off somewhere and everybody thought he was either dead or in bad trouble. Perch picked up the remote and surfed through the sports channels. He found a better game, Ohio State and Michigan State, two good teams who might provide some entertaining action. The Carolina-Georgia game would come on at 3:30, and he'd probably go to Bill's early to watch the first half before Boot and Mervin got there.

He sighed and took a slug of beer. How much should he tell them? Should he tell them anything at all? Skeeter had confided in Perch just enough so Perch didn't feel quite as concerned as the others. And he couldn't betray Skeeter's confidence. Still, Boot's phone call earlier had planted a worry in Perch that he couldn't shake.

He hoped Skeeter hadn't taken on more than he could handle. Hell, there wasn't much intimidation left in an old lawyer like Skeeter.

He'd probably have to tell Mervin and Boot something about what Skeeter was up to. But not everything. He wasn't sure. He'd think about it some more before he went to Bill's.

Mervin came through the door from the carport and found Becca in the kitchen pouring iced tea into two tall glasses.

"Good timing," Mervin said.

"I heard you pull up," Becca said. "Did she have meatloaf?"

"She had it, but I got you fried chicken instead."

"Then you better go back out that door and try again."

Mervin laughed and placed the big plastic bag filled with their Styrofoam lunch cartons on the table. He opened it, took out the one with *Meatloaf* scrawled across the top, and set it at Becca's usual spot. He placed his carton at his spot across the table from Becca.

She brought over some knives and forks, went back and got the tea, sat and asked, "So what is it you have to tell me?"

Mervin opened his carton and marveled at the amount of chicken bog Jessie Mae had heaped in there. He scooped a forkful into his mouth and savored it. The rice was perfect, not gummy at all, as were the chunks of chicken and slices of smoked sausage. He chewed slowly, swallowed, and Becca waited.

"We can't find Skeeter," he said.

Becca stared at him. "What do you mean you can't find Skeeter?"

"He didn't come to the bar yesterday. Boot said he hasn't seen him since Tuesday and he's not at home."

Becca was holding her fork in mid-air and studying Mervin's face. She could tell he was worried.

"How do you know he's not at home?"

Mervin tucked into his chicken bog, butter beans, and sweet potatoes, and between bites he told Becca the whole story of how he and Boot went out to Skeeter's place, searched the house, found his phone in the woods, and went straight to the police station when they got back to town.

"Skeeter's truck was in the driveway," Mervin said. "His wallet and keys were on the dresser in his bedroom. I have his keys."

"You've got his keys? Why do you have his keys?"

"I don't know," Mervin said. "It just seemed like I should. You know, in case somebody found them and stole his truck."

"That's dumb," Becca said.

Mervin looked away. "I know," he said.

"You need to call that Sergeant Lowrie and tell her you've got Skeeter's keys."

"Yeah, I will," Mervin said.

They ate in silence for a while until Becca said, "You're worried, aren't you?"

"Of course I am. This ain't like Skeeter."

"He's gone off before," Becca said.

"But he always lets us know for how long and when he'll be back."

They finished eating and Becca got up to start clearing things away.

"You gonna eat the rest of that okra?"

Becca smiled and dumped her remaining okra into Mervin's carton.

"I swear, I'm gonna get you a treadmill for Christmas," she said. "I'm not sleeping with a big ol' fatso rubbing all up against me."

"C'mon, Becca," Mervin said. "I'm not in that bad of shape."

"I mean it, no nookie for you until you slim down."

Mervin laughed when he saw Becca grinning, but she looked back over her shoulder and said, "I'm serious!"

Mervin polished off the okra anyway and helped Becca finish cleaning up. They refilled their teas and went through to a big den filled with a fireplace, his-and-hers sitting chairs on either side of a magazine-laden table, and one of those lamps with swivel-styled cone lights. A large television was suspended on the wall opposite the fireplace.

"Speaking of exercise, are y'all playing golf tomorrow?"

The concern over Skeeter's whereabouts had monopolized Mervin's mind, and he'd completely forgotten about their weekly round at Preston Country Club. They were as devoted to that Sunday tee time as they were to Bill's happy hour.

"I hadn't even thought about it," Mervin said.

He picked up his phone to call the club and ask the head pro, Benny Martin, if Skeeter had booked a tee time for tomorrow after last Sunday's round. But before he could tap Benny's number, his phone rang and startled him so bad he almost dropped it.

The ID said *unknown caller*, but Mervin answered anyway.

"Mr. Hayes?" a female voice said, sounding distant and outdoors. "This is Sergeant Lowrie. I'm out at August Ellington's house."

"Hey," said Mervin. "Thanks for calling. Did you find anything."

"It's mostly like y'all said. Nobody's here. I went all through the house. His truck is here like you said, but I didn't find any keys. I guess he has them on him."

Mervin started to come clean and tell her he had them in his pocket, but for some reason he didn't.

"Probably so," Mervin said. "Were you able to get inside the truck anyway?"

Becca was watching Mervin from her chair and listening intently to his side of the conversation.

"Yes, I got into the truck," Lowrie said, "but before I tell you about that I need to ask you a couple questions."

"Shoot," Mervin said.

"Did August, or Skeeter like you all call him, did he have a lady friend?"

"No," Skeeter blurted out. "No way. We'd have known."

"Are you sure? Maybe he was seeing some single mom who had a small kid?"

"What? Where is this coming from?" Mervin said. "Skeeter didn't know any single moms. Well, I can't say for sure he didn't know any, but I'm damn sure he wasn't involved with one. What makes you ask?"

"Underneath the bed in the guest room down the hall from Skeeter's room, I found a kid's backpack filled with coloring books, crayons, and a few drawings like they might have been done in school," Lowrie said. "When I got into the truck, I found a pair of kid's socks, balled up and stuck underneath the seat."

"I don't know what to say," Mervin said. "I have no idea where those things could have come from or why they were there."

"One more question," Lowrie said. "What kind of gun does Skeeter own?"

"Gun? Skeeter doesn't have a gun. He hates the things."

"Well, there's a lockbox in the back of his closet, and I'm pretty sure it's the kind where guns are kept."

"No, that can't be right," Mervin said. "It must be where he keeps important papers or something like that. He was a lawyer, you know. It might be records that he has to keep for a certain number of years. You know, like tax returns."

"Okay," Lowrie said. "I can't find a key to the lockbox, but I'm still looking. If I can't find one, I might have to take it to the station and see if we can open it there. You stay in touch with me and let me know if you hear from Skeeter."

"Absolutely. Of course I will," Mervin said.

"You sure you don't know anything about Skeeter being involved with someone?"

"No, Sergeant Lowrie. I promise you, I don't."

Mervin ended the call and set his phone on the table next to his chair as gently as if it was a bomb.

"Tell me," Becca said.

He told her everything.

CHAPTER EIGHT

MERVIN HAD TO CIRCLE THE BLOCK around Main and Fourth Street before he found a parking spot. It was no surprise that Bill's was busy. It was Saturday, college-football game day, and just a few weeks until Christmas.

Perch's truck had been parked on Fourth Street and Mervin spotted him at their usual spot at the far end of the bar, a half-empty bottle of Miller Lite in front of him. He was gazing intently at one of the big flatscreens behind the bar and didn't notice Mervin sliding onto the stool next to him.

"Doesn't look good," Mervin said.

Perch turned, startled. "Oh, hey. Nah, but nothing unexpected. Could be worse."

Georgia was up 21-7 and driving for another score. Mervin looked around the room and took in all the hustle and bustle in Bill's. Most folks sported South Carolina Gamecock paraphernalia but there were a few wearing Georgia Bulldog sweatshirts and baseball caps.

It was a large room with entrances on both Main and Fourth. A long hardwood bar ran along one wall, and the opposing wall was lined with booths. Tables for two sat in the big windows facing Main where department store displays had been located years ago.

Bill's Corner was known for its barbecue sandwiches, hamburger steaks smothered in onions, and some of the best chili in town. The alarming rate of heart disease in the region had prompted Bill to add some salad entrees.

It was almost five-thirty as darkness settled over Preston. Boot came through the Fourth Street door behind Mervin and Perch, walked over and clasped each of them on the shoulder.

They turned and smiled. "Watch it, boy!" Perch said.

"Who you callin' boy?" Boot shot back.

"You, fool," Perch said. "And you would be wearing that damn Tiger Paw hat."

"You know it," Boot said.

A couple next to Mervin obligingly moved down the bar so Boot could squeeze in. He had the faint smell of charred wood about him, so Mervin figured Boot had spent the afternoon by the fire pit, probably partaking of some of his fine homegrown weed.

"This place is busy," Boot said. "I had to park in the next block. Guess everybody wanted to get here early to watch the Clemson game."

"Funny," Perch said.

Boot grinned. He couldn't help winding up Perch.

Bill came over, greeted the new arrivals, and asked if they were having their usual. They were, and Bill went to fetch the beers and another for Perch.

"How many you had?" Boot asked.

"None of your business," Perch said.

"That many?" Boot shook his head.

Mervin sat in the middle, so Boot and Perch turned their chairs slightly to face him. He started recapping his and Boot's morning adventure.

Perch listened silently then said, "What do y'all think? I mean, something's seriously not right if you found Skeeter's phone out in the woods."

"There's more," Mervin said. His two friends leaned in closer.

He told them about the phone call from Sergeant Lowrie, about the kid's backpack in Skeeter's guest bedroom, about the socks under the truck seat.

Boot leaned back and crossed his arms across his chest.

"What the hell is she talking about?" he said. "A kid's backpack filled with school drawings? In Skeeter's house? Don't make no sense, man."

"I know," Mervin said. "But that's what she told me."

A loud moan went up in the room when Georgia scored again, and Perch took a deep slug of beer. He was looking up at the TV, wondering what he should do. It was now or never. He had to tell them.

"I might have an idea about what's going on," he said. "But I can't be sure."

Boot and Mervin faced him, surprised.

"What do you mean, Perch?" Mervin said. "If you know something you better tell us."

Perch took another hit off his beer and started in.

"Two years ago, one of Skeeter's old clients came to him for help. She had a daughter who was in an abusive relationship and couldn't find a way out. The husband was manic, violent. They feared for her safety and the safety of her three-year-old daughter.

"Skeeter tried to get her to go to the police, but the woman said her daughter refused because one of her friends had reported that her boyfriend beat her, and the police did nothing. In fact, the boyfriend beat her again for going to the police. Apparently, these men have friends on the force who turn a blind eye to what they call 'domestic squabbles.' Not the whole force, she was told, just a few bad apples. But it was enough to scare her. Skeeter met the girl and was shocked at the state she was in, bruises on her arms and legs, and barely able to put any weight on one leg. And the three-year-old was clearly traumatized.

"So, Skeeter took them to Urgent Care to get them checked out, and while he was there, he got to talking to this woman doctor who said she saw this kind of thing all the time. Skeeter and this doctor came up with a scheme to help the woman. She and her kid would stay at Skeeter's for a few days while the doctor, her name's Carol Baxley, would find a spot in a women's shelter far enough away so the husband wouldn't find them. Then she could file for divorce or whatever from there.

"And that's what they did. They found a place for them in Columbia. Skeeter snuck 'em down to the bus station one day and off they went," Perch said. "But that wasn't the end of it. The doctor told Skeeter that it was an epidemic, that wives and girlfriends were coming in all the time with broken noses, dislocated shoulders, concussions. Some would end up in the hospital. Skeeter was disturbed but wasn't sure what else he could do."

"But what about the husband?" Boot asked. "What did he do? I bet he didn't just let it go."

"No, and that's the rough part," Perch said. "He never found his wife or learned what Skeeter and Carol were up to, so he took it out on the woman's mother, Skeeter's old client. He almost beat her to death."

"Damn," Mervin said. "Surely she pressed charges."

"Nope. Like her daughter, she didn't trust them. She was terrified." Perch took another swig of beer.

"So anyway, the sight of that beaten-up woman made Skeeter so mad he decided he had to do something. He and this Carol Baxley got together, and they figured that since their scheme to get that first woman and kid to safety worked so well, why couldn't they do the same for other women? And that's what they've been doing this past couple years, running a sort of underground railroad for abused women and their kids, getting them out of harm's way so they can start a new life. So far, I think they've helped six or seven women get out of here and find shelter somewhere else. And they're not all just from Preston. They're from all around here."

"Damn," Boot said.

Mervin and Boot sat there quietly, drinking their beers and digesting all Perch had told them. There was an unspoken question hanging in the air and Perch spoke up before it could be asked.

"Skeeter confided in me because, well, he and I have done business before, and I still have some banking and insurance connections. Boot, he just didn't want to get you mixed up in this, and Mervin, he knew that you and Becca are so close that you'd need to tell her about it and—"

Mervin cut him off. "It was right that he told you," he said. "You were in a better position to help him than we were."

Mervin wasn't sure he believed that, but he wanted to clear the air, make sure Perch knew there were no hard feelings.

"What did he want you to do, you know, just in case?"

"He's been leaving written records with me of all the cases," Perch said. "No names of the women, of course, but all the men and what action they took. He also gave me some personal papers, his will, unopened letters, passwords . . . things like that."

"I need a shot," Boot said. "Bill!"

Bill looked their way from down the bar and Boot held up three fingers then made a capital T with his hands.

Bill walked down, placed three shot glasses in front of them, and filled each with tequila. Mervin, Boot, and Perch clinked glasses and knocked back the shots.

"So, what do we do?" Boot said. "Should we tell the police?"

"I don't think so," Mervin said. "Not yet anyway. Skeeter might've just needed to disappear for a while, and he might turn up."

Perch nodded.

"There's one more thing," Mervin said. "Sergeant Lowrie said she found a lockbox in Skeeter's closet that looked like it might have held a gun. I told her Skeeter hated guns and didn't have one. I don't think she believed me."

"No way!" Boot said. "All those times I tried to get Skeeter to go hunting with me? He wouldn't have anything to do with it. Said he didn't even want to be around guns."

"I don't know, man," Perch said. "Things might have been getting heavy. He might have had a change of heart."

They sat there, arms crossed, watching the television. It was dark and getting close to supper time.

"One more?" Mervin asked.

"One more," Boot said.

CHAPTER NINE

HAZEL'S PREDICTION CAME TRUE. WeirdoCat managed to record only three of their four songs, but the results were better than expected. The band mates were excited during playback, all of them clustered around the control panel while Hazel conducted some preliminary mixing. She told them it would sound even better when she had time to dig into it some more.

They were laughing and talking as they packed up their gear to leave, and they thanked Hazel profusely on their way out the door.

Back to Lumberton and on to stardom, Hazel thought. She always tried to nurture these dreams as best she could. She'd had them once herself.

WeirdoCat's session exceeded the band's number of paid hours, but Hazel let it slide. They would be back for the mixing and mastering and things would balance out. She checked to make sure all the amps were off and switched off the lights in the studio. Then she backed up the tracks on the control room's computer and shut everything down.

She walkd down the hall to reception, turned out the lights there, and then stepped through the glass door onto the sidewalk and locked the door behind her. It was dark and getting colder. A few cars were in front of the Fluff 'n' Fold, and the parking lot in front of the Mexican restaurant, *Las Camadres,* was packed. It was run by two strong Mexican women, thus the name, and Hazel thought about walking down and getting something to go. But she was anxious to get home and check on Carol.

Something was going on and Hazel really needed to talk to her. Times had changed and even in Preston two women could live together happily without fear of too much disapproval. Nevertheless, Hazel and Carol kept mostly to themselves and certainly didn't flaunt their relationship. Besides, folks in Preston loved Carol. She had helped most of them— or at least a friend or family member—at some time or another at the Urgent Care, and her kindness and knowledgeable treatments had not gone unnoticed. It wasn't surprising when a farmer would leave a sack of sweet corn, tomatoes, or a bushel of butter beans on Hazel and Carol's front porch as a show of thanks.

It was Saturday suppertime, traffic on 301 was heavy, and the highway was illuminated brightly by the signs at filling stations and burger joints. Hazel punched the keychain button to unlock her Jeep Cherokee, opened the passenger door, and tossed her laptop inside. Just as she closed the door, the headlights of a mud-splattered pickup at the far corner of the parking lot came on, and the truck idled slowly over to the parking spot next to Hazel's Jeep.

The driver left it running as he climbed out. A big man, beard, coarse hands, dressed like he'd been deer hunting.

"You Hazel Owens?" he asked.

"Who's asking?"

"My name's Ronnie. That's all you need to know. I'm looking for your friend, Carol Baxley."

"You sure know a lot about me, Ronnie."

"I know enough," he said. "Enough to tell you to pass along a message to your roommate that if my wife's not home by midnight, it ain't gonna be pretty."

The way he said "*roommate*" made Hazel shiver, a feeling she'd felt many times before. But she wasn't intimidated.

"Well, Ronnie, I'm sorry if you're having marital troubles, but I can assure you it's got nothing to do with Carol. Or me."

The man stepped towards Hazel. She slid a key between the fingers of her right fist and stood right up to him. She was as tall as him, nose to nose.

"You just tell her," Ronnie said as he turned and climbed back into his truck. He gunned it, backed out of the parking space, roared across the parking lot, bounced over the curb onto 301, and barreled off to the north.

Hazel was shaking. She released the grip on her keys and walked slowly around to the driver's side door, took a deep breath, and climbed in.

This is bad, she thought, *real bad*. She fired up the Cherokee and headed home.

Barbara Lowrie was tired. It had been a long day. All she wanted to do was go home, crack open a beer, throw a frozen pizza in the oven, and watch an old movie on the classic movies channel.

She'd informed Chief Holt and one of the department's two investigators, a stand-up guy named George Stanton, about her trip to Skeeter Ellington's place, what his friends had said, and what she'd found. Stanton said he knew Skeeter and would come in first thing after church tomorrow and open a missing-persons case file.

It was after 8 p.m. when the phone on her desk rang.

"Barbara, this is Hazel Owens."

"Hey, Hazel. I'm beat. I'm going home. I hope this can wait."

It's often said that everybody knows everybody else in a small town, but of course this is far from the truth. But Barbara did know Hazel Owens mostly by her punk-rock reputation. When she first started seeing Hazel around town years ago, she asked her old boss, Chief Moody, about the strange, tall, and athletically built woman who was always dressed in black. He told her Hazel's story, and it intrigued Barbara so much that she got to know her. To be honest, she was a bit in awe of Hazel's semi-celebrity past. They were by no means close friends, but they respected each other enough to occasionally get together over a cup of coffee.

Hazel told Barbara about her confrontation with a man named Ronnie in the parking lot. She said she just got home and Carol wasn't there.

"I gotta admit, I'm kind of freaking out here, Barbara."

Well, shoot, Barbara thought. *How many more people can go missing in Preston today?*

"You've got no idea where she might be?" Barbara asked.

"No idea. She should be home. She was supposed to be working an early shift and said she'd be home by seven. I called down there and one of the nurses said Carol called in another doctor to cover for her because she was going to the beach for the weekend. Going to the beach, she said. That's absolutely nuts. No way Carol would just up and go to the beach without me. Or at least telling me."

Hazel added the last part because she knew Carol's work was often so stressful she would need to get away on her own for a couple days. But they always gave each other the details of where they'd be when they had to be apart.

Barbara thought for a second. "Look, keep trying to call her. Stay inside and lock your doors. If this Ronnie turns up, call my cell. I'm only five minutes from your house. And call me tomorrow if Carol still hasn't come home. That's all I really know to do."

Hazel couldn't argue with that. She ended the call and went about making sure the house was locked up. She didn't think she'd have any more trouble from that Ronnie dude tonight, but not knowing Carol's whereabouts was another matter. That had her uncharacteristically scared, and she snuggled down into the sofa with their old Labrador retriever Rufus curled up on her feet.

She tried to watch an old movie to take her mind off things, but it didn't work.

CHAPTER TEN

BY THE TIME MERVIN LEFT BILL'S, the place was packed, and Clemson was kicking the crap out of Wake Forest. Perch left a half hour earlier, and as usual he was a little wobbly when climbing off his barstool. Mervin and Boot made the obligatory offers to give him a ride home or call him a cab, but Perch insisted, again as usual, that he was fine and would see them tomorrow.

Mervin told them he'd called Benny Martin, and Skeeter had booked their regular Sunday tee time after last week's round. After a short discussion, they decided they might as well play. Shoot, Skeeter might be there on the first tee waiting for them. *That would be nice*, Mervin thought, but he knew it wouldn't happen.

Boot said he was going to stay and eat a barbecue sandwich and watch the second half of the game. It was a good time to be a Clemson fan. Mervin slapped him on the back, said he'd see him in the morning at the country club and he'd better bring his A-game. Boot just laughed. He knew he had no chance of beating Mervin.

Gingerly making his way through the tables to the Main Street door, Mervin realized he'd had a shot or two too many. He stepped outside and the brisk late-November air was a relief. Christmas lights had already been strung across Main Street at every block, and their multi-colored flickering gave Preston a warm-and-cozy atmosphere as if the town had transformed into a little-known holiday destination.

More like lipstick on a pig, Mervin thought, but he immediately regretted it. He knew it wasn't fair. Preston was no different from hundreds of other small towns in the South. Progressive change was always slow to reach these rural outposts, but no matter how frustrating life became, the people were resilient and tried to make the best of things. Unfortunately, they often directed their anger and frustration at the very people and institutions that could help them.

Mervin felt there was little he could do about it. He'd just go in the voting booth and vote his conscience. Let the next generation and the ones after that figure it out. Maybe they could fix things. Mervin doubted it.

"Not my circus, not my monkey," he mumbled to himself. He laughed. What did it matter to him? He was retired and playing golf in the morning.

"Hey, Mr. Mervin!"

The voice made Mervin jump and he turned to see the Black man he'd met at lunchtime at Jessie Mae's.

"Hey. Mr. Goins, right?"

"Cedric. Just call me Cedric. Sorry, I didn't mean to scare you."

"You're all right. Going to Bill's?"

"Yeah, thought I'd have a couple beers. Listen, I don't mean no trouble, but I recognized you today at Jessie Mae's 'cause I've seen you in here drinking with your friends and I noticed yesterday there was one missing."

Surprised, Mervin shook his head to clear some of the whiskey fog.

"You're right. Ol' boy named Skeeter Ellington always drinks with us, but he wasn't here yesterday."

"Well, that's the thing I wanted to talk to you about. This might not mean nothing at all, but I saw him Thursday around midday out at Curry's Cross Roads on Highway 9. He was standing outside Gator's Mini-Mart and he didn't look so good. Looked like he'd been digging ditches or something, all dirty and wore out. I said hey when I walked by going inside but he didn't say nothing."

"You saw him Thursday out at Gator's? Was his truck there? Did you see a white Toyota Tundra?"

"No, I didn't see a truck. Just this fellow I always see drinking with you all. Like I said, he looked rough and like he might be waiting for somebody. I was working and just stopped in real quick to get a Mountain Dew and a hot dog. So I didn't have time to talk to him."

Mervin's head was spinning. *Skeeter was out at Gator's? By himself with no truck?*

"I just put two and two together. I saw him out there and then he wasn't in here with y'all yesterday. I thought you might wanna know."

Cedric was anxious to get inside Bill's.

"Yeah, man, thanks," Mervin said. "I gotta tell you, we've been a little worried about Skeeter, so thanks for telling me this. I mean it."

"No problem," Cedric said. "I hope everything works out all right. I'll see you around."

He turned and hurried into Bill's. Mervin stood on the sidewalk and stared at the Christmas lights, his truck keys in his hand. He wasn't sure what to do next.

———⌣———

Ronnie Dixon's phone rang precisely at 9 p.m. He looked at the screen.

"Damn."

He took a deep breath and answered.

"Hey man, what's up?"

"Did you go see her?"

The voice was thin and reedy with a scratchy hint of smoker's hack.

"Yeah, I went by there," Ronnie said. "Waited almost an hour for her to come out."

"What'd she say?"

"She said she didn't know anything about Louise. Said neither she nor Carol Baxley had anything to do with Louise being gone."

"Of course she did."

"Nah, man, look. I believe her. At least I believe she ain't had nothing to do with it. Not sure about the other one. Carol Baxley."

"What'd you tell her?"

"Said if my wife wasn't home by midnight there'd be hell to pay."

"What you gonna do?"

"Man, I don't know. Think I'll just leave it for a couple days."

"You want me to talk to her? Give her a nudge?"

"No!" Ronnie said too strongly, then added more gently, "No, man, it would just come back on me. Let's give it another day or two."

"I'm disappointed in you, Ronnie."

"Hey, it's all good. I'll be in touch."

Ronnie quickly ended the call. He never wanted to get in touch with this dude again, but he knew eventually he might have to.

Man, why did I even talk to this guy? he thought. Ronnie had treated Louise badly, smacked her around a few too many times, but he missed her. Swore to himself he'd never hurt her again if she came home. Ronnie popped the top on another beer and plopped down in front of the TV.

It was never supposed to get this complicated. Ronnie and a few of his buddies had gotten together a month ago like they always did out at Earl Tyler's place to shoot some pool, smoke pot, and drink. Earl lived on the edge of town near the turnoff for the state park. His house sat at the end of a long drive, had a big front porch, and was surrounded by trees and soybean fields. This particular night Luther Peacock brought along a friend no one else knew.

He was a small man but wiry and strong. You could tell he'd handle himself in a scrap. Sharp features, sunken cheeks, and tousled black hair.

Three days' worth of whiskers speckled with gray. About late forties or thereabouts, and he was dressed differently from the others. His plaid, button-down shirt was tucked into a pair of pleated slacks, but his dress shoes had long lost their shine. In fact, everything he wore looked old, not shabby, but like he'd had them a long time.

Luther introduced him as Harold Cephus, but said people called him Deacon. Someone laughed and asked if he was some kind of religious nut. The man just grinned and said he did the Lord's work whenever he got the chance. He said it like he was joking, and everyone laughed. But Ronnie didn't like it. He heard something menacing in the words and was surprised when he glanced around and no one else seemed to pick up on it.

Well, he couldn't blame them really. The fellows who gathered at Earl's weren't exactly former members of the Beta Club. In fact, they'd never been members of any kind of club for that matter, although they had their opinions about things.

They weren't a chapter of the Klan or a cadet branch of the Aryan Brotherhood or anything like that. They were just good friends, all in their early thirties who'd gone to school together, had dead-end jobs, and were just pissed at the world in general. They felt victimized by all the *rights* being given to other people and wondered why they weren't getting any help. Their manhood was important to them, and they weren't feeling very manly these days.

At one point during the evening, Ronnie and Luther were out on the front porch taking a smoke break when Luther asked how Ronnie and his wife were getting along. Ronnie said he was trying to keep her in line, although she was threatening to leave. Luther's friend, the wiry visitor, and a cop named Mark Rogers stepped onto the porch and lit up, too. Ronnie had seen them inside earlier, off to one side of the room, heads together and talking earnestly. He had no idea what they'd been discussing but it bothered him just the same.

The wiry dude who went by Deacon flicked his cigarette off the porch and said he hadn't meant to eavesdrop but had overheard Ronnie talking about his marital woes. He told Ronnie he had some experience with that sort of thing, and if Ronnie ever needed help he should give him a call. Ronnie mumbled thanks but in the back of his mind he hoped he would never have any reason to make that call.

But things have a way of getting weird. Two days ago, Ronnie came home from work and Louise's old Toyota banger wasn't in the driveway. He went inside and found her closet empty. She had left and didn't even leave a note.

He called around to some of her friends to ask if anyone had seen her. Word spread, and it was Mark Rogers who called Ronnie late that night to say he'd given his number to Harold Cephus who would be calling Ronnie later. Mark said he'd spent some time with Cephus who'd helped him deal with some anger issues brought on by a messy divorce.

"He'd be a good guy for you to talk to right now," Mark said. "He's been there, man."

Ronnie wasn't so sure, but he thanked Mark and said he was sorry about the divorce.

When Harold called, Ronnie was cordial and heard him out. He said to call him Deacon and explained how he'd had a wife at one time who'd lost her way and turned his life upside down. He was still getting over it, he said, and hoped that Ronnie wouldn't have to go through the same thing.

Deacon said he'd met a couple other men in Preston who told him their wives had become difficult before up and leaving without a trace. It was a travesty, he said, and he'd come to suspect that a doctor at the Urgent Care had something to do with it. He thought she might have had help from a retired lawyer who lived out by the river.

Ronnie asked him how he knew this, but all Deacon would say was he kept his ear to the ground.

"Look, Ronnie, I'm not trying to get all religious or anything, but it says in the Bible that women should obey their husbands. Plain and simple, you've got the right, and responsibility, to keep her in line."

Deacon suggested that Ronnie should confront the doctor from the doc-in-a-box to see what she knew. If he couldn't find her, he could ask her significant other, a woman named Hazel Owens who owned a recording studio.

Ronnie had humored Deacon long enough to get off the phone without upsetting him. He even agreed that he would confront either the lady doctor or Hazel Owens. Thus, his parking lot encounter with Hazel a few hours earlier for which he had nothing to show.

Now Ronnie slouched deeper into his chair to watch the late college game from the West Coast on ESPN. He needed to come up with a strategy to deal with this Deacon dude. Hopefully, it would be a plan that let him save face and avoid personal injury. Ronnie knew it might come to that. He wasn't scared, but now he had a new, multi-pronged dilemma. He wanted to get Louise back, but he didn't want to piss off the Deacon any more than he already had.

So much for local initiative, Deacon thought. He was disappointed in Ronnie Dixon, but he wasn't surprised. These Preston boys talked a good game but mostly they were all bark and no bite. All they cared about was preserving their Southern heritage, which Deacon knew was a crock of shit. Preserving their White privilege was what it came down to, and Deacon had no interest in that. White, Black, Brown, yellow, what difference did it make?

He sat in his black Dodge Ram pickup outside the abandoned hunting lodge deep in the woods near Reedy Creek and contemplated his next move. The Dixon boy was useless, and he could probably be scared into keeping quiet. Deacon hoped so anyway.

At least the cop, Rogers, seemed dependable, and the one inside watching the woman was somewhat reliable. After all, he was the one who'd introduced him to the cop, who in turn had turned Deacon on to this miserable backwoods shack and then helped him put new locks on the doors.

Deacon sat for a few more minutes then made his decision. Drastic measures were needed. He had an idea. He would need inner strength to shove aside any self-doubt and do the Lord's work. Thank goodness Louise Dixon had made a stop at the Dollar General on her way out of town, and even better, she'd parked on a side street behind the store. Grabbing her had been easy, and her old Toyota would still be parked there.

He went inside and told Luther he'd take the woman back into town and drop her off at her car. He'd give her a good talking to, tell her to get in line. Their point would be made. Luther could go home and get some sleep.

Luther was glad to hear that, and Deacon saw the relief on his face.

CHAPTER ELEVEN

MERVIN AND PERCH SAT in their golf cart in the middle of the fifth fairway, a short par four. They were waiting for the foursome on the green ahead of them to finish putting out. A groan went up when a portly old boy in a bucket hat missed a three-footer.

"Chump," Perch said.

"Be nice. You've missed your share."

Perch grinned because he knew it was true. It was a busy Sunday on the golf course, but Mervin, Perch, and Boot didn't mind. While they enjoyed being outside on such a chilly but pretty day, they couldn't help feeling a bit down about Skeeter's absence. It was like they were missing a member of the band.

Mervin told them earlier about running into Cedric Goins last night when he was leaving Bill's, and what Goins said about seeing Skeeter Thursday afternoon standing by himself outside Gator's Mini-Mart.

"No, Goins said his truck wasn't there," Mervin said when Boot asked. "He said it looked like Skeeter could have been waiting for somebody." Boot and Perch shook their heads in bewilderment and continued loading their clubs on their golf carts.

Now Boot was by himself in a cart just off the fairway near a row of pine trees where his tee shot ended up. He'd assured Mervin and Perch that he didn't mind riding solo. He tried to lighten the mood by saying he might play better since he didn't have to constantly listen to Skeeter's instructions. The mood didn't lighten.

They waited in silence as the last member in the group ahead lined up his putt.

"I read something wild in a magazine this morning," Perch said. "It was an article about the worldwide refugee crisis."

"What'd it say?" Mervin asked as he watched the players ahead place the flag back in the hole and head off the green.

"It said there were more than sixty million displaced people in the world. Sixty million! Can you believe that? Sixty million people with no place to live. That's depressing as hell, and it got me thinking about how great we have it compared to a lot of other folks. Look at me. I live in a big house with all those empty rooms while a family of four in Syria might be living in a burned-out car."

"What you gonna do, Perch? Adopt a family from Syria?"

"I might. Why not? Maybe they could cook and clean. Besides, I'd like the company."

"I don't think they'd be cooking collards and macaroni and cheese," Mervin said. "And you don't speak Syrian."

"That's not a language, Mervin. They speak Arabic."

"Well, something tells me you don't speak Arabic either, smart guy."

Mervin climbed out of the cart and motioned over to Boot to hit away. Boot's lie was lousy, and his approach shot fell short of the green. Perch hit it thin and watched his ball scamper across the green and disappear behind it. Mervin flushed an eight iron that landed fifteen feet from the flag.

"Nice shot, asshole," Perch muttered. Mervin grinned, floored the pedal, and off they went down the fairway.

"Are you lonely, Perch?" Mervin asked.

"No, man, I'm okay."

"You still miss Janice, don't you?"

"Every single day."

Mervin brought the cart to a stop on the cart path near the green.

"You've still got me and Boot," he said.

"And Skeeter."

"Yes, and Skeeter. Now chip it close and save your par. Like Skeeter would."

They climbed out of the cart, grabbed some clubs, and headed for the green.

"Hey Boot!" Mervin yelled. "Perch is going to adopt some Syrians."

"Good idea," Boot called, not missing a beat.

Perch chipped it fairly close and rolled in a five-foot putt for par. He, Boot, and Mervin walked back to their golf carts in silence.

***

Three hours later, Mervin stored his clubs securely in the back of his truck, climbed into the cab, and reached across to retrieve his phone from the glove box. They'd made a no-phones-on-the-golf-course rule years ago, and it made their rounds much more enjoyable. Not that these old geezers spent a lot of time on their phones, but at least the distraction was eliminated.

Mervin saw two texts from Becca. The first said Sergeant Lowrie was trying to get in touch with him, and the second told him to check his voice mail. He did and immediately heard Lowrie's voice saying she'd tried calling him several times and needed to talk to him right away. Could he please come by the police station as soon as he got this message?

Bad news, has to be, Mervin thought. He didn't want to face it alone.

He jumped out of his truck and hurried around to Boot's big King Ranch F-250. It was idling with a deep-throated rumble, Boot behind the wheel. Mervin made a motion for Boot to lower his window.

"We've got to go to the police station," Mervin said. "Sergeant Lowrie wants to see us."

"Why?" Boot asked.

"I don't know."

"Perch needs to go, too."

"You're right," Mervin said. "Blow your horn!"

Boot tooted the truck's horn twice while Mervin waved his arms above his head at Perch's truck leaving the parking lot. The brake lights came on, then the back-up lights, and Mervin sighed with relief.

They headed into town in a three-truck convoy. The two-lane highway wound through corn fields, dipped through a couple of Carolina bays, and eventually intersected with Preston's Main Street on the south end of town. It was quiet in downtown Preston on a late Sunday afternoon, and the three senior golfers parked next to each other in diagonal spots in front of the police station. Theirs were the only vehicles on the block.

Mervin had texted Lowrie earlier to tell her they were on their way, and she met them at the door.

"Thanks for coming," she said. "I've been trying to reach you all day."

"Sorry," Mervin said. "We've been on the golf course."

"So I heard," Lowrie said.

She led them through reception and the squad room to a small conference room at the back of the station. Mervin, Boot, and Perch were surprised when they walked in and found Chief Holt and Detective George Stanton already seated at the table with laptops and notes in front of them.

Introductions were made, they all shook hands, and Mervin, Boot, and Perch sat directly across from the officers. Lowrie took a seat at the end of the table to their left. Mervin hoped the mints he'd passed out on the sidewalk concealed their beer breath, and when he sneaked a glance at Boot, he could tell he was a little high.

"Thanks for coming in on a Sunday, fellows," Chief Holt began. "We've got some information about the disappearance of August Ellington. Not much, but we needed to ask y'all some questions. Sergeant, if you could give the details."

Lowrie told them how they managed to force open the strongbox found in Skeeter's closet.

"There was an indentation that told us it contained a weapon at some point, although there was no weapon inside. Most likely an automatic handgun. We also found three zip-lock bags, each containing five hundred in cash, a contact list for emergency services in a five-county area, and the phone numbers and email addresses of your friend Skeeter and that of Dr. Carol Baxley."

She stopped and silence filled the room.

"This has us concerned," Detective Stanton said. "Can y'all shed any light on what this might mean?"

Mervin and Boot instinctively glanced at Perch.

"I think my friend Henry Gordon here can shed some light on it," Mervin said.

Everyone at the table looked at Perch. He cleared his throat and calmly began to relate the entire story about Skeeter and Carol Baxley's attempts to help abused women escape their tormentors. When he finished, there was an even longer silence in the room. Sergeant Lowrie shook her head and asked why they hadn't come forward with this information earlier.

"We just found out about it last night," Mervin said. "Or at least me and Boot just found out about it."

"Skeeter made me promise not to tell anyone," Perch piped. "But I know it's all changed now with Skeeter missing and everything, and I thought they needed to know."

"And we didn't?" Stanton asked a bit angrily.

"Actually, there's more," Mervin said a bit sheepishly, and he told them about his conversation with Cedric Goins.

Stanton let out a loud sigh of disgust.

"Okay, thanks for telling us this. Now we know," Holt said, diffusing the tension in the room. "But I need Sergeant Lowrie to bring y'all up to speed on another case that, as it turns out, connects to the disappearance of Ellington."

Barbara Lowrie told Mervin, Boot, and Perch about her call from Hazel Owens. About how Carol Baxley had asked another doctor to cover her weekend shifts so she could go to the beach. And now no one, including Hazel, knew Carol's whereabouts. She decided to hold back the information about the bearded man named Ronnie who threatened Hazel in the strip mall parking lot.

"Shit," said Mervin.

"Damn," said Perch.

"No shit," said Chief Holt, summing up the situation. "We'll be coordinating with the sheriff's department, and the State Law Enforcement Department has been notified. We've got several leads to follow up, but for now we just need you three to monitor your phones and let us handle things."

Detective Stanton was itching to add his two cents.

"Look, we appreciate that Mr. Ellington was a close friend of yours, but the last thing we need is y'all poking your nose in and playing amateur detective. So don't go back to his house, don't go out to Gator's, or do anything else that might hinder our investigation."

"We just want to help," Mervin said.

"I get it," Stanton said, "But no offense, y'all don't exactly look like a SWAT team. Let us do our jobs."

Mervin felt Boot bristle next to him and he kicked Boot's leg under the table to keep him quiet. Boot had a prideful streak that sometimes prompted him to get in someone's face.

"Don't worry about us," Mervin said. "We're just really worried about Skeeter. If you could keep us informed about what's going on, we'd really appreciate it."

"We'll do that," Holt said. "Again, thanks for coming in on a Sunday. We'll be in touch."

That signaled the meeting was over, and Mervin, Boot, and Perch got up and followed Sergeant Lowrie back through the police station to the front door.

"That son-of-a-bitch Stanton needs to watch his mouth," Boot muttered loud enough for Lowrie to hear.

She smiled and said, "He's just like most men, needs to dog his spot every now and then. Don't worry about him."

"I ain't worried about him," Boot said, "but he might need to worry about me."

Lowrie laughed, held the door, and followed them onto the sidewalk. "Calm down, tiger," she told Boot. "I know how much Skeeter means to you. I really do. And with what you said about his connection to Carol Baxley and what they were doing, I'm going to do my best to get to the bottom of this. It sounds like they were doing some good. I'll keep in touch with y'all."

Mervin liked this Lumbee Indian police officer.

"Thanks, Sergeant," he said. "Let us know if there's anything we can do."

Lowrie went back inside, and Mervin, Boot, and Perch were left on the sidewalk in the deep gloaming of the evening.

"I don't care what Stanton says, I ain't sitting around on my ass while Skeeter's got himself all mixed up in this," Boot said. "We gotta find him."

"I agree," said Perch.

"I hear you," said Mervin. "But we gotta keep it on the down low. It won't do Skeeter any good if we get locked up."

The three men took turns giving each other a strong hug before they climbed back into their trucks. They might be long in the tooth, but one of the advantages of getting older was you had much less to lose. Stanton and Holt might disapprove, but Mervin, Boot, and Perch were not going to sit on the sidelines while Skeeter was out there in the wind.

CHAPTER TWELVE

IN ALL HER FORTY YEARS, Jodi Mercer had never loved a job as much as she loved working at the Urgent Care. Her years there were two of the most meaningful in her life.

Sure, all she did was check patients in, answer the phone, and file insurance claims, but she felt like she was helping people. The doctors and nurses were nice, too, and they never made her feel like she was a less important member of the team.

Jodi repaid their confidence by always getting to work early, turning on all the lights, and making sure everything was ready when doors opened to clients at 7 a.m.

When she pulled into the parking at six-thirty on Monday morning, she noticed a weather-beaten Toyota Corolla parked in front. Jodi circled around and parked at the rear of the building, but instead of going in the staff entrance at the back, she walked to the front to see if someone in the Toyota was waiting to see a doctor. Healthcare options were few in these parts, and sometimes folks in the rural areas would get up early and drive miles for help.

The car was covered with morning dew, so it must have been in the lot for hours. Despite the mist on the windows, Jodi could see a woman with long hair behind the wheel. *She's reclined the seat and must be asleep,* Jodi thought.

Jodi knocked on the window.

"Hey. Good morning."

The woman didn't move so Jodi knocked harder.

"Hey! Are you okay? Do you need some help?"

Still no response, so Jodi tried the door. It was unlocked and when she opened it, the woman's left arm fell limply to her side. Jodi knew right away.

"Oh, god."

She fumbled in her bag for her phone and called 911. Then she called Wanda Bethea, the nurse who was scheduled to work that morning. Wanda told her to stay with the woman until the police arrived then to go inside and get things ready for business. She was on her way.

The police arrived in less than five minutes, roaring up in one of the department's new Ford Explorer squad cars. Jodi didn't recognize the two officers, but they were nice enough. One told her to go inside, and he would speak to her later. But she lingered just long enough to hear the other officer say, "We need to call Stanton. Look at those bruises."

Jodi managed a quick peak over the shoulders of both policemen who were hunched over and peering in at the dead woman. A thin blue bruise almost completely encircled her throat.

"Oh, god," Jodi said again, and she hurried off in the direction of the Urgent Care's back door.

Preston was a small town, and for the most part fairly quiet. But the events of the past three days had Barbara Lowrie wondering just how much anger, violence, and bodily harm might be occurring behind closed doors. She knew she shouldn't entertain the thought because Preston was a good town with good people.

But she also knew that domestic violence was a big problem in South Carolina. Up until a couple years ago, the state led the nation in the number of deaths of women at the hands of their husbands or boyfriends. The politicians finally got their act together and passed stronger laws, but South Carolina remained near the top of this depressing statistic.

Barbara watched as the paramedics lifted the dead woman from the Toyota and placed her on a stretcher. She felt anger swell up inside. As she looked out over the flashing lights atop the ambulance and all the cop cars, she wondered how many other women were suffering abuse, terrified of coming forward, and searching for a way out. Her anger was tempered by a newfound respect for Carol Baxley and Skeeter Ellington, wherever they were.

Chief Holt walked over.

"The car is registered to a Louise Dixon," he said. "According to DMV records, she lived out on Deerwood Lane near the high school. Shump thinks she's Ronnie Dixon's wife."

Shump was Sergeant Pete Shumpert, one of Preston's longest-serving officers and a treasure trove of local history and familial connections.

"Ronnie?" Barbara said.

"That's right. I think we might have identified your Ronnie from the other night. See if you can find Hazel Owens. We'll bring Ronnie Dixon in as soon as we find him."

She walked to her squad car, another shiny new Ford Explorer, calling Hazel on the way. The call went to voice mail and Barbara left a message.

"I'm on my way to your house," she said. "It looks like we've identified Ronnie but it's not all good news."

Barbara glanced again over the busy, sorrowful scene in the parking lot and knew that in a matter of hours the good people of Preston would be abuzz about the dead woman found in her car at the Urgent Care.

CHAPTER THIRTEEN

MERVIN SWUNG HIS LEGS over the side of the bed and sat up. Slowly but surely, he stood and waddled to the bathroom. Relieving himself, he could barely see the little fellow over his beer belly. Becca was right. He needed to lose weight. *Easier said than done these days*, Mervin thought.

He groaned as he slipped an old zip-up hoodie over his flannel PJs. His back, knees, and hips were sore at the best of times, but on Mondays after Sunday golf, they throbbed more than usual. Growing old was not for the timid, but Mervin tried not to think about it. He liked to pretend he was still only thirty-five or maybe forty. But there was no pretending on mornings like this.

The aroma of fresh coffee wafted down the hall and Mervin made his way to the kitchen. Becca stood looking out the window, a cup nestled in both hands as if she was making a morning offering to the backyard. She was immaculately dressed and ready to do battle with thirty third graders at Haden Elementary.

The school was on the less affluent side of Preston, a poor town to begin with. Median family income in Preston was around $28,000, and a third or so of the town's population lived below the poverty line. The kids Becca taught wore the same clothes to school almost every day and they devoured their free lunches like ravenous birds of prey. They might be poor, but you could never tell by their energy, laughter, and typical third-grade shenanigans.

Becca's class consisted of eight White kids, six Hispanic kids, and sixteen Black kids. She cared for each one of them, but there were two or three she'd come close to strangling on occasion. "Figuratively speaking," she would always add.

"Thanks for saving me some coffee," Mervin said. He poured a cup and sat at the kitchen table with another groan.

"You're welcome, old man," Becca said. It was 7:30. She would have been up for at least an hour.

Becca walked around behind Mervin, draped her arms around his neck, and kissed the stubble on his cheek.

"I'm out of here," she said. "Try to stay out of trouble today. And text me if you hear anything about Skeeter."

She was going through the backdoor to the carport when she turned and said, "You left your phone on last night. It's over there on the counter. I heard it buzz a little while ago."

"Thanks, babe," Mervin said. "Have a good day."

Becca closed the door, and for the ten-millionth time Mervin marveled at how he could have been so lucky. Like the old Dire Straits song said, he was crazy for the girl.

He jumped when the door opened suddenly and Becca stuck her head back inside.

"By the way, if you run into Boot today, ask him if he's got any pot to sell. We're almost out."

Mervin grinned. "I'm sure I will, and I'm sure he does."

Becca closed the door a second time and about a minute later, Mervin heard her car start and back out of the carport.

He sat and sipped his coffee for a while, taking time to wake up. When he fetched his phone from the kitchen counter to check his messages, he saw a text from Boot.

"Speak of the devil," Mervin said.

Boot's text read, *Waffle House, 9 a.m. Be there. It's time to act, Sherlock!*

Mervin laughed but choked it off when it caused a back spasm. He looked at the Kit-Kat Clock above the sink and saw it was ten minutes to eight. He better get moving if he was going to make the Waffle House by nine.

He texted Boot, *See you there, Watson. The game's afoot!*

―――――――⌣―――――――

Hazel opened the living room curtains and was greeted by a gray, dreary morning. There were projects on her laptop that needed her attention, but she knew it would be hard to work today. All she could do was worry about Carol.

The worry turned to dread when she saw a police Ford Explorer pull up in front of the house. She stepped out onto the front porch and watched Barbara Lowrie walk around the truck and cross the front yard.

"Did you get my message?" Barbara asked. She was dressed in her crisp, navy-blue uniform and shiny black boots. Hazel wore old sweatpants, flip-flops, and a plaid flannel shirt. Rufus stood next to her on the porch, his tail wagging like crazy at the sight of Barbara.

"No, I just got up a few minutes ago," Hazel said.

Barbara saw the fear on Hazel's face and quickly said, "No word yet on Carol, I'm afraid, but we've had a development downtown. I need to talk to you for a minute. Can I come in?"

"Yeah, yeah, of course," Hazel said, flustered but relieved. "I haven't made coffee yet. You want some?"

"That would be great," Barbara said. She scratched Rufus on the head and followed him and Hazel through the house to the kitchen.

Hazel took down a bag of ground coffee and a box of filters from an overhead cabinet, leaned against the counter, grasping it with both hands, and let her shoulders sag. Her spiky black hair was plastered flat on one side from sleeping.

"You look like a cross between a Deadhead and a punk," Barbara said.

Hazel was strong. She took pride in her ability to keep her emotions in check. But when she laughed at Barbara's joke, it came out as a hiccupping sob.

"I'm sorry, Sarge," Hazel said. "All this has been too much. I don't know what to do. I feel helpless."

"I know," Barbara said. She slid a chair out from the kitchen table. "Here, sit down. "I'll make the coffee."

Hazel took a seat and Rufus padded over and rested his chin on her leg, a look of concern on his furry black face. Barbara busied herself with the coffee and talked as she worked. She told Hazel about Louise Dixon being found in her car outside the Urgent Care. She told her that Louise's husband was named Ronnie, and at this very moment, both Preston police officers and county sheriff's deputies were out looking for him.

"Ronnie?" Hazel asked. "You're thinking it's the same Ronnie from the other night outside the studio?"

"I guess it could be a coincidence," Barbara said. "There are other Ronnies in town, but not that many. I'm pretty sure this is our man."

"What do we do now?"

The coffee maker gurgled as java began to drip into the carafe. Barbara took down two mugs from hooks underneath a cabinet and placed them on the counter.

"We have a cup of coffee," she said. "And wait."

Barbara and Hazel sat at the kitchen table, drank coffee, and chatted, Rufus curled up at their feet. Barbara asked how things were at the studio, and Hazel told her business was good. She was looking forward to a band from Charlotte coming to town this week for a couple days of recording. They were called The Suburbs of Hysteria and were supposed to be pretty good.

"From Charlotte?" Barbara said. "Why would a band from Charlotte come to Preston? But I'm not saying you won't do just as good a job as anybody up there," she added, backtracking.

Hazel smiled. It was a legitimate question.

"They said they wanted to get away from their familiar surroundings and come here just to create," Hazel said. "They said they'd heard good things about Clarke Studio and even remembered Purple Hazel."

Barbara heard a note of pride in Hazel's voice, and she smiled over the rim of her coffee mug. At that moment, her phone on the table gave a shrill ring and she picked it up to look at the screen.

"It's Chief Holt," she told Hazel.

"Lowrie here. Yes, sir. I'm at Hazel Owens' house."

Hazel clutched her mug and listened to Barbara's side of the conversation.

"That's great." Barbara listened some more and then said, "How about this. You all give us a ten-minute head start, then bring him through the front door of the station. Hazel and I'll be across the street where she'll have a clear view."

Barbara looked over at Hazel in her flannel shirt and flip-flops and said, "Chief, if you could, make that a fifteen-minute head start. Okay. Great. Thanks."

"What?" Hazel said.

"They found Ronnie Dixon. He was at his house getting ready to go to work like nothing was wrong. I asked Chief Holt to wait awhile before they headed back downtown and to bring Ronnie in through the Main Street door. We'll be sitting across the street where you can get a good look at him."

"What if he—"

"He ain't gonna see you," Barbara said. "Now get up from there and get moving. I'll clean things up in here while you get dressed."

"And pour some food in Rufus's bowl," Hazel said on her way down the hall. "It's over in the corner."

Twenty minutes later, Barbara angled the Explorer into a parking spot on Main Street across from the police station. The pawn shop in front of them hadn't opened for business, but the florist on one side and gift shop on the other both had the lights on and OPEN signs on their doors.

The Explorer's passenger seat next to Barbara was occupied by a mounted laptop, its screen dark. Hazel had ridden into town in the backseat and now she was hunkered down and peeking across the street at the police station's front door.

"Can you see okay?" Barbara asked.

"Yeah, no problem."

They sat quietly and waited. The sky grew darker as clouds moved in from the southwest.

"Supposed to rain today," Barbara said.

"And get colder tonight," added Hazel.

"Fine by me. I'm ready for some wintertime weather."

At that moment, two police cars came down the street and parked next to each other across from Barbara and Hazel. Holt had spotted Barbara's Explorer and parked far enough away from the station's door to give the women a clear view.

Car doors were flung open and a large, bearded man was escorted by Holt and three other officers down the sidewalk and through the police station's large glass doors, which were being held open by two other policemen. The man's crestfallen face and plodding walk spoke of immense sorrow. He wasn't handcuffed.

"Is that him?" Barbara asked.

Hazel didn't hesitate.

"That's him," she said, "without a doubt."

"Okay, hold on for a couple minutes then I'll run you home."

Barbara texted her chief, *Positive ID*. His text came back almost immediately. *Great!*

Barbara let him know that she was taking Hazel home and would be back in fifteen minutes. *Don't start without me!* she wrote.

"Something has me worried," Hazel said from the backseat as they pulled away. "If this guy came looking for me Saturday night so I could warn Carol, that means he doesn't know where she is either. I don't think he'll be able to help us find her."

Barbara cranked the Explorer, looked over her shoulder, and started backing out of the parking space.

"Don't start overthinking things," she said. "We won't know how much he knows until we sit him down and let him sweat a little bit. We'll find out if he knows anything about Carol. Now let's get you home."

CHAPTER FOURTEEN

RAINDROPS PELTED THE WINDSHIELD of Mervin's truck as he pulled into the Waffle House parking lot. He looked for a spot near the door but had to settle for an empty space near a dumpster in the back. The joint was jumping on a Monday morning.

He found Boot in a booth next to the windows at the end of the room and slid in across from him. Mervin ordered coffee, two scrambled, and a pecan waffle from the waitress who was already standing there, pen and pad at the ready.

"You're not hungry, are you?" Boot said with a smirk.

"As a matter of fact, I am," Mervin said, peeling off his jacket.

Boot ordered a western omelet with smothered hash browns and asked for a coffee refill.

"So what's got you all worked up?" Mervin asked. "Shot a ninety-two yesterday and now you're all full of yourself?"

"I'm coming for you, Merv, you know it. It's only a matter of time."

"Yeah, but how much time have we got?"

They both laughed and Boot leaned forward.

"I've been thinking," he said.

"That's a first," said Mervin, slurping his coffee.

Boot ignored him.

"I can't help feeling Skeeter is out there hiding somewhere or being held somewhere or maybe even something worse. Since Perch told us about what he and this Carol Baxley were up to, it's obvious he's found trouble with some pissed off husband or crazy boyfriend. But the thing is, Skeeter's smart. He knew something bad could happen. Why do you think he bought a gun?"

"Well, he might've bought one," Mervin said, "but I doubt he knows how to use it."

"That don't matter. What does matter is what kind of trouble he's in and where he's at."

"Behind the at," Mervin said.

"Shut up, Mervin. This is serious."

Boot was right. It was serious. They hadn't seen or heard from Skeeter for five days.

Mervin set his coffee mug down. "You're right. I'm sorry. Tell me what you think we should do."

"I'm not sure what we should do, but anything's better than sitting around worrying while that asshole Stanton sits behind his desk and twiddles his thumbs.

"I see it this way. An old client needs help and gets in touch with Skeeter. He and this doctor from the Urgent Care end up helping her and her daughter. But then Skeeter's old client gets herself almost beat to death by the daughter's husband. This really pisses Skeeter off, so he and Carol Baxley, the lady doctor, start helping other women, but they bite off more than they can chew. Someone got wind of their rescue operation and told a husband or boyfriend, or maybe two or three husbands, and they went after Skeeter and Carol.

"So, I think we go back to the first one," Boot said. "That first one is a violent son of a bitch. I think we should find him."

Their waitress appeared with an armload of plates. She sat the food down in front of Boot and Mervin, refilled their coffees. "Thanks, Charlene. You're amazing."

The waitress took a good-natured swing at Boot, missing by a mile, and hurried off to another table.

"Charlene?" Mervin said. "You're amazing? Boot, that woman is thirty years younger than you, at least. And all those tattoos!"

"A man can dream," Boot said and tucked into his omelet.

Mervin sat there and studied his friend. Folks often underestimated Boot Pearson, and Mervin had been guilty of it many times himself. But he learned long ago that whenever he was in a tight spot, Boot was who he wanted by his side.

"Here's what I'm thinking," Boot continued as he squirted ketchup over his smothered hash browns. "We sneak back out to Skeeter's place, break in if we have to, and go through all his old files. I'm sure they're in that study of his. See if we can find out who the woman was who came to Skeeter for help in the first place."

"Boot, we don't have to go looking through Skeeter's files. Perch said they kept records of everything, remember? We can just ask Perch," Mervin said.

"Oh yeah! I forgot about that."

"Besides, we wouldn't have to break into Skeeter's house."

"What do you mean?"

"We wouldn't have to break in because I've got Skeeter's keys."

"You've got Skeeter's keys?" Boot said gaping wide-eyed at Mervin. "How have you got Skeeter's keys?"

Mervin told Boot the whole story of how he'd lifted them from Skeeter's dresser Saturday morning when he went back into the house. He said he wasn't sure why he did it. It just felt like the thing to do.

Maybe he thought he was protecting Skeeter's property, but that was just Mervin rationalizing. He'd told only Becca. Except now he'd told Boot, who continued to stare at him.

"That was a dumb thing to do, Mervin," Boot said. "But I'm glad you did it. You old dawg!" He held up a fist for Mervin to bump above the table.

"And, you know, it might not be a bad idea to go back out there and look around some more. Hell, Skeeter might be hiding under the house."

"So, when do you want to go? Right now, after breakfast?"

"Slow down, Boot," Mervin said. "Let's think about this thing. We need to be prepared before we go out there. Maybe we can go early tomorrow morning. In the meantime, I want to get in touch with Hazel Owens, the woman the cops told us about who lives with Carol Baxley. Maybe if we compare notes with her, we might discover something."

"I've heard of her," Boot said. "She runs that recording studio out on 301, the one the Clarke boy started years ago."

"You never cease to amaze, Boot," Mervin said, and they finished breakfast buoyed by an action plan and a new sense of purpose.

———⌣———

The rain had stopped but the sky was still gray and heavy with more rain to come. Boot and Mervin stood on the wet, asphalt parking lot and listened to the steady hum of traffic from the interstate.

"You going to find Hazel Owens?" Boot asked. "I think her studio is in that little strip mall with the Mexican restaurant."

"I know where it is," Mervin said. "I'll probably head over there this afternoon. I've got some things to do around the house this morning."

"Well, call me tonight and let's make plans to go out to Skeeter's tomorrow."

"Okay," Mervin said, and they headed off to their respective trucks.

"Hey, hold up, Boot!" Mervin called and he started walking back to where Boot had stopped. "Becca wanted me to ask if you had any pot to sell."

"Becca wanted you to ask?" Boot said with a grin. "So it's for Becca and not for you."

He laughed at Mervin's exasperated expression and said, "Come on, I think I've got a little bit in the truck."

They climbed into the cab of Boot's pickup, which was considerably higher off the ground than the cab of Mervin's truck, and Boot began rummaging around in the console. He pulled out a small prescription bottle that contained two or three fat buds.

"Here you go," he said. "Y'all can have this until I get some more."

"No, Boot, I'll pay you for it," Mervin said. He could see that there was enough pot in the bottle to last him and Becca two or three weeks, given the little amount they smoked. It was nice to have a hit or two in the evening while they watched TV, plus, it really helped them sleep.

"Don't worry about it," Boot said. "And I oughta let you sample it just so you'll know it's okay."

He produced a joint from an inside jacket pocket, and before Mervin could say that it was too early in the day for him, Boot had fired it up. He took a long toke and handed the joint to Mervin who did the same. It would have been impolite to do otherwise.

After one more hit each, Mervin signaled he'd had enough, so Boot snuffed out the joint and put it in the ashtray.

"Damn," Mervin said.

"I know, right?" said Boot.

They sat for a while, buzzing and gazing out across the split-rail fence that separated the Waffle House parking lot from a field filled with row after row of dried-up cornstalks. Boot cranked up the truck and the cab was filled with music from the stereo, a melodic electronic drumbeat pulsing beneath a synthesizer and what sounded like a harp and an acoustic guitar.

"What the hell is this, Boot?" Mervin asked.

"Chill-hop, man. It mellows me out."

"Chill-hop? Where in the world did you hear chill-hop?"

"There's this thing called the internet, Mervin. They've got this thing on there called YouTube. You should check it out."

"You blow my mind, Boot, you know that?"

"Blow your mind? Seriously? This ain't *Easy Rider*, Mervin. It ain't the 1960s "

They both laughed so hard tears filled their eyes.

"This is good stuff," Mervin was finally able to say. "Becca will be pleased."

"Do I need to drive you across the parking lot and drop you off at your truck?"

"That would be nice."

Before Boot could shift the truck into reverse, his phone buzzed. He removed it from his pocket, looked at the screen, and reached over to turn down the music.

"It's Perch," he said. "Hey, man. What's up?" He listened for a few seconds then said, "What? Outside the Urgent Care?"

Mervin sat up, alarmed, and watched Boot.

"Do they know who she was?" A few more seconds passed and Boot said, "Yeah, okay. Yeah, Perch, I get it. I'm with Mervin now. We just finished breakfast at the Waffle House. We'll talk to you this afternoon. Just go home and don't freak out. We'll see you later."

Boot ended the call.

"What?" Mervin said.

"Perch said he went downtown a little while ago to the Ace Hardware and one of the old boys in there told him they found a dead woman in her car outside the Urgent Care this morning. A woman who works in there, Jodi somebody, told a friend of his she'd been strangled."

"Holy crap," Mervin said. "This changes everything, Boot. We've got to let the police handle this. Becca would never forgive me if I went out looking for Skeeter and got strangled."

"Shut up, Mervin. We don't even know if it has anything to do with Skeeter. And if it does, it means we need to move quickly. I told Perch we'd hook up with him later."

Boot drove around to where Mervin's truck was parked behind the Waffle House, and Mervin opened the door and climbed out.

"Man, talk about a buzz kill," he said.

"I heard that. Go find Hazel Owens and talk to her, and let's me, you, and Perch get together at Bill's for happy hour."

"What are you gonna do?"

"I'll tell you later," Boot said, and he roared off after Mervin shut the door.

Mervin climbed into his Silverado and tucked the bottle of pot into the glove box. He was still really high, and he sat there for a few minutes trying to get a handle on things. Boot was right. Perch's call about the dead woman at the Urgent Care was ominous. Mervin had been fighting against the notion, but now he admitted that Skeeter might be dead, too.

CHAPTER FIFTEEN

THE SILENCE IN MERVIN'S TRUCK was deafening. He sat there and breathed slowly. He could feel his heart thumping. The whole thing with Skeeter and Carol Baxley and all those women getting beat up, it was a lot to take in, especially after two hits of Boot's magic bud.

One thought kept rising above all the others racing around in his head, the thought that he might never see Skeeter again. The two men had shared so many interests through the years, cars, girls, and guitars, and not necessarily in that order. In high school, Skeeter had introduced Mervin to Jimi Hendrix, and Mervin returned the favor by helping Skeeter restore an old Ford Bronco.

Skeeter played guitar. Mervin worked on cars. Boot played baseball and a little basketball. Perch . . . well, Perch was Perch, sort of a bookworm. None of them played football, and that was one of the reasons they'd bonded as friends. In a small Southern town in the 1960s, every able-bodied teenage male was expected to at least try out for the team.

Mervin played one year of junior varsity football in ninth grade. He was a second-string defensive back. One day during practice, the offense ran a sweep and Mervin was the only defender on the corner who had a shot at tackling the 190-pound tenth grade running back who had a full head of steam. It was like getting run over by a small truck. Mervin turned in his pads the next day.

The rain started again, and Mervin knew he should head back into town. He also knew he should probably call Boot and tell him they should forget about going out to Skeeter's house. It was borderline criminal activity, and it might be dangerous as well. But he knew it wouldn't do any good. Boot was hardheaded. When his mind was made up, there was no stopping him.

Mervin remembered the time in the winter of 1972 when they were high school seniors. Mervin had saved up and bought a 1969 Chevelle SS-396, electric blue with white leather interior. He loved that car, and it was fast. Pure Detroit muscle.

He'd heard about a lonely stretch of highway up in North Carolina above Maxton where races were held for money on Saturday nights. Mervin started going up there to try his luck. Every now and then, someone got the best of him, but for the most part Mervin blew away the competition. Some didn't take it so well.

Mervin started getting nervous and thought it was best to put an end to his late-night highway racing. But he heard about a big-money race coming up a few weeks later, so he decided one more wouldn't hurt. To be on the safe side, he asked Boot and Skeeter to go with him.

He didn't hold anything back, told them all about the dirty looks and bad karma he'd felt at his last race. Skeeter had reservations, but Boot was raring to go.

On a Saturday night in December, the three long-haired eighteen-year-olds piled into Mervin's Chevelle and headed north. They blasted through the backstreets of Preston, Boot in the backseat and Skeeter up front next to Mervin. The Allman Brothers' *Idlewild South* eight-track blasted from the stereo.

"You got it, run it!" Boot chortled every time Mervin approached a stop sign or red light, and Mervin would drop the Hydromatic transmission down a notch, punch it, and pin them to their seats.

"*Wooooo!*" Boot yelled from the backseat while Skeeter hung on for dear life.

Half an hour later, they were on a dark stretch of North Carolina highway and could see red taillights in the distance. Mervin pulled in behind three or four cars lined up along the side of the road, got out, and walked over to a group of teenagers standing in the headlights of one of the cars. He recognized one of his main adversaries, a Native America boy from Lumberton named Albert Oxendine.

Albert fancied himself a real tough guy, and he drove a bright red Dodge Charger. He was a formidable opponent. Mervin could sense that Albert had convinced his buddies to place money on him, assuring them he would beat Mervin. A loss would not be taken lightly.

Mervin approached, frosty greetings were exchanged, and a monetary value was assigned to the race. It was a lot, just as Mervin hoped. He felt nervous as he agreed and handed over his stake, but he hadn't come all this way to back down now.

He returned to the Chevelle, climbed in, and said, "You guys be ready. I might need you at the other end."

Mervin rolled up to a white line painted across the highway. Albert brought his Dodge alongside. Both cars sat there growling like hungry tigers waiting to pounce on the first thing that moved.

The race was three-quarters of a mile, mostly straight but with one dip and a gentle curve. More kids were waiting at the finish line to verify the winner.

Mervin, Boot, and Skeeter were strapped in with their seatbelts across their laps, and Mervin revved the Chevelle and watched a kid with shaggy blonde hair who stood in the middle of the highway with his arm raised. His arm came down and Mervin floored it.

"Woooo-hoooo!" screamed Boot.

The Chevelle shuttered at every gear change and the engine's high-pitched hum was music to Mervin's ears. For the first quarter mile, the two cars flew through the night side by side. Then Mervin started to pull away. Coming out of the curve with a quarter mile to go, Mervin put it to the floor and left the Charger in the dust. He blasted across the finish line a good three seconds ahead.

"That's what I'm talking about!" yelled Boot as Mervin slowed, swung into a big U-turn, and headed back to the finish line to collect his winnings.

Mervin got out of the car and walked over to where Albert and two of his friends stood with an older guy who was holding the money.

"Good race, Albert," he said. "Tough luck on that last stretch."

Albert wasn't pleased.

"Your car's not legal," he said. "If you want that money, you're going to have to take it."

"What do you mean?" Mervin asked. "My car's as legal as yours. I'll take that money right now, if you don't mind."

"I do mind," Albert said as his two friends stepped to his side.

Mervin heard a car door slam behind him as Boot and Skeeter flanked him. Even at eighteen, Boot was five inches taller than anyone there and he possessed an air of invincibility. For his part, Skeeter crossed his arms and tried to look mean.

"Problem, Mervin?" Boot asked.

"I don't think so."

They all stood there, waiting for someone to make a move, two American muscle cars idling nearby. Finally, the older guy handed the money to Mervin and said, "You won it, man. Fair and square as I saw it."

He looked at Albert, who clinched his fists but didn't say anything.

"Thanks," Mervin said. "Y'all take care."

He pocketed the money, more than $500, and he and Boot and Skeeter walked back to the Chevelle. Calmly, they pulled back onto the highway and drove past Albert, his friends, and the Dodge Charger. When they were clear, Mervin floored it and they sailed back to Preston. He grinned at the Chevy's raw power. No one needed to know he'd removed the standard 396 V-8 and installed a more powerful 427.

When they got home, he split the money three ways with Skeeter and Boot. Boot didn't want to take it, said he wouldn't have missed that ride for the world. Mervin knew right then that these two fellows were his brothers. And being an only child, he relished the feeling.

How did we survive all that? Mervin's pot-addled mind drifted back to the present, and he smiled and squeezed the pickup truck's steering wheel. The Silverado was a nice Chevy, but it was no Chevelle SS. He turned the key and the truck came to life. Mervin sat remembering what Skeeter told him that night on the way back to Preston.

"I looked over at you halfway through the race. You looked so confident, so relaxed. All the fear just left me. I knew we'd win."

Mervin turned on the headlights and windshield wipers and backed the truck out of the parking space behind the Waffle House. He spun through the parking lot and heard the tires bark when he hit the highway back to town.

"I'm gonna find you Skeeter," he said aloud. "I'm gonna find you and we'll make this right."

CHAPTER SIXTEEN

HAZEL UNLOCKED THE DOOR to the studio, stepped inside, and quickly locked it behind her. After all she'd been through, she wasn't taking any chances. She stood for a second and gazed through the large, plate-glass window out across the parking lot to make sure no one followed. Then she closed the blinds.

"Chill out, Hazel," she told herself. "Nobody's stalking you."

She started turning on lights as she walked through the studio—through reception, the control room, and the studio with its amplifiers stacked in corners, forest of microphone stands, and an upright piano pushed against one of the walls. It was chilly in the studio, so she turned up the heat at a thermostat in the hall.

Hazel was planning to mix the WeirdoCat project and do the final mastering of a full-length recording by a gospel singer from rural Horry

County. If she had time, she'd do the prep work for the band from Charlotte, which was due in the studio the next day. She had a full day's work ahead and was glad she did. Hopefully, it would take her mind off the tragedy of Louise Dixon and the worry she had about Carol's whereabouts.

She took a seat and fired up the console, computer, and monitors. She pulled up the WeirdoCat tracks in her ProTools recording software and the first song boomed from the speakers. Hazel adjusted a few levels and experimented with a couple effects. She felt a certain artistic license with this band and thought she could surprise the kids from Lumberton with various unexpected touches.

Midway through the second song, Hazel began to hear a weird knocking that was out of synch with the beat and strangely hollow in its timbre. She zeroed in on the drum tracks, bringing down each one individually to isolate the rhythmic offender. But there was nothing. She scratched her head and decided to go back to the beginning of the song and start over. In the silence of the control room, the knocking started again. Hazel froze. Where is that coming from?

She got up and walked through the open soundproof door and into the studio. It was silent, but then the knocking exploded louder. It was coming from the studio's backdoor that opened onto an unpaved alleyway behind the strip mall. That door was almost never used. The only things in the alley were a couple big garbage dumpsters.

"Who's there?" Hazel shouted. She took out her phone, ready to dial 9-1-1.

"It's me," a voice croaked. "Let me in."

Hazel hesitated. The voice sounded familiar, but she couldn't be sure. "Who's me?"

"Damn it, Hazel, open the door. It's me, Carol."

Hazel almost tripped over a microphone stand in her haste to get to the door. She twisted the deadbolt, pulled open the door, and there was Carol, looking like she'd been on a training mission with the Navy Seals.

"Dear god," Hazel said and pulled Carol into her arms. "Look at you. Where have you been?"

They stood in a long embrace, then Hazel pushed Carol away and said, "What the hell, Carol? I've been going insane!"

She pulled Carol back into a long hug, kissed her, then led her inside and latched the deadbolt on the backdoor. They walked hand-in-hand to the control room and Carol collapsed on the tattered old couch along the back wall. Hazel sat next to her.

"You don't have to tell me everything right now," she said. "Just tell me you're all right."

"I'm fine. Tired, hungry, kind of scared, but I'm okay."

Hazel put her arm around Carol and felt her shiver.

"Come on, let's go home. I'll fix you a cup of tea and something to eat. We've still got some of that vegetable soup I made."

"No! We can't go home," Carol said and tightly gripped Hazel's arm. "It's not safe. They could be watching the house."

"They? Who's they?"

"These men. Or maybe just one man. Friends of a fellow named Ronnie Dixon. I don't know."

Hazel knew Carol was a grounded, pragmatic woman, a doctor of significant intellect and empathy. This didn't sound like her at all. Something awful must have happened to instill this kind of paranoia.

Reading Hazel's mind, Carol said, "Look, I know I'm sounding delirious, but just give me a few minutes. I'm not psychotic, I promise."

"That's the last thing I'd ever accuse you of being. Stretch out here for a while. Catch your breath. I'll fix a pot of coffee and we can decide what to do. I've got a few things to tell you, too."

As Hazel stood up to go make coffee, someone began lightly rapping on the front door.

"Oh, shit!" Carol said. "Don't go. Just stay in here."

"Don't worry. I can peek out and see who it is, but they won't be able to see me."

Hazel leaned slowly into the hall, peeked with one eye, and could make out an older man with gray hair over his ears wearing a baseball cap. Average height and a bit pudgy in jeans and a fleece jacket. He knocked again.

Hazel leaned back into the control room and said, "It's some old guy. He doesn't look scary."

Carol got up and with her hands on Hazel's shoulders, leaned out and peeked down the hall, too.

"I think I know him," she whispered. "He looks like a friend of Skeeter's. That hat he's wearing, I've only seen him from a distance, but he was wearing that same hat. TaylorMade. It's some kind of golf thing."

"Are you sure? What do you want to do?"

"Go out to reception. Don't unlock the door but ask him if his name is Mervin."

"What if it's not?"

"Then hold up your phone so he can see it and say you're calling the police."

Hazel followed Carol's instructions, walking slowly down the hall and into the front room. Mervin saw her through the blinds and raised a hand in greeting.

Hazel called out, "Is your name Mervin?"

"Yes, that's right. Mervin Hayes."

"What do you want?"

"I'm looking for Hazel Owens." Mervin was almost shouting. He wasn't sure how well he was being heard through the glass door. "I've been told she's a friend of Carol Baxley's. Are you her?"

"Who told you that?"

"A policewoman. Sergeant Lowrie."

Hazel stood there for a moment then went to unlock the door. Before she did, she asked, "What do you want to talk to me about?"

For some reason, Mervin looked up and down the sidewalk to make sure no one was within earshot all the while knowing he was the only person standing in the cold outside the studio.

"I know that Carol Baxley and my friend Skeeter Ellington were working together, and now we can't find Skeeter. We're worried and thought you might know something."

Hazel unlocked the door and Mervin stepped inside. Carol appeared behind Hazel and said, "What do you mean you can't find Skeeter?"

"Who are you?" Mervin asked.

"I'm Carol. I really need to talk to Skeeter."

Mervin was dumbstruck. "Do you know how many people are looking for you?" he finally managed.

Hazel stepped around Mervin and locked the door. She closed the blinds completely and said, "Y'all go on down the hall and I'll fix some coffee."

Mervin followed Carol to the control room door, but he took a few more steps and peered into the studio, checking out all the musical equipment. He retraced his steps to the control room and marveled at the spaceship-like interior with its control panel and subdued lighting.

"This place is cool," he said. "I've never been in a real recording studio before. All those knobs and buttons and switches and stuff!"

Mervin sounded like a teenager but didn't care.

"It gets the job done," Hazel said from behind him. "Here, take a seat." She swiveled the captain's chair from in front of the sound board around for Mervin. She sat next to Carol on the couch.

"So, where's Skeeter? Why can't you find him?" Carol said.

"We haven't seen him since Tuesday. A Black guy named Cedric Goins said he saw Skeeter out at Gator's Mini-Mart on Highway 9 last Thursday afternoon. He said he looked kind of rough. That's the last we've heard of him."

"I was supposed to pick him up at Gator's on Thursday," Carol said. "He said he'd get someone to drop him off there so he wouldn't have to leave his truck. We were planning to use my car."

"Use your car for what?"

Carol hesitated then said, "We had to take someone to the bus station." She paused again. "The bus station in Florence."

Florence was thirty-five miles away.

"Look, Carol," Mervin said. "We know all about what you and

Skeeter have been up to. He confided in one of our pals, a fellow named Henry Gordon."

"Perch," Carol said.

"That's right."

"He told me all about you and Perch and Boot," Carol said. "He said if there was ever any trouble or I felt threatened or scared, I could count on any of y'all for help."

Mervin felt a rush of emotion at the thought of Skeeter's trust in him and his friends.

"So why Gator's?" he said. "And why Florence?"

"Gator's isn't all that far from Skeeter's house, and we've been trying to be unpredictable in our movements. That's the reason for going to Florence. Just trying to keep certain folks off the scent. We thought someone might be keeping an eye on the bus station here.

"I was going to pick him up and then we were going to pick up a woman named Louise Dixon and take her to Florence. She was going to meet us at the post office on Main Street. I'd arranged for her to take a room in a women's shelter in Savannah. But neither Skeeter nor Louise were where they were supposed to be. I've been looking for Louise for three days."

Hazel and Mervin looked at each other.

"What?" Carol said.

Mervin nodded at Hazel.

"They found Louise this morning," Hazel said quietly. "She was in her car in the parking lot at Urgent Care. She'd been strangled."

Carol's face went white, and she rocked forward on the couch.

"Oh, god, I knew something like this might happen."

Hazel put her arm around Carol and they rocked gently together back and forth. Carol began to cry. No one spoke for a minute or two.

"I have something to tell you," Hazel said once Carol had cried herself out. "Louise's husband, Ronnie Dixon, threatened me here in the parking lot night before last. He was looking for you."

Carol's tear-streaked face filled with shock.

"He *threatened* you? How?"

Hazel pulled her close and told her the whole story about her encounter with Ronnie, the support Barbara Lowrie had given her, and how the police had apprehended Ronnie just a few hours earlier.

"He's in custody right now," she said, and Carol sagged into her, a mixture of relief and exhaustion.

"I never figured Ronnie Dixon would have the balls to do something like that," Carol said. "He always seemed to be a blowhard. A good ol' boy, but all mouth and no trousers."

The tension eased and Mervin shifted anxiously in his seat, ready to leave.

"Carol, I'm really glad you're okay," he said. "I'm really sorry about Louise Dixon and I don't mean to be callous, but none of this gets us any closer to finding Skeeter."

"I know," Carol said. "I'm sorry. I don't know what to tell you."

"What will you do now?"

"Don't worry about us," Hazel said. "We'll be okay. And we'll help you find Skeeter."

Mervin appreciated Hazel's determination but didn't think it would make much difference. The death of Louise Dixon changed everything. Someone out there was filled with rage and hell bent on revenge. *None of us are safe now*, Mervin thought.

He told Hazel and Carol to be careful and to stay in touch. He made sure they had his phone number and those for Boot and Perch. He walked down the hall, stepped outside, and heard Hazel lock the door behind him. Zipping up his fleece jacket, Mervin sighed and saw his breath turn into a cloud. It was getting colder.

CHAPTER SEVENTEEN

LIKE MOST SMALL TOWNS, Preston had seen its share of tragedy and heartbreak. The murder cases Barbara Lowrie had worked were mostly shootings during convenience store robberies, arguments in bars that escalated to gunplay, or gang nonsense that was increasingly taking the lives of Black teenagers.

Wives and girlfriends had been severely battered in Preston by their significant others, but those tragic events ended quickly when the men were caught or turned themselves in and readily confessed.

But something about the murder of Louise Dixon shook Barbara to her core. The victim had not been beaten or tortured. Besides the thin bruise around her neck, there were no visible injuries. She had looked peaceful, almost like she was sleeping.

And yet there was an aura of evil about the killing that gave Barbara a sense of foreboding she couldn't easily explain. Louise Dixon had been murdered somewhere else, driven in her car to the Urgent Care, and placed gently behind the wheel. It was obviously a message intended to intimidate Carol Baxley. But it was also an act of such brazen arrogance that it made Barbara frightful of what might lie ahead.

Given the evidence they'd gleaned from Hazel Owens and Henry Gordon, Barbara and her colleagues had felt certain that Ronnie Dixon was responsible for his wife's death. But after a full day of being interrogated, Ronnie steadfastly denied killing his wife. He'd confessed to all sorts of physical and psychological abuse of Louise, but he said he could never kill her. He said he loved her.

Barbara had watched the interviews, seen the anguish on Ronnie's face, and she eventually started to believe him. She'd also watched the reactions of Chief Holt and Detective Stanton when Ronnie admitted the abuse, and while they listened closely and were clearly concerned, Barbara got an unsettling notion that they didn't completely get it. Surely they wouldn't condone a man knocking his wife around, but at the same time, maybe they didn't think it was any of their business. It gave Barbara an insight as to why women were reluctant to report abuse to the police.

Barbara hoped her ideas about Holt and Stanton were misplaced, and to be honest, she had every confidence in them to work hard on the case. Besides, this was a question of murder, not just spousal abuse.

And that brought Barbara back to the central question. If Ronnie didn't kill Louise Dixon, who did? Who else would have a motive for killing her?

Perch lived in one of the old antebellum homes on Preston's downtown streets. Its two white columns, wide front porch, and ornate hardwood stairs that led to the second floor had reminded Janice of *Gone with the Wind*. She always joked about needing a horse and carriage to complete the effect. Perch would laugh and admit it might not be a bad way to get around town.

But he had settled for a Ford F-150, the same one he was backing down the driveway behind the house to a two-car garage, an addition from the 1980s. He got out, hoisted the garage door open, and lowered the truck's tailgate. The truck's bed was filled with bags of mulch and wood chips, a few gallons of paint and a new shovel.

Perch and Janice had worked hard restoring the old house, and they'd had fun doing it. But recently Perch had let things go. He just couldn't muster the energy since Janice wasn't there to pick paint colors, light fixtures, or decide whether to plant red tips or camellias in the spacious lawn.

But he'd put things off long enough. It was time to get some projects done. Besides, his doctor had been telling him to stay busy, lose some weight, and stop self-medicating with booze.

"So what are you saying, Doc?" Perch once asked. "You're saying I'm depressed and have anxiety issues? Wow. That's a brilliant diagnosis." He'd apologize for the sarcasm then head to Bill's for a couple drinks.

But things were different now. All the nonsense with Skeeter and the battered women and the death of Louise Dixon had forced his hand. Perch needed to get moving. He would do a little landscaping along the front of the house this morning and paint the downstairs bathroom after lunch.

He walked back to the truck to fetch his phone from where he'd tossed it on the passenger's seat, and just as he opened the door it began to buzz.

"Hello."

"Mr. Gordon, this is Detective Stanton. We met yesterday at the police station."

"Right," Perch said. "What's up?"

"We've had a development and I need your help."

"Louise Dixon."

"You've heard," Stanton said. "News travels in this town."

"I was downtown at the hardware store this morning, and well, you know how word gets around."

"Yeah, I do. Look, when we talked yesterday, you said you had some kind of records of what your friend and Carol Baxley were doing. I need to see those and was hoping you could drop them off at the station."

"Sure, no problem," Perch said. "I kind of figured they might help so I pulled them out last night. There are six cases in all, including the first one that got this whole thing started." Perch paused. "I should tell you, the first victim wouldn't report her husband because she thought he had friends in the police. She was scared to go to you all."

Stanton was quiet for a second. "That's a serious allegation."

"I ain't allegatin' anything," Perch said. "I'm just telling you what the woman told Skeeter."

"I'll take it under advisement," Stanton conceded. "When can you get here?"

"Give me a little while. I just got home and need to unload this stuff from the hardware store. I'll be there in an hour or so."

"Thanks," Stanton said and abruptly hung up.

Sheesh, thought Perch. *What have I gotten myself into?*

He started unloading the truck, stacking the bags of mulch where Janice's Honda Accord used to sit. "Old Reliable" they called it. She drove it for twenty-one years.

When he'd finished, Perch closed the garage door, slammed the truck's tailgate, and headed inside to collect Skeeter's files to take to the police station. They didn't amount to much, just a few pages about each of the six cases. But they revealed in detail the abuses that had been inflicted on the women and the action Skeeter and Carol Baxley had taken to provide escape from the torment.

Perch read through them the night before and was shocked by the brutality of the abusers. He had zero comprehension of how a man could commit such physical violence against a woman he supposedly loved.

Even if love wasn't involved, the acts perpetrated by these men were heinous and merciless and made Perch shudder. Just the thought of someone raising a hand to Janice made his blood boil. Sure, they'd had arguments and yelled at each other, but they always calmed down, made up, and usually ended up laughing about whatever they'd been arguing about.

Perch had heard all the psychological reasons why frustrated men vented their insecurities and inadequacies by beating up their women, but he wasn't buying it. Such men were messed up. It was more than a chemical imbalance or synaptic malfunction. They were just plain mean.

It reminded Perch of something Skeeter said months ago. They were out at Skeeter's house in early summer, watching a Braves game and having a few beers. Skeeter said, "You know, Perch, ninety-five percent of the men in Preston County love their women, cherish them even, and wouldn't dream of hurting them. But the other five percent, they're hateful. They have no qualms about beating up a woman, so they'll feel better about themselves. I'm no psychiatrist but I know an evil act when I see it. It scares me."

Skeeter had a right to be scared, and now Perch was too. He feared something dreadful might have happened to his friend, and he worried that his role in all this might have dragged him into harm's way.

"Can't dwell on that," Perch said aloud as he extracted the files from a locked drawer in his desk. "It's time we took the fight to the bad guys."

CHAPTER EIGHTEEN

HAZEL FINALLY CONVINCED CAROL that they would be safe if they went home and called Barbara Lowrie. They should tell her everything.

"She'll protect us," Hazel said. "She'll make sure no one can get to us."

Carol wasn't so sure, but she allowed Hazel to lead her outside to the Jeep Cherokee and climbed in the passenger's seat while Hazel held the door.

"Where's your car?" Hazel asked.

"Over there," Carol said, pointing to a far corner of the parking lot past Las Camadres.

"Let's just leave it there for now," Hazel said. "It'll be okay."

It was mid-afternoon and 301 was busy. Traffic backed up at every red light, and Hazel could sense Carol's anxiety every time a car rolled up and stopped next to them. But a few minutes later, they turned off the busy thoroughfare and were rolling down the quiet streets on their side of town.

Hazel turned into the two dirt ruts that passed for a driveway at their house and she and Carol climbed out of the Cherokee. Their next-door neighbor, a woman named Vickie Vanderhall, came out her front door. Vickie was raising two kids fathered by two different men.

"Hey, ladies. Y'all doing all right?" she called. "Haven't seen you in a while."

"It's all good," Hazel said. "How's Stephon? He doing better in school?"

"Yes, ma'am. I appreciate you talking to him."

"Excellent! Tell him to come over this weekend and I'll take him to the studio."

"He'll love that," Vickie said, waved and headed for her most recent car, a slightly worn Chevy Blazer that still sported the paper tags from a used-car dealership.

Hazel and Carol had watched with fascination as Vickie pulled up to her house in a different car every four or five months. Probably because of wobbly family finances, they thought, but not for lack of trying.

They knew Vickie had worked all morning serving biscuits through a drive-through window, and now she was off to do a shift behind the register at a Mini-Mart out on 301. Vickie doted on her two boys, thirteen-year-old Stephon and six-year-old Delancey, and they loved her. Stephon wanted to be a musician and he loved hanging out with Hazel.

Her brief chat with Vickie lifted Hazel's spirits. In fact, it had given her a shot of optimism. Hazel and Carol had cool neighbors.

Their other next-door neighbors, an old couple named Roger and Mildred McLean, had not known what to make of the black-leather-clad woman with spiky hair at first, especially when the lady doctor moved in with her. Roger had worked at the long-shuttered carpet factory and Mildred was a quiet-but-tough housewife and staunch churchgoer.

It had taken a while, but suspicions thawed and now they all got along like family. Mildred was always bringing over a pie or leftover casserole for Hazel and Carol. The home cooking was always gratefully received.

They'll look out for us, Hazel thought, *just like we'd look out for them.* Vickie, too. And meeting Mervin Hayes earlier had given her the same feeling.

Hazel unlocked the front door and led the way into the house. Carol followed and was knocked onto the living-room couch by a joyous Rufus, who jumped atop her and began to lick her face. His tail thumped the sofa cushions so hard puffs of dust plumed. Carol basked in the unconditional love, her arms around Rufus and a big grin on her face.

"I'm glad to see you, too, boy," Carol managed to sputter, "now get down. Get down!"

It took a minute to calm Rufus and get him off the couch, but his tail was still thumping as he stretched out on the floor. Hazel smiled. The family was back together.

"I'm going to call Barbara Lowrie," she said. "Tell her that you're home."

Carol pulled her feet up underneath her and smiled.

"She likes you, you know."

"And I like her," Hazel said. "But it's not like that."

"I know."

Hazel flopped into a big easy chair and began unlacing her hiking boots. It was good to be home.

"How much should we tell her?" Carol asked.

"She knows pretty much everything. She knows about Ronnie Dixon and how he beat Louise. She knows about what you and this Skeeter guy were up to. They're out looking for Skeeter. So is the sheriff's department."

"They don't know everything," Carol said, her eyes staring into space. She shook herself, started to get up off the couch. "I need to call the clinic. I know they're probably run off their feet." She stood. "And what about you? I know you've got a lot going on at the studio. I don't want to keep you from your work."

"Babe, don't you worry. I've got it all under control," Hazel said, not bothered by her little white lie. "Let's just get through this thing."

"Poor Louise. Such a sweet girl. Dammit Hazel! We need to make somebody pay."

Hazel stood, putting her arm around Carol's waist and spinning her like a ballroom dancer. "That's the kind of talk I like to hear."

———⌣———

The squad room bustled with phone calls and witness statements being sorted, assignments being made. Not a single Preston patrol officer had dared punch out at 6 p.m., and even the senior officers and county deputies showed no signs of packing up for home.

Formerly an exclusive club for white men with guns and badges, the Preston police station now buzzed with more than a dozen Black officers and three women in addition to Sergeant Barbara Lowrie.

Barbara watched it all from behind her desk where she had just finished reading the post-mortem report on Louise Dixon. It confirmed that death was due to strangulation. It also revealed bruising and vaginal tearing, indicating that Louise had been raped. *Add that charge to the bastard's rap sheet,* Barbara thought.

She walked out to reception, looked through the glass doors, and saw three television crews from regional stations getting ready to go live for the evening news. Their spotlights illuminated reporters who were checking their notes and casting long shadows across the sidewalk.

"It'll take this town a long time to get over this," Barbara said. She sensed Jimmy Glover at her shoulder.

"It's gonna take a long time for me to get over it," he said. "Boss wants to see you. They've finished going over that stuff Henry Gordon dropped off."

"You mean Perch?"

"Yeah, Perch," Jimmy said and grinned.

Barbara went back to the squad room and saw Chief Holt, Detective Stanton, and a State Law Enforcement Department agent in the conference room. Holt waved her over to join them.

"We're working through the notes kept by August Ellington that identify six men who abused their partners during the past twenty-four months," Holt told the group. "Three of them are from Preston, one from

Nichols, one from Mullins, and the sixth is an old boy who lives out in the middle of nowhere between Lake View and the state line. We've tracked down five of them, and quite frankly, it wasn't that hard. Even the old boy out in the woods was easy to find. Officers have talked to them and it's becoming fairly conclusive that none of them had anything to do with the death of Louise Dixon. They were contrite, regretted their past actions, and a couple even said they missed their wives."

"Yeah, right," Barbara muttered under her breath.

"Who's the sixth man?" Stanton asked.

"Name is Silas Conn. He happens to be the first offender Ellington acted on. Conn no longer lives in Preston, and we have no idea where he is."

"We'll track him down," said the SLED agent, whose last name was Mankey, Barbara remembered.

"Thanks," Holt said. "It's too bad we can't connect any of these men to Ronnie or Louise Dixon, but we're still following up on a few things. There's forensic evidence from Louise Dixon's car that has to be processed, but I'm not hopeful. We're running out of ideas. Any suggestions?"

"There was one thing," Stanton said. "Ronnie Dixon told us about an individual named Harold Cephus who contacted him about helping him with his problem wife. Called himself the Deacon. Dixon said the guy was, and I quote, 'weird in a scary way.' But he said he didn't have any contact with him after that last phone call. Dixon said he was introduced to the guy weeks ago by someone named Luther Peacock."

"I know Luther," Barbara said. "He's spent the night in the drunk tank a couple times. I say let's bring him in and find out about this Harold Cephus."

"That's the weird thing," Stanton said. "We've already run every ID check you can think of, and there's no mention of a Harold Cephus. Nothing. No birth certificate. Nothing with the Motor Vehicles. Nothing."

"That is weird," Holt said. "But I agree with Barbara. Let's bring in Luther and see what he can tell us about this Cephus character. I'll tell Pete Shumpert to find him. In the meantime, let's double down on finding Ellington and Carol Baxley. I believe they're key to finding out who murdered Louise Dixon."

"And raped," Barbara said.

"Yes, sorry." Holt's voice softened. "You're right, Barbara."

"I'll follow up with Hazel Owens and Mervin Hayes," she said. "If nothing else, I feel we should keep them in the loop."

Stanton frowned, but Holt agreed and told her to relay any new information as soon as she gets it.

"This has been a stressful day," he said. "We all need to get some rest." He rubbed the stubble on his cheek and seemed lost in thought for a moment. "I've got to admit. Ellington and Carol Baxley were doing good work. That system they put together to help those women is so simple and efficient, it makes you wonder why something like that couldn't work in more official channels."

Jimmy Glover poked his head into the room.

"Sorry to interrupt, boss, but two of those TV reporters want to talk to you."

"Tell them I'll be there in a few minutes." Holt rose from his seat. "Thanks, everybody. I'll see you in the morning."

Notes were gathered and chairs pushed back under the table. Barbara went to her desk, logged off the computer, and locked her regulation sidearm, a Glock .9 millimeter, in a desk drawer. Like every other Preston police officer, she had other weapons.

As she turned to leave, the phone on her desk began to ring.

"Sergeant Lowrie," she said, exhaustion in her voice.

"Barbara, is that you?" Hazel said. "You don't sound good."

"Hazel, what's going on? I was just about to leave. It's been a long day."

"Can you come by the house on your way home?"

"I'm really tired, Hazel. Can it wait?"

"Carol's back."

"What?" Barbara glanced quickly around to see if Holt or Stanton were still in the room.

"Please, stop by and see us. Just you. Carol's shook up but she has a lot to tell you."

Barbara saw Stanton talking to the SLED agent as they headed for the backdoor to the parking lot. Holt would be out front in the glare of a spotlight talking to a TV reporter.

"I'll be there in fifteen minutes," she said. She unlocked the desk drawer and holstered the Glock.

CHAPTER NINETEEN

LUTHER PEACOCK COULDN'T BELIEVE Louise Dixon was dead. He'd checked on her before he left her with Deacon at the shack Saturday night. She was scared but seemed to be okay despite the duct tape around her ankles and wrists. He told her everything would be all right and that his friend would take her back into town. Louise had nodded and tried to smile. At least Luther thought she tried to smile.

Now there were TV reporters in Preston, search crews in the woods, and every cop in the world was out looking for whoever killed Louise. Luther didn't know what to do, but he was certain Deacon had killed Louise, and he was damn sure there was enough evidence out in that dilapidated shack that would point back to both him and the Deacon. He couldn't call Ronnie because he was still being held at the police station. He wasn't about to call Deacon because, quite frankly, he was scared of that nutcase. Maybe he should go back out there and burn down the shack. Then he could pack a few things and get out of town for a while.

"Shit, shit, shit," he said, standing in his doublewide's cramped little kitchen, both hands on his head while a pot of canned chili simmered on the stove. "What have I gotten myself into?"

Luther went to pour the chili into a bowl, but before he could pick up the pot, the intro to Marshall Tucker's *Take the Highway* chirped from his phone on the table. He checked the number, took a deep breath, and answered.

"Hey, man. What's happening? Where you been?"

"Did you kill her?" asked the harsh, ragged voice.

Luther was shocked.

"Did I kill her? What are you talking about? That's crazy. You were there. You know she was fine when I left the other night to go back into town. I left her with you."

Luther cringed.

"Well, I didn't kill her," Deacon said.

"I sure as hell didn't kill her."

"Somebody did."

Luther quaked with panic. He wanted to get off the phone.

"I think we should burn that shack down," he said. "There's bound to be all kinds of evidence of us and her in that place."

"Nah, it'll be okay. They'll never find it."

"I don't know, man. A few of those Preston cops know all the back roads."

"Don't worry about it. Just stay calm and go about your business. Act like you don't know anything because you don't know anything."

Luther knew this wasn't true, but he wasn't going to argue.

"Sounds good. You're right. We can't tell them anything. We don't know who killed Louise."

"That's the time. Now be cool and I'll call you in a couple days."

"Right. That sounds great. Take care of yourself."

Luther ended the call and wondered how he'd ever thought this guy was someone to befriend. When Deacon had showed up at the shack Saturday night, the quiet intensity that Luther had mistaken for charisma had become something far more menacing.

Luther's chili was boiling out of control on the stove, but it didn't matter. No longer hungry, he took the pot off the burner and turned off the stove. He turned off the light in the kitchen and hurried to his bedroom where he grabbed a large duffel bag and filled it with clothes. He went in the bathroom and tossed his razor, toothbrush, toothpaste, deodorant, and a hotel sample bottle of shampoo into a shaving kit.

He got down on his knees and slid an old wooden box out from under the bed, removing the Smith & Wesson revolver his daddy had given him. He put it and a box of bullets next to the shaving kit on top of the clothes in the duffel. He pulled on a hooded sweatshirt and his hunting jacket over that. Luther made sure all the lights were off then stepped out of the doublewide and locked the door behind him.

"Just get to the interstate, just get to the interstate," he chanted as he pulled open the door to his Ford Ranger, tossed the duffel inside, and climbed in after it. Luther had a cousin in Florida who he got along with, and he knew he could crash down there for a few weeks.

Luther cranked the Ranger, circled through the yard, and was turning onto the two-lane road in front of his trailer when he saw the headlights of a big, black Dodge Ram pickup on the opposite shoulder.

"Damn! He was calling from outside the house," Luther said and he floored it and tore down the road that led to the highway that intersected with I-95. *Just get to the interstate, just get to the interstate.*

The Ranger's headlights threw a cone of light off the white lines of the middle of the road and lit up the tall pine trees on both sides. The truck shuddered because it wasn't used to going so fast, but it was no match for the powerful Dodge right on its bumper.

Luther was blinded by the headlights in his rearview mirror, and he knew he had no choice. He slowed and eased onto the side of the road. The big Dodge pulled in behind him. Luther looked in his side mirror and saw the driver's side door swing open. He reached into the duffel bag and gripped the Smith & Wesson.

Becca found Mervin in the den in his chair, tears running down his face.

"Did you get news of Skeeter or are you crying at the Andy Griffith Show again?"

The familiar whistling theme song filled the room.

"I can't help it," Mervin said. "It was the one where Opie accidentally kills a mama bird and Andy makes him raise her chickadees."

"Winkin', Blinkin', and Nod."

"That's them. Anyway, when they're grown, Andy tells Opie he has to open the cage and set them free. He does it then gets sad because the cage seems so empty."

"And Andy says—"

"'But don't the trees seem nice and full.' It gets me every time."

Mervin looks like he might puddle up again.

"Come on, Gomer. We've got pork chops and tater tots."

Mervin lifted himself out of the chair with a grunt and followed Becca to the kitchen. She poured glasses of tea, and they tucked into their supper. Becca recounted her day with the third graders, and Mervin told her about his visit to Hazel Owens' recording studio and meeting Carol Baxley.

"Whoa," Becca said, a tater tot suspended in midair on her fork. "Thank goodness she's okay. Where's she been?"

Mervin told her that Carol and Skeeter were trying to help Louise Dixon get out of town and away from an abusive husband, but neither Louise nor Skeeter were where they were supposed to be at a pre-arranged time on Thursday.

"She was freaked out and decided to lay low until she knew what was going on. I don't know where she's been hiding, but she turned up at the back door to Hazel's studio this morning."

"Wow," Becca said. "So she doesn't know where Skeeter is?"

"No, and that's the sad part."

They ate in silence for a few minutes then Becca asked, "Did you have breakfast with Boot?"

"Oh, yeah," Mervin said. "We met at the Waffle House."

"And?"

Mervin waited a couple beats, sighed dramatically, and said, "Yes, I got you some weed. It's good, too."

"You tried it?"

"It was offered, and I certainly didn't want to offend Boot. It was the courteous thing to do."

"Mervin Hayes, I'm gonna have to find you a job. I can't have my husband cruising around town stoned out of his gourd on a Monday morning."

"You're right. I'm sorry. I'll take the pot back to Boot and tell him I need to go on the straight and narrow."

Becca bent her fork back and flipped a tater tot at Mervin. It smacked him in the forehead and left a ketchup spot the size of a nickel. They were laughing so hard they almost didn't hear the tapping on the back door.

Mervin got up and pulled aside the curtain on the door's window.

"It's Perch," he said and opened the door. "Hey, man, what's up? Come on in. We're just finishing supper. Becca, is there another pork chop over there?"

"I've already eaten but thanks all the same," Perch said. "Hey, Becca. How was your day with the kids?"

"Okay . . . you sure you won't have anything? A glass of tea?"

"That sounds good."

Becca got up to pour a glass of tea and Perch took a seat at the table.

"Mervin, you've got a splotch of ketchup on your forehead."

"She's been molesting me again, Perch. I don't know what to do about it."

"I'm worried. Becca," Perch said. "How long has this been going on?"

Becca set the glass of tea on the table in front of Perch and stared down at him.

"Perch, you wouldn't believe what I have to endure," Mervin said.

"She's either hitting me in the face with ketchup-covered tater tots or humiliating me for crying at the Andy Griffith Show."

"That's cruel, Mervin. I cry at Andy Griffith reruns all the time."

They couldn't hold it any longer and laughter erupted in the kitchen. When he finally caught his breath, Mervin wiped the tears from his eyes and said, "But it's true, Perch. Becca doesn't understand why I get so emotional during Andy Griffith."

"Okay, that's it," Becca said. "You guys can sit here and talk about Andy Griffith all you want. I'm going next door to talk to Amy Sue. Perch, good to see you as always. Try to keep him in line."

"Don't worry, Becca. If he gets all weepy, I'll slap him around."

"You and Amy Sue go easy on the wine," Mervin said as Becca went out the back door. He and Perch sat at the kitchen table and talked. Mervin told Perch about meeting Hazel Owens and Carol Baxley, and Perch related his trip to the police station to drop off Skeeter's files.

"I don't know, I didn't get a sense of any progress when I talked to that Stanton guy," Perch said. "He just took the files and said they'd let me know if there was any news. This little town, man, sometimes I just want to pack up and get out of here."

"This little town ain't no different from any other little town," Mervin said. "Except maybe we're in the South so we're fat and dumb with little motivation to change, but we still do the best we can."

"That's bullshit. If we did the best we could, we wouldn't be fat and dumb, and we might be motivated to make things better. At least we might be motivated to look outside our meager existence and find something more fulfilling."

"Meager existence, I like that. It's one of the reasons me and Becca like living here."

"Come on, Mervin. Don't go all New Age on me. You know what I'm talking about."

Mervin knew exactly what Perch was talking about. Years ago, he'd often dwelled on the insular, limited lives led by the people in Preston. He wondered how they maintained any sense of purpose and optimism.

Then he and Becca made a trip to Ireland—she'd always wanted to visit the "old sod" as she called it—and Mervin sat in pubs and talked to local folks in villages who had the same range of life experiences as people in Preston. It was a revelation. He realized that people all around the world were anchored in tight, close-knit communities and would never experience anything else.

You live your life and make the best of it, he decided. You don't worry about what might be or what might have been. You sell cars or insurance. You grow soybeans or pot. Whatever it is, you just get on with it.

But Perch had a point. In times like these, it would be nice to have a little more technical know-how and intellectual savvy in the people who were out looking for Skeeter.

"Well, now that Carol Baxley has reappeared, things might start moving faster," Mervin said. "Maybe we'll get some news tomorrow."

"Have you talked to Boot?"

"We had breakfast at the Waffle House, but I haven't heard from him since. Damn! We said we'd call you and meet up at Bill's for happy hour. I completely forgot."

"You should call him," Perch said.

Mervin brought up Boot's number on his phone and touched the screen. Boot answered right away.

"Hey, Boot, I'm sorry I didn't get back to you about going to Bill's."

"No worries. I just got home anyway."

"Where've you been? What's going on?"

"Nothing much, but I did have an interesting afternoon."

"What have you been up to?"

"Let's just say I've got a lead on some places the police might not have looked for Skeeter and Carol Baxley."

"Carol Baxley came home today," Mervin said. "But she doesn't know where Skeeter is."

There was silence on the phone then Boot said, "That's good news and bad news. Get in touch with Perch and let's meet at Bill's at four-thirty tomorrow."

"Perch is right here. We'll see you there."

Mervin set his phone down on the kitchen table.

"Boot's been roaming around," he told Perch. "I think he's on to something."

"So, we're getting together tomorrow?"

"Yeah, four-thirty at Bill's."

They sat in silence for a while. Then Mervin said, "You want a drink? I've got some fifteen-year-old Dewar's."

"I can't say no to that. Just a couple of cubes in mine."

Mervin got up, fetched the bottle from one cabinet and two glasses from another and poured a nice measure in each. He and Perch sipped the whisky and sat in silence with their thoughts.

"This is good," Perch said.

Mervin nodded. He lifted the bottle to freshen their drinks.

Carol was still on the couch with Rufus curled up next to her when Barbara Lowrie rang the doorbell. Hazel showed Barbara into the living room, and Rufus jumped down to greet her.

"Carol, are you okay?"

"I'm fine. A lot better now that I'm home."

Barbara sat across from Carol and Rufus pushed his head into her hand for some attention. Barbara obliged and started scratching his chin.

"So many people have been worried about you," Barbara said. "I'm glad you're all right."

It was heartfelt and Carol and Hazel felt it. The shock from seeing the body of Louise Dixon twelve hours earlier was still evident in the lines around Barbara's eyes. *She fears the worse for Carol,* Hazel thought.

"I've got work to do," Hazel said. "The band from Charlotte texted me a while ago and said they're looking forward to getting here tomorrow and seeing the studio."

"You go ahead," Carol said. "I'll talk to Barbara."

Hazel thanked Barbara for coming on her own then went down the hall to fetch her laptop and do some preliminary work for The Suburbs of Hysteria.

"So what happened, Carol? Where've you been?"

Rufus hopped back onto the couch and Carol put her arm around him. She told Barbara about the escape plan she and Skeeter had put together for Louise, and how neither Skeeter nor Louise turned up at the appointed time to put it into action. She had waited at Gator's Mini-Mart as long as she dared before hightailing it out of there.

"Something was wrong. I had a terrible feeling something bad had happened or was about to happen. Turns out I was right."

"Where did you go when you left Gator's?"

Carol curled up tighter and scratched Rufus behind the ear. He closed his eyes and let out a deep moan of appreciation.

"I went to one of the women's shelters that's been helping us," Carol said quietly. "But that's all I'm going to tell you. You'll understand why these places depend on discretion."

"Don't worry, I get it."

Barbara told Carol about Louise Dixon's death, the apprehension of Ronnie Dixon, and how she felt he wasn't responsible for the murder.

"I agree," Carol said. "From what Skeeter and I could tell, Ronnie was an asshole, but he wasn't a killer. However, he might have gotten mixed up with some other men who are capable of violence, maybe even murder."

"Like who?"

"I'm not exactly sure. But there was a group of them who hung out together and they had a ringleader, some fellow who kept 'em stirred up."

Barbara debated how much she should tell Carol about Ronnie Dixon's mention of a man named Harold Cephus who'd contacted him about Louise. Before she could decide, Carol continued.

"Skeeter had a run in with a man at a filling station last week. This guy walked up and asked if he was Skeeter Ellington then just turned and walked away. It scared Skeeter. He felt like it had something to do with me and him and what we've been doing."

"Did Skeeter tell you who he was?"

"He didn't know him but said not to worry about it. Said the guy was 'all talk and no bottle.' I wasn't so sure Skeeter believed that."

"Carol, you do realize that Louise Dixon's body was left at the Urgent Care to intimidate you?"

"I know that. Someone's trying to scare me and Skeeter. But I don't care. Bring it on. I hid out for three days and I didn't like it. I'm going to work tomorrow."

"You're also coming down to the police station to give an official statement."

"No problem," Carol said.

"And another thing. What you and Skeeter were doing is out in the open now. Lots of people know you were involved. So as far as I'm concerned, you're under police protection. I'm gonna look out for you. I give you my word."

"Thanks, Barbara. That means a lot," Carol said and she squeezed Rufus tighter.

CHAPTER TWENTY

PETE SHUMPERT POUNDED on Luther Peacock's door but was pretty sure no one was home. Luther's truck wasn't parked out front and there was no sound from inside.

Pete walked down the steps and circled the doublewide. A busted-up kayak, old boat trailer, and a mountain-bike frame with no wheels were scattered across a backyard that was only fifty-feet deep before giving way to thick woods. The blinds were closed on all the windows so there was no way to see inside.

Nothing to do but head back into town and ask some of Luther's friends where he might be, Pete thought. He walked past his squad car, a Ford Crown Vic he'd driven for years, down the dirt driveway. Monday's rain left the ground soft, and Pete saw a set of tire tracks that clearly turned left away from town when they hit the two-lane blacktop. The tires had thrown some dirt, too, so whoever it was had really punched the gas.

Pete climbed into the Crown Vic and turned left onto the road. Five minutes later, he saw an old red-and-white, two-tone Ford Ranger parked on the shoulder and knew right away it was Luther's. He pulled in behind it and left the squad car running.

The Ranger's hood was cold and the cab empty, so Pete slipped on a latex glove and tried the driver's side door. It opened with a creak, and Pete peered inside.

"Ah, damn," he said and stepped back quickly.

The seat, door, and window on the passenger's side were splattered with blood and what looked like specks of bone and small chunks of meat.

Pete stood for a few seconds outside the truck, his hand raised to cover his mouth. Then he hurried back to the Crown Vic and called Jimmy Glover at dispatch on the radio.

"Jimmy, this is Pete, come in, over."

"Hey, Pete. What's up? Over."

"I'm on County Road 15 a couple miles or so past Luther Peacock's place. You know it?"

"I know it," Jimmy responded.

"I'm outside the city limits so you need to tell Chief Holt to call Sheriff Whittington and for both of them to get out here. I've got a crime scene. Tell them to look for my car on the right side of the road."

"Will do. Over and out."

Pete cradled the microphone in its clamp on the dashboard and leaned against his car to wait. It was quiet on the lonely stretch of highway except for the birds calling to each other as they flitted around looking for some breakfast. The sun was getting higher, hitting the trees and throwing shadows across the road.

"Damn it, Luther," Pete sighed. "Looks like you really screwed up this time."

The Suburbs of Hysteria held a closing chord, the drummer did a brief run, and the song ended with a cymbal crash.

Hazel gazed through the large glass window at four inquiring faces, punched on the studio mic, and said, "Very cool! I loved the middle part when you dropped into a minor key. Your guitar tones are great, too, by the way."

The four musicians in the studio visibly relaxed, thanked Hazel, and started recapping their performance.

Hazel was enjoying herself. This band was good. They were well-rehearsed, and their material was smart and engaging. She thought of DJ and how he would have loved working with these guys. She wished he could be smiling down, getting off on the music being made in his studio, but Hazel didn't believe in that sort of thing. She just took comfort in the fact that she'd kept DJ's dream alive, and on days like this, it was especially meaningful.

One of the guitarists, a guy named Ryan, poked his head into the control room and said they wanted to take a short break before starting another tune.

"Absolutely," Hazel said.

"I'm going to pop down the road to a convenience store I saw and get some beer. You want anything?"

"There's a better selection at the one across the highway," Hazel said. "But you'll need to cross the road at the stop light on the corner. And still be careful. I'll take a bottle of Fiji water," and she reached in her backpack for some money.

"Nope, it's on me," Ryan said, and he was gone.

Hazel picked up her phone and decided to give Carol a call. They'd made a pact early on to avoid calling each other at work, but recent circumstances called for a suspension of that rule. Her call went straight to voice mail.

"Hey, just thinking about you and wondering how it went at the police station and how it's going at work. No need to call me back. Love you."

Within ten seconds, Hazel's phone buzzed.

"I'm glad you called," Carol said. "It went fine at the police station. Barbara was great and the police chief seemed okay. He agreed that I needed protection, so don't be surprised if there's a police car outside the house when you get home."

"How's work? I bet they were glad to see you."

"Oh, god, you wouldn't believe. Lots of hugs and crying. And poor Jodi Mercer. Finding Louise Dixon's body like that has really traumatized that poor girl. They said it didn't hit her until later and she became really emotional. Joyce Young, one of the nurses, told Jodi she could take some time off, but she wanted to come in. When I walked through the door, she burst out crying all over again. But I think she'll be okay. How are The Suburbs of Hysteria?"

"Really good," Hazel said. "Nice guys and very talented. I think you'll like their stuff. It's kind of jangly with a little edge. Reminds me a little bit of those early records by the Psychedelic Furs with a touch of country thrown in."

"I can't wait to hear it," Carol said. "Look, I've got to run."

Hazel knew what that meant in Urgent Care speak.

Ryan the guitar player came through the door and handed Hazel a bottle of water.

"There's some old Black dude outside who says he wants to talk to you. I told him I'd let you know."

Hazel thanked him and walked down the hall and stepped out the front door where she saw Jerome straddling his bicycle in the parking lot.

"Hey, Miss Hazel. I sure don't mean to be bothering you."

"That's okay, Jerome. You all right?"

"Yes, ma'am, I'm fine. It ain't really none of my business, but I thought I ought to tell you that a pickup truck been parking out here in front of your place. I seen it a couple times. It's got those tinted windows so I couldn't see inside. It just sit for a while then start up all of a sudden and leave. I just thought you oughta know."

"Thanks, Jerome. I appreciate that. What color is it?"

"Black. Shiny, too. One of those new Dodge trucks."

"Did you see the license plate?"

"I didn't get the number, but I did notice it wasn't a South Carolina plate. It was from Florida."

"That's good to know. I'll keep on the lookout," Hazel said. "You been playing that guitar?"

"Oh, I get it out every now and then, sing a song or two at the kitchen table."

"I'm telling you, Jerome, you just say the word and we'll make a record."

Jerome laughed. "I don't know about that," he said. "I'll think about it. You take care of yourself, you hear?"

He started to pedal off and Hazel called after him, "You take care, too."

Jerome waved a big hand behind his head and kept pedaling.

———◡———

Mervin pulled into the lot at the golf course and parked just a few spaces from the clubhouse. Not many cars were scattered about. The course was usually quiet on Tuesday afternoons, and this was no exception. It was a chilly but sunny day. Mervin could walk nine holes in two hours and easily make it to Bill's by 4:30.

Walking was how golf was meant to be played. It made the game much more relaxing than when riding in a cart. For Mervin, walking alone gave him a chance to slow down, think, and put things in perspective. It could be considered meditative, but he didn't want to get too carried away.

He put on his golf shoes, strapped his bag onto his pushcart, and rolled around to the first tee. He poked his head in the clubhouse door and asked Benny Martin if it was okay if he teed off. Benny was seated behind the register at the check-in counter, and he waved his hand like he was shooing away a mosquito. Mervin grinned and told him thanks.

After some stretching and a few practice swings, Mervin teed a ball at the right side of the tee box. The first hole was easy, a short, straight par four. Mervin took his stance, calmed his breathing, waggled his driver a couple times, and laced a beauty that started left and faded gently back to the middle of the fairway.

He slid his driver back into the bag and started off down the fairway, pushing his clubs in front of him. It felt good to be outside on a quiet afternoon. He walked at a deliberate pace and let his mind wander. It veered from the unease in Preston after the death of Louise Dixon and the plight of Skeeter to the direction the breeze was blowing and his next shot. It looked like it would be a stock pitching wedge.

Mervin caught his breath for a couple seconds then hit a solid approach that went a little long and landed with a thud into the back of the green. *Oh well, at least I'm dancing*, Mervin thought as he pushed his cart toward the green.

And so it went for the next two hours. Mervin would hit a shot, study the result, then let his mind take off to parts unknown while he walked to the next shot. He seldom solved any problems during these nine-hole therapy sessions, but somehow at the end he always felt lighter in spirit.

If I could only feel lighter in bulk, he thought as he puffed his way up the hill to the ninth green. But it was an afternoon well spent, especially after he watched a twenty-five-foot par putt curl across the green and drop into the cup on the difficult ninth.

It gave Mervin a sense of satisfaction. He felt better and began thinking Skeeter might be okay. *He's smart. He knows what he's doing.* Buoyed by these thoughts, Mervin rounded the clubhouse to the parking lot in time to see the taillights of a white Toyota Tundra pulling onto the highway. It was a truck just like Skeeter's, and Mervin took it to be a good sign, an omen.

He hoisted his cart and his clubs into the back of the truck. It was after four o'clock. He needed to get moving if he was going to meet Boot and Perch at Bill's. He looked forward to seeing them and maybe lifting their spirits, too. That, plus lifting a few cold beers.

CHAPTER TWENTY-ONE

BOOT AND PERCH WERE IN THEIR USUAL SEATS, beers in front of them. Mervin slapped them on the back as he passed before sliding onto the stool next to Perch at the end of the bar. He liked being the farthest from the front door.

Bill walked over, tossed a coaster in front of Mervin, and placed a frosty Miller High Life on it.

"Thanks, Bill," Mervin said.

"You been playing golf?" Boot asked.

"I went out and walked nine. It was a gorgeous afternoon."

"Why didn't you call me?" said Perch.

"Perch, you can barely walk from this bar to your truck," Boot said. "Ain't no way you gonna walk nine holes on the golf course."

"You don't know that," Perch said testily.

Mervin grinned and took a slug of the High Life.

"I'll call you next time, Perch. It was good to get out there away from everything. And a strange thing happened. When I was loading up to leave, I saw a white Tundra like Skeeter's pulling out of the parking lot. It gave me a good feeling, like Skeeter might be alright."

"It might have been a white Tundra, but it wasn't Skeeter's," Boot said.

"What makes you so sure?" Perch asked. He was still smarting from Boot picking on him for being out of shape.

"Because I was out at Skeeter's place yesterday and his truck was still there in front of his house, all locked up and everything."

Mervin and Perch both turned and looked at Boot.

"What were you doing out at Skeeter's?" Mervin said.

"Just wanted to check something."

"Check what?" said Perch.

Boot looked up at the TV above the bar and avoided their stares. Finally, he turned and said, "I took Jack and Joe out there to do some tracking. I figured it couldn't hurt."

"And?" Mervin said, leaning over the bar to look down at Boot.

"I found one of Skeeter's old ball caps stuffed under a seat on the jon boat and was able to set 'em pretty good on its scent. You know, Jack and Joe are good trackers."

"Yeah, we know, Boot," Perch said. "So what happened?"

"Well, they took off down that trail we took to the river. They were wide open 'til they hit the riverbank. I think Skeeter had a kayak or a canoe down there and he went off down the river."

They sat and studied that idea for a moment. Mervin lifted his empty bottle and waved it at Bill down the bar indicating another round for everyone.

"That ain't all," Boot said. "I got Jack and Joe back in the truck and we rode down to Grayson Road, you know, the one that crosses the river upstream near the state park?"

Perch and Mervin nodded that they knew it.

"Well, anyway, there's a bunch of old logging roads that branch off back there. Some of them nothing but a couple of ruts running through the woods. I stopped on the other side of the river, set the dogs again, and I'll be damn if they didn't take off. Not as open as before but they definitely had a scent. After about half an hour, they were whining and chasing their tails, so we loaded up and went home."

"So what are you saying?" Mervin asked.

"I'm saying I think Skeeter is hiding out somewhere in those woods. There's all kinds of abandoned farm houses, fishing shacks, and huntin' lodges back in there. Hell, if you circle far enough around the state park, there's an old, dilapidated church back there with a graveyard and everything."

"I remember that place," Perch said. "We used to hike to it when we were on Boy Scout camping trips. It was scary then."

Bill appeared with fresh beers and Mervin said, "I need a shot. Fellows?"

Boot and Perch agreed, and Bill turned to pour the drinks, Irish for Mervin, bourbon for Perch, and tequila for Boot. They clinked glasses and knocked them back.

"You know, this kind of makes sense," Mervin said. "It's obvious that something spooked Skeeter. He'd just finished breakfast. He was still in the kitchen. The backdoor and the trail to the river were his most immediate means of escape. He didn't even take time to go upstairs and get his wallet and keys."

Once again, they took a few seconds to study on things. Then Mervin broke the silence.

"So if that's the case, what do we do?"

"I say we go back out there tomorrow and check out some of those old logging roads," Boot said. "We go as deep as we can into those woods."

"Should we take Jack and Joe?" Mervin asked.

"Nah, I don't want to have to keep up with them. We'll just take my truck and run those roads. Hey Bill, another shot," Boot said. He was getting excited.

"What time you gonna pick me up?" Mervin said.

"What about right after lunch, say around one. I got some stuff to do in the morning. That sound okay to you, Perch?"

Perch twisted his beer on the coaster.

"Y'all go ahead and let me know what you find."

"Come on, Perch, you need to go with us," Mervin said.

"Man, I'm sorry about saying you couldn't walk nine holes," Boot said. "Come on and go with us."

"It ain't that," Perch said. "I've got some projects in the works at the house, and besides, I'll just hold y'all back. Get out there and beat the bushes. Call me when you get home."

Boot and Mervin made eye contact.

"Okay," Mervin said. "We'll call you as soon as we get back."

They sat in silence for a few seconds, each in their own thoughts.

"Damn, that last shot went down smooth," Boot said, flashing a wicked grin and slapping Perch on the back. He held up his glass. "Bill," he called. "Three more on me."

Perch and Mervin glanced at each other.

"He's got the bit between his teeth," Mervin whispered.

Barbara Lowrie was reading the Charlotte Observer's online coverage of the events in Preston. It wasn't much, just a wire story under their regional news tab that said combined forces from multiple agencies were investigating the disappearance of August Ellington and the death of Louise Dixon.

She closed the piece, landed back on the newspaper's homepage, and was about to log off when she noticed a headline that read *South Carolina is one of the worst states for women, study finds*. Barbara didn't need more bad news, but she clicked on the piece anyway.

The study ranked the states best to worst based on factors that contributed to women's life experiences, such as health care and economic opportunities. South Carolina landed at No. 46.

At least we're not at the bottom, Barbara thought, then she saw another category based on homicides of women. South Carolina was No. 43, but when Barbara looked further, she saw that the last seven states, almost all in the Deep South, were virtually tied at No. 43.

"That's just great," Barbara muttered and logged off the machine. A weight seemed to settle over her. She was tired and angry. What could she do? She couldn't write or pass laws to address such an awful situation. All she could do was enforce the laws on the books, as inadequate as some of them might be, and try to catch the scumbags who were harming women.

She started gathering up her things to go home and felt someone coming up behind her desk. Pete Shumpert circled around and plopped in the chair opposite.

"Hey, girl," he said.

"Hey, bubba."

It was their usual greeting.

"I hear you had an exciting morning," Barbara said. She could see fatigue in Pete's face.

"You could say that." He sighed and stretched his legs out in front of him. "I just got a forensic report on the truck. That was blood, bone, and bits of brain splattered on the passenger's side. Oh, and it was Luther's truck. We ran the tag."

"You think that was his blood and brains?"

"Most likely, unless someone else was driving his truck. The way I see it, he pulled off the road, someone pulled in behind him, walked up to the window and pop."

They sat quietly for a few seconds. Barbara liked Pete. He was a dedicated, blue-collar cop. Loved the job, never sought promotion. And he was honest. He was the father of two grown daughters and had a wife pestering him to retire. Barbara figured he would within the year.

"Any news on that list of men y'all got from Perch Gordon? I heard you found and cleared all of 'em except for that asshole Silas Conn. I remember that case. He was an evil bastard. I had a bad taste in my mouth for weeks after we couldn't lock him up."

"Well, you wouldn't believe," Barbara said.

"What?" Pete sat up in his chair.

"We were finally able to trace him. He moved from here to Conway to Georgetown to Myrtle Beach. Stanton was on the phone with a detective down there all afternoon. They finally confirmed that a Billy Conn who was working as a maintenance man in an oceanfront hotel was the same Silas Conn who used to live here. They had DNA, fingerprints, the works."

"What do you mean had?"

"Billy Conn is dead," Barbara said. "He was drinking late one night in a bar on Highway 17, and when he left, he was hit by a truck while trying to cross the highway. A couple who were in the parking lot said he just stepped out in front of the truck, a big eighteen wheeler. Didn't look or anything, just walked out into the lane."

"Suicide?"

"Who knows? It was ruled an accidental death."

"So, from all those names on Skeeter's files, not one could have killed Louise Dixon?"

"I'm afraid so," Barbara said. "Plus, we can't find any record of someone named Harold Cephus, the man Ronnie Dixon told us about."

"Yeah, I heard that. But since Ronnie said he met him through Luther Peacock, that has to mean something, right, given what's happened this morning?"

"It has to, or we're back to square one."

Pete sat up in his chair, rubbed his face, then gazed into space. Barbara could sense that Pete needed to talk about something.

"What's on your mind?" she said.

Pete sighed. "Oh, I don't know. It's probably nothing."

"What's probably nothing?"

Pete sat up, leaned forward, and put his elbows on his knees.

"I heard there was something in those notes Skeeter Ellington kept that said one woman was scared to come to us because her husband had friends in the police. Is that true?"

"Yes, there's a mention of that from the first victim." Barbara hesitated then said, "And Carol Baxley told me off the record that she heard the same thing from a couple others."

"Do you believe it?"

"Do I believe a couple of these men might be acquainted with police officers? Sure I do. It's a small town. But I don't believe for a second that a Preston policeman would be involved or turn a blind eye to assault and battery."

She heard the hollowness in her voice, and Pete heard it, too.

"Why are you bringing this up?" Barbara asked.

"Well, when I got back to the station this morning I went looking for Jake Rainey and Mark Rogers because I know they're pals with Luther and might know where he is or what he's been up to. I found them in the breakroom, and when I told them about finding Luther's truck with the blood splatter and everything, they were visibly shaken.

"We sat down and talked for a couple minutes, and they said they hadn't seen or heard from Luther since early last week when he called Jake to see if he wanted to go quail hunting."

"It's understandable that they'd be upset after hearing about Luther's truck," Barbara said.

"Yeah, I know that, but when I asked them if they knew anything about a Harold Cephus who Luther was supposedly hanging around with, I sensed something. They seemed to tighten up a little bit, especially Rogers, and I saw him glance at Jake with a look that, I don't know, it gave me a funny feeling."

"You think they know something?"

"I don't know. Maybe, maybe not. I know Jake and Mark hang out with Luther and Earl Tyler and—"

"And Ronnie Dixon," Barbara finished.

"Yes, Ronnie, too, and a few others. They're all around the same age. Some are married, some aren't. They go huntin' and fishin' together and sometimes they gather out at Earl Tyler's place and get a little wild. I got called out there one Saturday night a few months ago when two of 'em got in a fight and one ended up in the hospital. Jake was there and he was drunk. We talked and he said they were just blowing off steam and I should let it go. It was all over by the time I got there. The one who went to the hospital wasn't hurt that bad and didn't want to press charges. So that's what I did, just let it go."

"Sounds like you've been thinking about this a lot," Barbara said.

Pete just sat there staring at a corner of Barbara's desk. She could tell this was hard for him, having doubts about the integrity of fellow officers.

"Look, I hear you, Pete," she said. "And I think you're probably right. Your instincts have never let us down and I know you respect the job enough to be worried."

Pete relaxed, thankful for Barbara's vote of confidence.

"We've got to cut Ronnie Dixon loose in the morning," she continued. "Let's just keep an eye on him and see how it plays out."

Pete looked up and smiled. "That sounds like a good plan," he said. "I'm beat. I'm going home."

He walked back around Barbara's desk and squeezed her shoulder as he passed.

"Thanks, girl," he said quietly.

"Get some rest, bubba," Barbara said.

For more than one hundred years, cotton was the number one cash crop in South Carolina. *King Cotton* they called it. But when the 1950s arrived, a new agricultural monarch ascended to the throne. Tobacco soared past cotton in the number of acres grown and the amount of revenue earned. It continued this way until the 1990s when smoking was proven to be a major health hazard and millions of people kicked the habit.

Preston had been smack in the epicenter of South Carolina's tobacco boom, and remnants of that thriving agricultural past still existed on the west side of town. Abandoned tobacco warehouses, some that covered half a block, were lined along streets near the railroad tracks.

Once upon a time, mounds of cured tobacco would stretch in rows from one end of these warehouses to the other and auctioneers would lead buyers from the big cigarette companies up and down the aisles, chattering a hypnotic cadence while bids were issued with the tilt of a cap or a trademark shout.

They were exciting times, good times. Farmers earned a substantial living and Preston rode a wave of economic prosperity. But those days were long gone. Now the warehouses loomed like empty cathedrals to a forgotten religion. Cracks ran through the brick walls and the metal roofs were bent and rusted. Some were being used as storage facilities and one was home to a farmers' market in summer. But at this time of year, especially at night, they were mostly large empty shells, silhouetted in the moonlight.

In front of the side door of one of these warehouses, a black Dodge truck idled with its headlights off and driver's door open. A figure dressed in black quickly opened a combination padlock and slid the large, sheet-metal door open, its runners greased in advance so it wouldn't make a sound.

Deacon hurried back to the truck, pulled it inside, and closed the warehouse door, locking it from the inside. It was strange living in an open space that was almost half an acre, but he had gotten used to it. In fact, he found it somewhat liberating after the tight confines of his most recent domicile.

There was a large, clean mattress on the concrete floor. A Honda generator provided power for a couple of lamps, a mini-refrigerator, and a laptop computer that sat on a makeshift desk of pressboard and cinder blocks.

It's home, but not for much longer, he thought. Deacon pulled the starter cord on the generator, but it didn't start. He was tired. The past seventy-two hours had been draining. He'd never killed anyone before. After he'd strangled Louise Dixon, he looked at his hands and wept for the woman's soul, wondering if he'd relinquished any chance for salvation. But gradually he recovered and realized that leaving her in her car at the Urgent Care had felt right. It sent a message. People needed to learn that men could be harsh masters. *But they are masters! Masters of the marriage, masters of the family.*

Deacon fetched a bottle of orange juice from the mini fridge. He needed sustenance, he needed fortitude. Out loud, he recited his favorite passage from Ephesians, "Wives, submit unto your own husbands, as unto the Lord. For the husband is the head of the wife, even as Christ is head of the church."

It calmed him, helped him focus. His old preacher down in Florida had taught him well. Deacon yanked again on the generator's starter cord. It sputtered, caught, and suddenly a small corner of the cavernous warehouse became a home with lamps burning and the beep of a laptop coming to life.

He was surprised that the second killing had been so easy. He'd liked Luther, he really had. The ol' boy didn't deserve to die that way, but Deacon couldn't take chances. Luther was the only link between him and Louise Dixon, so he had to go.

But it was all right. Deacon had allies. The lawyer and the lady doctor had eluded him so far, but he would find them. He would complete the mission. Then he could go home.

CHAPTER TWENTY-TWO

MERVIN MADE A SHOW of looking at his watch as he climbed into Boot's truck on Wednesday afternoon.

"Sorry I'm late," Boot said. "Some business took longer than I thought it would."

Mervin just frowned and buckled his seatbelt. He'd been worried for months that Boot might be expanding his pot dealing beyond Preston. It was a bad idea, but Mervin didn't say anything.

"You know we've only got about two-and-a-half hours of daylight left," he said.

"Plenty of time. Look in the back."

Mervin turned and saw a soft cooler sitting on the backseat of the king cab and a 12-gauge pump in the gun rack on the window.

Boot grinned, gunned the big F-250 and backed out of Mervin's driveway, almost clipping the mailbox at the street. They headed out of town on Highway 9, turned onto Grayson Road, and followed it for a couple miles past the entrance to the State Park. Boot had tried to put a Rush CD in the stereo, but Mervin nipped that in the bud. When Boot refused to play the Drive-By Truckers, they settled on Neil Young and ended up howling along to *Powderfinger*.

"*Shelter me from the powder and the finger,*" they belted with gusto. "*Cover me with the thought that pulled the trigger.*"

Boot swung the truck off Grayson onto a road of packed red clay, and after passing several acres that had been cut for timber, they were plunged into thick woods. Light from the sun low in the sky filtered through the trees.

"I'm pretty sure there are some old hunting cabins back here," Boot said. "We're not too far from the river, and I think Reddy Creek joins up with it about a mile that way."

Boot flung his hand in front of Mervin's face and pointed out the passenger-side window. Mervin had no idea if he was pointing north, south, east, or west.

For the next hour they bounced through woods, along fence lines, and around irrigation ponds. They found two decomposing tobacco barns, an abandoned farmhouse, and two old hunting shacks, both rundown and deserted. It was getting late, and Mervin was getting restless. He'd had three beers from the cooler and didn't want another. They were sitting outside the second shack, truck idling, and Mervin said, "Let's go home. If Skeeter went down the river and hid out back here, he'd be long gone by now."

"Maybe," Boot said. "But let's follow this road a little more. I think there's another old house farther in near the creek."

Boot didn't wait for Mervin to agree, just turned on the headlights, shifted the truck into four-wheel drive, and drove deeper into the woods.

The sky was burnt orange on the horizon and the sun was setting in a hurry. Ten minutes later it was pitch black except for the high beams bouncing off pine trees, ancient oaks, and occasionally the eyes of a possum or raccoon.

They eased around a muddy curve and came upon an old house on the left. Boot pulled up to the front steps and the headlights bounced off something bright and shiny on the porch.

"That's weird," he said.

He hopped outside, leaving the door open and the truck running. Mervin followed, but he gently closed his door. As they approached the porch, they could see the light was reflecting off a brand new padlock on the front door.

"What do you think?" Mervin said.

"I think there ain't no reason to have a padlock on this pile of shit unless you're hiding something inside."

"What should we do?"

Boot didn't answer. He walked across the porch and tried the door. It was solid. A sledgehammer could bust it open, but they didn't have one.

"Let's check it out," Boot said. He retraced his steps to the truck, switched it off but left the headlights on. He grabbed a powerful, halogen flashlight and began to circle the house. Mervin followed, not sure if he liked this idea.

They found a backdoor that was equally secure and continued on around the house. A window on the far side had termite damage in the sill, and Boot was able to kick it loose and slide it open.

"Are you going in?" Mervin asked.

"We got to," Boot said. "Give me a boost."

Mervin linked his hands together, hoisted Boot through the window, and passed him the flashlight. Boot stuck out a hand and pulled Mervin inside.

"God almighty," Mervin said and put his hand over his nose. "Smells like an outhouse in here."

Boot swung the flashlight's beam around the room. It revealed folding chairs, a kerosene heater, and a soiled mattress covered with an equally dirty sheet. A Confederate flag draped one wall, and one of those yellow, *Don't Tread on Me* flags with the coiled snake adorned another.

Boot and Mervin stepped gingerly through the house as Boot played the beam back and forth. When they approached the front door, Boot swung the beam to the right and stopped. Something, a duffel bag or maybe an old burlap sack, was on the floor fifteen feet away. Then he saw the soles of a pair of shoes in the light and knew what it was.

"Oh, damn. Damn, damn, damn!"

Boot strode quickly over, Mervin at his shoulder.

"Oh, Skeeter," Mervin said, his voice choking. "Skeeter, damn it, man."

He couldn't look anymore.

"Hold on a second," Boot said. He dropped down on one knee and slowly turned the body.

"Oh, god," Mervin cried and backpedaled feverishly, looking for a way out of the house.

"Calm down," Boot said. "This ain't Skeeter."

The head on the corpse was obliterated, most of the face and skull blown away. But there was enough of the chin and all of the body to see that the man had been much younger than Skeeter.

Mervin sank to his knees in a far corner and vomited the beers and the rest of his stomach contents onto the dirty floorboards. Boot came over, put his hands under Mervin's armpits, and lifted him up.

"Let's go," he said.

They stumbled back through the house, helped each other climb through the window, and made their way back to Boot's truck.

"I'm calling Barbara Lowrie," Mervin said.

"Okay," Boot said. He was breathing hard, his arms outstretched as he leaned against the truck.

"Where the hell are we?" Mervin asked.

"Just call her. I'll talk to her."

Mervin tapped her number and when Barbara answered, he dove in. "Sergeant Lowrie? This is Mervin Hayes. Me and Boot went looking for Skeeter and we found a body that's not him, but it's a long way out here and y'all need to get here—"

Barbara cut him off. "Mr. Hayes. Slow down. Take a deep breath. Where are you?"

Boot held out his hand for the phone and Mervin passed it to him.

"Sergeant Lowrie, this is Boot Pearson. You got a pen and paper?"

For the next few minutes, Boot did his best to describe the scene and give Barbara directions. When she finally felt good about how to get there, she ended the call and Boot handed the phone back to Mervin.

"They're on their way."

"Boot, they ain't gonna find us way the hell out here. Shit, man, I have no idea where we are. I just want to go home and sit down to supper with Becca."

Boot smiled at Mervin, reached in the truck, and cranked it up to save the battery.

"You better call Becca and let her know you're going to be late. We gotta wait here for the police."

"Why don't we drive out to the main road and show 'em how to get back here?"

"Barbara Lowrie said we should wait here. Relax, Mervin, it's going to be okay. Look on the bright side. That ain't Skeeter in there and that means he might still be okay. I'll grab us a couple beers while we wait."

Just as Boot was reaching into the truck, they heard a loud pop, and something whizzed over their heads.

"Holy shit!" Mervin cried and he dropped to the ground.

Boot passed on the beers, grabbed the 12-gauge instead, and turned off the truck's headlights.

"Where'd it come from?"

"From over there, I think," Mervin said. "The other side of the road. Farther down, toward the creek."

Boot pumped a shell into the chamber, and, squatting low, he peeked around the front end of the truck. Another pop was followed by a loud *pang* when the bullet hit the truck's right front fender.

Mervin heard Boot mutter, "Yeah, I saw you, you son of a bitch."

In a flash he was up and firing into the woods across the road. *Boom! Pump. Boom! Pump. Boom!* Each blast from the 12-gauge sounded like thunder echoing through the trees, and Mervin felt himself pressing tighter against the side of the truck.

Boot spun back around and sat down next to Mervin. They didn't budge for a full two minutes, then heard the faint sound of a vehicle coming to life and driving away. The sound was distant and fading.

"I think we're okay," Boot said. Nevertheless, they sat still for another five minutes.

"How about those beers?" Mervin finally said.

"Better not," said Boot. "Here comes the cavalry."

Mervin stood slowly and could see flashing blue lights in the distance, bouncing up and down and creating a weird halo effect in the trees.

"I better call Becca before they get here," Mervin said. "While I've got the chance."

"Damn you, Mervin Hayes," Becca said, sniffling and wiping tears. "You gotta promise me you'll never do anything like this again."

"Becca, I'm fine. Boot's okay. And I promise I'll be more careful next time."

She flashed an angry look.

"Check that," he said. "I promise there will never, ever be a next time."

It had been back and forth like this since Mervin got home. He had told her briefly what had happened, and when he got to the part about the gunshots, Becca lost it. But she was finally starting to calm down, and Mervin convinced her that he and Boot never intended to get in a gunfight. They'd just gone out looking for Skeeter.

Becca whimpered, blew her nose, and looked up at Mervin. He put his arms around her and pulled her close. She was only five-foot-two and the top of her head snuggled perfectly under his chin.

"I love you, punkin," he said.

"Promise me."

"I promise."

They stood in the kitchen holding each other tight and it felt good. Mervin whispered in her ear, "I'm kind of hungry, baby."

She punched him in the stomach and told him to sit. He obeyed and

Becca switched on the microwave to heat a plate of squash casserole, string beans, and yellow rice.

"You missed out on the biscuits," Becca said.

"That's okay. I'll just have a slice of wheat bread."

Becca sat the plate in front of Mervin, poured him a glass of tea, and sat down with him at the table.

"So, tell me everything," she said.

Between bites of the supper he didn't deserve, he did just that. He told her about roaming all across the countryside with Boot and about finding the rundown shack after dark. He was delicate in describing the finding of the body, but he expanded on his earlier version of the gunplay, making a big deal about Boot's heroic action that "certainly saved our lives."

"Y'all weren't high, were you?"

"No, baby, we'd had a few beers, but we didn't smoke any pot."

She glared at him, but he continued. He told her about the arrival of the police and how they cordoned off the house, searched the area, and questioned him and Boot for what seemed like hours.

"Who were they?" Becca asked.

"It was Barbara Lowrie and Pete Shumpert in one car, and Chief Holt with a cop named Jake Rainey in another car. It made me feel good that the chief of police came. And a deputy sheriff was there, too, I guess because we were way out in the county. They all seem to be working hard on this thing."

"So y'all got questioned."

"And Boot didn't hold anything back," Mervin said. "He told them he'd seen a muzzle flash in the woods and fired three times with his shotgun. They said they'd need to confiscate his weapon, and Boot didn't hesitate, just gave it to them."

Becca shook her head in disbelief. "This is insane," she said. "So, what now?"

"I'm pretty sure they know who the body in the house is . . . or was," Mervin said. "Me and Boot have to go to the police station in the morning to give a statement."

"Should we be worried?"

"What? No, Becca, whoever was shooting at us doesn't know me or Boot. We just stumbled onto something at the wrong time. They got no idea who we are."

Becca wasn't sure about that, and she could see that Mervin wasn't either. They sat quietly while Mervin finished his supper.

"This casserole is good," he said. "Did you make it?"

"No, it's from Amy Sue, leftovers from her Sunday dinner."

"Mmm," Mervin said as he forked some more into his mouth. "You want to watch a movie later?" he asked.

Becca gave him an exasperated look. "Yeah, I guess so." She smiled. "Only if you make love to me later."

Mervin almost choked on the casserole. "I'll do my best," he said.

CHAPTER TWENTY-THREE

BARBARA LOWRIE WAS AGITATED. No, make that angry. Two murders in two days in Preston. It was getting hard to keep things in perspective. She was a law officer. She took it personally. It was the feeling of being helpless, of not knowing what to do.

It's a feeling investigators have all the time, she rationalized. *We need to focus. Just work the case,* she told herself.Maybe she should ride up to Pembroke and recruit the old Lowrie gang. Those outlaws would find the bastard. Maybe their ringleader, old Henry Berry Lowrie, was still out in those woods. Maybe he heard those shots and could lead her to the killer.

Focus, Barbara thought, *stop fantasizing.* She paced back and forth across the parking lot behind the police station and recapped the events of the past three hours. She could hear traffic on 301 even at this late hour, slowing for the stoplight at Main then gunning away when it turned green.

She had been just a few feet away when Pete Shumpert knelt to examine the body in the shack. He knew immediately it was Luther Peacock even though there was hardly anything left of the body's face. Chief Holt asked the deputy sheriff to call his department's forensic team while he put a call through to SLED.

The contents of the shack had been disturbing, especially the flags on the walls. They introduced a dreaded new element into the case that Barbara had hoped wouldn't be a factor. White supremacy, right-wing paranoia, that whole grab bag of hate.

An examination of the bed in the shack suggested it had been recently used. They found a duffel bag full of clothes that most likely belonged to the victim. There was a box of revolver bullets in the duffel as well.

The forensics team arrived along with two more Preston police officers, another veteran cop and a female officer. They searched the woods diligently and found shell casings, footprints, and tire tracks from a vehicle with the wheelbase of a large pickup truck. The evidence verified the stories of Boot Pearson and Mervin Hayes.

Those guys, Barbara thought and smiled. *They are something else.* But she had to give them credit for going all the way out there to look for their friend. Boot was running on adrenaline when she arrived, and Mervin was somewhere between shock and fear. He did admit to throwing up in the corner of the shack. Barbara understood. When she saw what was left of the victim's head, she almost lost it herself.

"Lowrie!"

Chief Holt was leaning out the backdoor to the station looking for Barbara.

"Yo, chief, out here."

"My office. Right now."

Barbara hustled back inside, went through the squad room, and into Holt's office. Pete Shumpert and Preston County Sheriff Darnell Whittington were sitting in chairs across the desk from the chief. Whittington rose to greet Barbara when she entered the room.

"Hello, Sergeant," the sheriff said. "I hope you're keeping well."

Whittington was a tall, broad-shouldered Black man with a shaved head and a quick wit. He and Holt had a good working relationship that was based on mutual respect.

Barbara admired the sheriff, too. She shook his hand and took a seat next to Pete.

"I appreciate the sheriff's willingness to join us at this late hour," Holt said. "We had a long talk the other day out on the highway where Pete found Luther Peacock's truck. He and I agreed that since city police are already investigating the murder of Louise Dixon and since we feel there's a connection to Luther Peacock, we'll continue to lead the investigation with his department providing any support we might need."

"And we're very interested in helping y'all find August Ellington," Whittington said. "As you probably know, he had an uncle who worked for the department back in the day. It sounds like he could be on this guy's hit list."

"That's likely," Holt said. "His friends think he was spooked and is hiding out somewhere, and that's why they were searching all those broken-down farmhouses and hunting shacks. I believe it's a plausible explanation, and we'll keep you informed every step of the way."

Whittington nodded his thanks.

"What we have so far is this," Holt continued. "Thanks to the initiative of Ellington's two friends, as foolhardy as it might have been, a body has been found in an abandoned shack near Reedy Creek. Shump says the body is Luther Peacock, and while we don't yet have any forensic confirmation, I'm inclined to agree with him. As soon as we get a time of death, we can form a timeline from when Luther left home, was shot and killed in his truck on the side of the road, and ended up in a shack in the middle of nowhere, however he got there."

"I think whoever killed him loaded up his body and duffel bag, and dumped him in that shack," Pete said. "How the killer knew about that shack is the question I have."

"But the bigger question," Holt said, "is who killed Luther and how is his murder connected to the murder of Louise Dixon. We know from

Carol Baxley's statement that she and Ellington were attempting to help Louise, so that makes the whereabouts of Ellington even more worrisome. But there's still a missing link between Louise and Luther."

"This Harold Cephus guy is the key," Barbara said. "He was acquainted with Luther, and he called Ronnie Dixon to discuss his problem wife. It's a clear connection to both murders."

She stared at Pete and Chief Holt, daring them to contradict her.

"Possibly," Holt said. "But we have no idea who this man is. As we've heard, there's no record of him on any regional database."

"But he exists," Barbara said. "Both Luther Peacock and Ronnie Dixon have laid eyes on him. And probably a few more of that crowd."

Barbara made brief eye contact with Pete to let him know she'd been thinking about their previous conversation.

"That's all we need to know," she went on. "We're police. We'll find him."

Pete grinned. "Right on, girl," he said. "Let's do it."

Holt sighed and managed a grin, too.

"I hear you," he said. "Damn it, it's almost midnight and I haven't called my wife. Let's get out of here. I'll see y'all in the morning."

Pete and Barbara saw the stress on their chief's face and realized he was feeling intense pressure to make an arrest, not so much to maintain his reputation but to calm the people in Preston.

The sheriff saw it, too. "Don't worry, Chief," Whittington said. "I agree with the sergeant. We'll catch the bastard."

They all stood to leave. Holt smiled his thanks and waved them away.

"Sure, why not," Hazel said when the drummer for The Suburbs of Hysteria asked if she'd like another beer. They were sitting in a circle in the studio, drinking, laughing, and talking about music and life.

It had been a fun two days and Hazel was enjoying the company of these four unassuming young men who made remarkably cool music. Plus, it didn't hurt that they were enthralled by her musical history and peppered her with questions about Purple Hazel's heyday.

She was about to launch into a fun tale about a double-bill gig with Devo in 1985 when she felt her phone buzz in her pocket. She took it out but didn't recognize the number.

"Hello?"

"Hazel? This is Mervin Hayes. We met the other day."

"Oh, yeah. Hey Mervin. What's up?"

"Nothing urgent, just wondered if I could talk to you sometime tomorrow. It's been a wild night and I thought I should fill you in on what's happening."

Hazel was alarmed. "Can't you tell me now?" The four Suburbs were watching her.

"It's best we talk in person. Nothing to worry about, I promise."

"Okay. I'll be here at the studio tomorrow afternoon. Say around three?"

"Perfect. You have a good night, and like I said, it's nothing for you to worry about."

Hazel ended the call and looked up into four inquiring faces.

"No big deal," she said. "Somebody just wants to book some studio time. Now where was I? Oh yeah, that gig with Devo in L.A. Now *THAT* was a wild night."

———◡———

Deacon closed the big sheet-metal door, locked it, and hurried around to his truck, reached in, and turned it off. The deep silence in the cavernous warehouse amplified the ringing in his ears from the gunshots.

He looked down and saw thick, dried mud on his boots. His truck was covered with the same mud, thrown up by the tires during his manic escape. He'd been lucky to find a logging track that led out of the woods to a main road.

He switched on the generator and turned on a lamp. Something scurried along a far wall of the warehouse two hundred feet away. Most likely a rat. He didn't care, just fetched a bottle of water from the mini-fridge and sat down calmly in a folding chair.

It was weird, the more the rage seethed inside him, the calmer he became. Psychologists probably had a term for this, and he'd be happy to talk to them about it, but not for a while. The rage was indeed seething, and it had found new targets tonight.

Deacon had come to this godforsaken town to enact justice on two individuals, people who had stuck their noses into the private lives of others and perverted a divine natural order. They had wrecked families and destroyed lives, but they would be dealt with, he was certain of that.

And now new offenders were on the list, including a female police officer, an Indian who was acting way above her station. And those two in the big Ford truck, they would have to go, too.

The world was filled with chaos and so many had gone astray. A great reckoning was coming. He knew it. In the meantime, if he could restore order to a small corner of God's creation, he would have done his part. He reached over and unzipped a large weapons bag, pushed aside an AR-15, and took out his Model Seven bolt-action Remington. He attached the infrared scope, polished it, and raised the rifle to his shoulder. Gazing through the scope, he saw two tiny red eyes reflecting from the far wall of the warehouse.

"I will smite them with the pestilence and destroy them," he mumbled, trying to remember the passage from the *Book of Numbers*, "and will make for thee a nation greater and mightier than they." He pulled the trigger. Click. It will be that easy.

CHAPTER TWENTY-FOUR

MERVIN LEFT A NOTE on the kitchen table for Becca telling her what he was doing and where he would be. It wasn't something he normally did, but given last night's circumstances, he felt it was the right thing to do.

He told her he was going to Hazel Owens' studio to tell her about his latest adventures, and he'd probably grab a beer at Bill's on the way home. He would call her from Bill's to see if she wanted him to bring supper home.

Hazel was glad to see him, and they sat and talked for almost an hour. He told her about going to look for Skeeter, finding a body in the shack, and getting shot at by someone in the woods.

Hazel shook her head in disbelief. "What's going on in this town?"

Mervin told her that according to Boot, the body wasn't Skeeter, so that was a good thing.

"Not to be disrespectful to that poor fellow's soul, but you hear what I'm saying?"

Hazel did and she, too, was relieved it wasn't Skeeter. She said Carol had told her all about Skeeter's zeal to help these women and how she'd grown to have tremendous respect for him.

"How is Carol?" Mervin asked.

"She's good. Back at work and staying busy. It's flu season and the Urgent Care is slamming."

They chatted some more about Skeeter and Carol and talked about being kind of scared. Hazel told Mervin they'd had a policewoman outside their house the past couple of nights. A really cool, powerfully built woman.

"I'm really sorry about Skeeter," Hazel said. "I know y'all must be going through hell. I sure was before Carol came home."

Mervin got a little misty when he told Hazel about how his friendship with Skeeter, Boot, and Perch had grown over the years. She saw it and changed the subject.

"Hey, are you into music at all?"

"Oh yeah," Mervin said. "I grew up on The Beatles, Dylan, Joni Mitchell, Led Zeppelin, Neil Young, all those geezers. I was into R.E.M. and The Clash, too. And I keep up with some of the new stuff. I like Drive-By Truckers, War on Drugs, North Mississippi All Stars."

Hazel was impressed.

"Let me play something for you," she said. "A really cool band from Charlotte was in here this week and they put down some interesting stuff."

She cued up The Suburbs of Hysteria and punched play. The control room filled with the dynamic interplay between two electric guitars, bass, drums, and a singer whose impassioned vocals landed somewhere between Jeff Buckley and Eddie Vedder.

They listened to the entire song, then Mervin said, "Wow. That's great. I mean that's really, really great."

Hazel almost laughed at Mervin's giddy, teenage reaction.

"Play another one," he said.

At that moment someone knocked on the studio's front door. Mervin and Hazel sat up, startled, and Hazel went to see who it was.

"It's him," she said. "Ronnie Dixon. Louise's husband."

Mervin pushed past her in the hall and opened the front door. The man outside was like a grizzly bear, almost a foot taller than Mervin, a beard that hung down to his chest, and a ball cap emblazoned with a Purina Chow logo.

He took off the cap and held it in front of him. "I'm sorry to disturb you," he said, "but is Hazel Owens here?"

"She might be," Mervin said. "Who wants to know?"

"My name's Ronnie Dixon. I was here the other night. I just need to talk to her."

Mervin studied the king-sized good ol' boy and determined he was more teddy bear than grizzly. He didn't sense any ill-will, so he led him into the studio.

Hazel eyed him warily, but as soon as he saw Hazel, Ronnie broke down and started apologizing. He sobbed and hiccupped, told Hazel he was so sorry about ambushing her in the parking lot and that wasn't like him at all, and he missed Louise so bad he couldn't stand it.

Hazel's cold expression thawed, and she invited him to sit down. They talked for a minute or two and she asked him why he'd done such a thing.

"There's this guy, Deacon, they call him . . . he put me up to it," Ronnie said. "To be honest, I was a little bit scared of him and just wasn't thinking right. Now Louise is dead."

"Do you think this Deacon killed her?" Hazel asked.

"I don't know. Maybe. It could've been somebody else."

"Like who?" Mervin said.

"I don't know, man," Ronnie said and sniffed, wiped the back of a big hand across his eyes. He looked at Hazel. "I just wanted to come and tell you I'm sorry. And I'm sorry for the way I treated Louise. I'll never forgive myself for that."

More tears rolled down into his thick bushy beard, and Hazel said it was okay. She led him out of the studio and gave him a hug on the sidewalk. Mervin marveled at the sight of a lesbian, former New York punk rock star hugging a big ol' Southern boy who could have been a roadie for Molly Hatchet. *Crazy old world*, he thought and watched as Ronnie pulled on his cap and walked to his truck.

"That was weird," Hazel said once she was back inside and had locked the door behind her.

"No kidding," Mervin said. "But do you believe him?"

"Yeah, I'm pretty sure I do."

Mervin nodded. He believed Ronnie was telling the truth, too. "I'm sure he told the police everything. So that's good, isn't it? It narrows things down. They'll be looking for this Deacon fellow."

"Yeah, I guess," Hazel said. "But you heard him. I'm not so sure only one person is behind all this."

"I know," Mervin said. "That scares me."

A stiff breeze gusted out of the north casting a chill over Preston. The gray sky grew darker, so Mervin turned on his headlights as he pulled onto 301. A mile later he turned onto Main Street and encountered a little traffic along Preston's main drag.

There were a few cars parked in front of the bank, several at the hardware store, and more than several in front of the Dollar General. He eased his way through the stoplights and pulled into a diagonal spot in front of Bill's.

It was quiet on a Thursday evening and Mervin took his usual seat at the end of the bar. A couple was talking quietly in a booth by the wall, and an old fellow at the other end of the bar was busy with a Budweiser and a barbecue sandwich.

"Wasn't expecting to see you in here today," Bill said as he walked over. "Miller High Life?"

"No," Mervin said. He deliberated for a second. "Let me have one of those Sweetwater IPAs."

"This is a surprising day," Bill said with a grin and went to pull the draft.

A gloomy mood had come over Mervin, and it had nothing to do with the weather. He'd been thinking about the night before, and the more he pondered it, the more disturbed he became. It wasn't just about being shot at, although that was a big part of it. It was about the sense of anger and paranoia he'd felt in that old rundown country shack.

The flags on the walls gave it away. And there was the fact that Louise Dixon had been left at the Urgent Care to scare Carol Baxley, who was gay. Mervin was seeing connections and they weren't about simple prejudice. *It's about hatred, plain and simple. Hatred of women? Hatred of gay people? Both?* He wasn't sure.

Bill set the beer in front of Mervin and his mood lifted a little. "That's good."

Bill was leaning against a cooler polishing shot glasses with a towel. Mervin thought for a second then started telling Bill about how he and Boot had gone looking for Skeeter. Bill didn't make eye contact, just listened, nodded occasionally, and kept wiping the glasses.

When Mervin got to the part about the flags, he said, "Bill, I need to ask you something."

Bill looked up and Mervin continued.

"Do you think there's a lot of that sort of thing around here or is this just about some lone wacko who's got a burr up his ass?"

Before Bill could answer, Mervin went on. "Look, I get it. I'm not naïve. This is South Carolina. I'm from here. I know we're still fighting the Civil War. Racism is part of our genetic code, we don't trust the fedrul gub'mint, and queers need to come to Jesus. But damn, Bill, aren't most of us past all that by now? Has it actually gotten worse?"

Bill tossed the towel onto the cooler and held up a hand for Mervin to wait. The old boy down the bar was waving his empty Bud bottle, and Bill went to fetch him another round.

When he came back, he leaned against the cooler. "Mervin, I see all kinds in here. Rednecks, bikers, bankers, rich farmers, poor farmers, liberal lawyers, conservative judges, and I'll tell you, I mean this seriously, what you saw out there in that shack is just the tip of the iceberg. Those flags represent the majority in these parts. I'm sorry to say."

It was a surprising confession. Mervin knew Bill was originally from Massachusetts, but he'd lived in Preston for almost twenty-five years. His wife was buried here.

"You nailed it when you mentioned trust," he went on. "It's sad, really, and you can almost feel sorry for these knuckleheads. They've been conditioned for decades to not trust anyone or anything connected to an established institution. And I'm not just talking about the government. They don't trust college professors, scientists, lawyers, women who speak their minds, or smart people in general. They think knowledge and wisdom are what elites use to manipulate and control their lives." Bill took a breath. "Like I said, it's kind of sad."

Mervin pondered Bill's words, took a long slug of the IPA. "Thanks," he finally said. "That cheers me up. I feel better now. There I was thinking it was only about the government taking their tax money and giving free things to lazy Black people. I see now that it's more than that. Could I get a shot of Jameson?"

Bill laughed and turned to pour the shot. Mervin took another swallow of beer and looked up to see Boot coming through the front door, moving like he had fire ants in his socks.

He sat beside Mervin, and breathing hard, said, "You ain't gonna believe."

"I ain't gonna believe what, Boot?"

"I'm telling you, you ain't gonna believe it."

Bill turned around, curious, and set Mervin's shot on the bar.

"I'll have one of those," Boot said.

"What? Jameson?" Bill said.

"Whatever."

"Boot, I'm about to smack you upside your head," Mervin said.

"I went out to Skeeter's place this afternoon. I figured I'd take Jack and Joe and try again."

Bill set the shot of Irish whiskey on the bar and Boot knocked it back. "You won't believe."

The look Mervin gave Boot said he was indeed on the verge of punching him in the face.

"His truck's gone," Boot said.

"What?"

"Skeeter's truck, his Tundra, it ain't there. I walked all around the house and even drove down to the boat landing. There's no sign of it anywhere and no sign of a break-in at the house. Did you take it?"

Mervin sat back and looked at Boot.

"What? No. I didn't take it. What's wrong with you?"

"Well, I know you got the keys."

Boot and Bill looked at Mervin.

"I swear," he said. "I didn't take Skeeter's truck. I haven't even been back out to his house." Mervin paused a moment. "This means it could have actually been him leaving the golf course day before yesterday. Or somebody else in his truck."

"Nobody else drives my truck," said a voice from the door to the kitchen.

They all turned to look.

"Wooo-hooo!" yelled Boot.

It was Skeeter, standing there with a dumb smirk on his face. Boot sprinted around the bar and grabbed him in a bear hug. Mervin was off the stool and waiting his turn. The other patrons in the bar were watching and wondering what the fuss was all about.

"Got dawg, Skeeter," Boot said. "I swear, man, you've had us in knots. Where you been?"

Mervin threw his arms around Skeeter, almost knocking his wire-rim glasses off his face.

"You ol' dipshit," he said, "where've you been?"

"We need to call Perch," Boot said. "He ain't gonna believe this."

"No, wait," Skeeter said. "I'm going over to Perch's house in a little while. We've got a few things to straighten out."

"Okay," Boot said. "But come on, man. Tell us where you've been."

Mervin saw Skeeter cast a quick glance at Bill and realized their favorite bartender had been unusually quiet during the celebration.

"You've been right here," Mervin said. "At Bill's, all this time."

"Well, it seemed like a convenient place to be," Skeeter said. "Probably the safest, too. There's a couple rooms and a bath upstairs, and Bill was kind enough to—"

"Look," Bill cut in. "When one of your most loyal customers is in a jam, you do what you can. That's all."

Boot's smile was so wide it almost cracked his face. "Bill, I always knew you were okay for a Yankee, and after all, you put up with us. But man, I never knew you had that kind of goodness in you."

He started around the bar to give Bill a hug.

"You stay on that side of the bar," Bill said, "or I'll throw you out." He said it like he meant it.

Boot froze and they all laughed.

"Well, one thing's certain," Boot said, eyeing Skeeter up and down. "You sure ain't lost any weight during your exile."

Skeeter's powder-blue, button-down oxford shirt was tucked into a pair of old brown corduroys and its buttons were strained to the limit.

"Yeah, I've run up quite a tab with the kitchen here," Skeeter said. "I have to say, I've gotten kind of spoiled."

Bill turned around and set four shots of Glenlivet on the bar.

"Wow, the good stuff," Mervin said.

"Just this once," Bill said. "And I want to remind you, they still haven't caught whoever's out there killing people. He might come after y'all next."

"I'm afraid that's true," Skeeter said. "We've got a lot to talk about."

"But first," Mervin said, lifting his glass. "To Skeeter, welcome home old friend."

"To Skeeter," and they all clinked glasses and drank their shots, savoring the Scotch.

"I need to get out of here before somebody sees me who shouldn't," Skeeter said.

"You going to see Perch?" Boot asked.

"Yeah, I need to get moving."

"We're going with you. Where's your truck?"

"It's out back."

"Go out there and wait," Mervin said. "I'll swing around and pick you up. Boot, meet us at Perch's house."

Bill reached behind the bar, grabbed a bottle of Johnny Walker Red, and stuffed it into a to-go bag.

"Just in case Perch is out," he said.

"Bill, you know I want to come back there and kiss you," Boot said.

"And it would be the last kiss you ever got. Now y'all get out of here."

CHAPTER TWENTY-FIVE

BOOT WISHED HE'D TAKEN A PICTURE of Perch's face when he saw Skeeter standing at his backdoor.

They laughed and pushed past Perch into the house, but only got as far as the kitchen where more hugs took place and maybe a tear or two glimmered in the corners of a couple eyes.

The band is back together, Mervin thought as he placed the bottle of Johnny Walker at the center of the circular hardwood antique kitchen table that had been in Perch's family for years. Perch went to the refrigerator and grabbed a six-pack of Miller Lite.

"Still drinking that thin beer, I see," Skeeter kidded as he took a seat at the table.

Unperturbed, Perch passed around the beers and Boot unscrewed the cap on the Scotch.

"You got glasses, Perch, or are we just gonna pass the bottle?"

Perch dutifully fetched four shot glasses from a cabinet and took a seat at the table.

"Okay, you old piss ant," Boot said, pointing his beer at Skeeter. "Tell us everything."

They sat quietly, like the Knights of the Preston Roundtable, waiting for Sir Skeeter to tell his tale.

"First, a shot," Skeeter said, and no one argued with that. "To good friends," he said.

The glasses clinked above the center of the table, the shots were knocked back, and Skeeter cleared his throat and began. He told them about the work he and Carol Baxley had been doing for the past year, the success they'd had leading up to the case of Louise Dixon.

"It was going smoothly like before," he said. "Carol was great. She had great contacts and made all the living arrangements. I provided money and any legal help we might need.

"But something strange happened last Wednesday afternoon. I was at one of the gas pumps at the Little Bear Pantry filling up my truck when this guy came up behind me and asked if I was Skeeter Ellington. I gotta tell you, it scared me, and I asked, 'Who wants to know?' He just grinned and said he was making sure, then turned around and walked away. I knew right then we were in trouble."

Mervin said that Carol had told him about Skeeter having an encounter with a strange man, and Skeeter nodded to confirm he'd told her about it. He said they decided to go ahead with their plan for Louise anyway.

Skeeter described how he was having a second cup of coffee after breakfast on Thursday morning, the day they planned to take Louise to Florence to catch a bus to Savannah, when he heard a vehicle pull up in his front yard. He went through the house, looked out the front window, and saw the same man from the gas station and another fellow getting out of a Dodge Ram pickup.

"There were two of them?" Mervin asked.

"Yes. I didn't get a good look at the second one. I was too busy running back through the house to get out of there."

Skeeter said he grabbed his phone and a pistol he'd recently bought, flew through the backdoor, and never looked back.

Turned out, Jack and Joe were on the money. Skeeter had hightailed it down the trail to the river, jumped in a kayak he kept there, and paddled upstream for all he was worth.

"I figured if I went downstream, they might be waiting for me at the boat landing."

"Good thinking," Boot said.

Somehow Skeeter lost his phone and gun in the excitement. He was pretty sure the gun went over the side of the kayak and was at the bottom of the Little Pee Dee.

"We found your phone by the trail," Mervin said. "There was a text to me, but it wasn't sent."

"I'd been thinking about what happened at the gas station and was getting more worried. I wanted to talk to you about it and was writing the text when I heard them pull up in front of the house. I have no idea how my phone ended where it did. I guess it flew out of my hand while I was running."

"I knew it," Boot exclaimed. "Jack and Joe are the best ol' coon dogs in the state."

"Calm down, Boot," Perch said. "Here, have another shot."

"Long story short," Skeeter continued, "I ditched the kayak near the bridge at Highway 9 and made my way through the woods and came out near Curry Crossroads. I was scared to get out on the highway, so I kept to the woods for about half a mile and came up behind Gator's Mini-Mart. I thought maybe if I hung around there for a while, I might be able to hitch a ride."

Mervin told him he was spotted by a Black fellow named Cedric Goins who works for the highway department.

"Yeah, I remember seeing him," Skeeter said. "But anyway, that's what happened. I was lucky enough to catch a ride with an old farmer who was going into town. He dropped me off, I snuck in the backdoor at Bill's, and I've been there ever since. Couple days ago, I convinced Bill to run me out to the house so I could get my wallet and truck. I felt guilty about not being able to pay for my meals and tip everybody. And I thought if Carol was brave enough to go back to work, why was I staying couped up?

"The house was locked but I had a spare key on a nail underneath the deck. I could tell the house had been searched and my wallet and keys were gone."

Boot looked at Mervin but didn't say anything.

"I guess the police have them," Skeeter said. "I had a spare credit card hidden in my desk and kept an extra truck key in a magnet lockbox under the rear bumper, so I got out of there pronto."

"Ahem," Boot said and looked at Mervin again.

"I've got your keys," Mervin said.

"You've got them? How?"

Mervin told Skeeter the story of how he and Boot went looking for him Saturday morning and how he took the keys, and no, he wasn't sure why he did it. "It just seemed like a good idea at the time. They're out in my truck. I'll go get 'em."

"No," Skeeter said. "You keep them for now. You never know what might happen, and besides, I've relied on your automotive instincts before."

Mervin smiled and nodded. They say quietly, each lost in his own thoughts.

"Damn," Perch said, breaking the silence. "That's a helluva story. You did good, Skeeter. Like Steve McQueen in *The Great Escape*."

"Yeah, good job, Skeeter, but we gotta find out who those two assholes are who came to your house," Boot said.

"How do we do that?" said Perch.

"I don't know," Boot said, "but we can't just hang around waiting for them to come after us."

That possibility gave them a start.

"I know who one of them might be," Mervin said. "A fellow named Deacon," and he told them about his encounter with Ronnie Dixon a few hours earlier at Hazel's studio.

"Deacon?" Boot said. "What is he a good ol' Baptist or something?"

"I don't know," Mervin said, "but we need to go to the police, tell them everything, and let them handle it."

"Yeah, like they've done such a great job so far," Perch muttered.

Skeeter had been listening and nursing his beer. He reached over, picked up the bottle of Johnny Walker, and filled his glass. He held the bottle aloft and his three cohorts signaled, sure, go ahead.

Skeeter took a sip of Scotch and said, "Bill's been keeping me up-to-date on what's happening. I'm heartbroken about Louise Dixon. She had such a good heart. I'll never forgive myself if what I was doing caused her to get killed."

"Skeeter, you were trying to help her," Mervin said. "No one could have seen this coming."

"That's not true. One of us should have seen it . . . me or Carol. Especially after all we've seen this year."

No one knew what to say so they didn't say anything.

"On the other hand, I'm proud of Carol for being out in the open and going back to work. She's flipping the bird at whoever killed Louise and Luther Peacock."

"Luther Peacock?" Boot said. "Are you saying that's who me and Mervin found the other night? The body in the shack?"

"Yeah, that's what they're saying."

"Who's saying?" Mervin asked. "How do you know this?"

"Cops drink in Bill's, too, you know."

"So, you know about me and Boot getting shot at the other night?"

Skeeter just nodded and lifted his glass.

They finished their shots and Perch asked who wanted another beer. No one did. Their alcohol-induced euphoria had waned. The reality of their situation had settled upon them, and they were just feeling drunk.

"Damn, I sold pot to ol' Luther a couple times," Boot said. "He wasn't a bad dude."

"Wasn't he a pretty good ball player back in the day?" Perch asked.

"Yeah, a shortstop," Boot said. "High school and American Legion ball."

The atmosphere at the roundtable was heavy. Skeeter felt it and tried to lighten the mood.

"I can't tell you guys how good it feels to sit here and have a drink with y'all. All that running and staying at Bill's, you know I never felt worried the whole time. I knew if worse came to worse, you rascals would have my back."

"No question," Mervin said. "You'd do the same for us."

"Absolutely," Perch said.

Boot reached over and slapped Skeeter on the back. "I wouldn't help you out of a hog trough, you old lawyerin' fool."

Skeeter leaned back and roared. Perch fist-bumped with Boot, and Mervin, in an act of ill-advised bravado, snatched up the Johnny Walker and took a hit straight from the bottle.

"That's the time," said Boot. "Hand me that bottle."

Mervin did, then said, "I need to get home. I can't wait to tell Becca you're okay."

"You've got to take me back to Bill's first," Skeeter said.

"What about the stuff you needed to straighten out with Perch?" Boot asked.

"Oh, yeah, I forgot about that. It's just record-keeping stuff."

"Stay here tonight," Perch said. "I'll take you back to Bill's tomorrow."

"We gotta decide what to do," Boot said, slurring his words a little.

"I'm calling Barbara Lowrie in the morning whether y'all like it or not," Mervin said. "We need to sleep on this, sober up, and be ready for what's next. I've got a feeling it's gonna get crazy."

"That's not a bad plan," Skeeter said. "We all need to be ready to answer a lot of questions. And I'd like to add, don't sell the Preston cops short. I think they might be getting closer than they realize."

The four sexagenarians rose unsteadily, high-fived, hugged, said good night, and Boot and Mervin left through the backdoor. Before Perch could close the door and lock it, Boot poked his head back into the kitchen.

"Has anybody booked tee times for Sunday?"

CHAPTER TWENTY-SIX

MERVIN SAT GINGERLY in a plastic Adirondack chair on the deck, gently placed his mug of coffee on the armrest, and waited for the pine trees in the backyard to come into focus. For the third time this week he told himself he needed to cut back on his drinking.

He had no memory of driving home and yet his Silverado was parked neatly in the carport. He did remember coming in the backdoor, blurting out to Becca that Skeeter was okay, and kissing her on the mouth. She was over the moon and wanted to talk to Skeeter, so they called Perch's house, and when Skeeter came on, Becca grabbed the phone, gushed about how happy she was, and said she couldn't wait to see him.

Mervin leaned against the wall next to the door to the den, drooling and grinning. He loved it that Becca loved his friends. She hung up and wanted to toast the return of Skeeter. Mervin couldn't possibly say no to that. They took the celebration to the bedroom and almost made love two nights in a row, but the little fellow wouldn't cooperate.

"He's too drunk," Mervin mumbled before passing out.

Mervin awoke in the morning with a groan.He was hurting. He looked at his watch and saw that it was almost 10:30. He needed to talk to Skeeter so they could synchronize their stories. Get on the same page. Should he call Perch or Bill's Corner?

Mervin took a sip of coffee and punched the number for Perch.

"What?" said a groggy voice.

"Put Skeeter on."

Mervin heard some shuffling and coughing then Skeeter's voice.

"What's up?"

"I feel like shit."

"Oh really, why's that?"

It wasn't funny. Mervin shivered, thought it was probably just the shakes.

"When should I call Barbara Lowrie to let her know that Skeeter Ellington, the creature from the black lagoon, has returned?"

"Wait until around noontime. I'm not feeling all that great myself. Perch is gonna run me down to Bill's in a few minutes. I want to shower and change clothes. And I need to call Carol Baxley."

"She's gonna be happy to hear from you."

"Yeah, I can't wait to see her."

"Okay," Mervin said, who felt like he might puke. "I'll call you at Bill's right after I hang up with Lowrie. It'll be a little after twelve. Be by the phone."

"Yes, sir, captain," Skeeter said and ended the call.

Mervin sat the phone on the armrest opposite the mug of coffee. It was a gorgeous morning. Bright sunshine and a chill in the air. Birds were calling to each other across Mervin's backyard.

Is Thanksgiving next week? He thought it was. December would be here a week later and maybe it would bring some wintertime weather.

Mervin doubted it. There wasn't much difference in the seasons in

South Carolina nowadays. It was brutally hot in the summer and not quite so hot the rest of the year. There might be a week or two of cold weather in January or February, but nothing to get worked up about.

Mervin looked at his watch again and saw that he could sit on the deck for another half hour. Then he would need to eat something and call Barbara Lowrie. He hoped he wouldn't have to go to the police station with Skeeter. He really needed to eat something, but in a little while.

———⌣———

Barbara Lowrie was sitting in her Ford Explorer in the 7-Eleven parking lot at the corner of Main and Highway 9. She was scrolling through emails about the case and saw that some interesting information had been uncovered.

The SLED agent, Mankey, had relayed the results of an FBI search on the name Harold Cephus. There weren't many, and almost all of them were so far away from South Carolina they couldn't have anything to do with the events in Preston.

Except for one. There was an evangelical preacher named Harold Cephus in Washington County on the Florida panhandle. He had a criminal record filled with assault charges, attempted rape, and the illegal possession of firearms. All this occurred before he found the Lord and founded his own church.

The disappointing part of the email revealed that Cepus had died in a boating accident six months ago, eliminating him from being the man who'd befriended Luther Peacock and Ronnie Dixon.

Barbara was pondering this new wrinkle when her phone buzzed. It was Mervin Hayes.

"Hello, Mr. Hayes. What's going on?"

"Good news. A key witness in your case will be arriving at the police station in about fifteen minutes."

"Who might that be?" Barbara asked, indulging Mervin.

"August Ellington, or to people who know and love him, Skeeter."

Barbara sat up and closed the laptop.

"Skeeter? He's okay? Where is he?"

"He's absolutely fine, and he's on his way to make a full statement. I suggest you be there."

The phone clicked off and Barbara scrambled to crank the Explorer. She tapped the number for Chief Holt, told him about Skeeter, and floored the gas pedal before she heard his reply.

It was like a mosh pit in the conference room. Skeeter was sitting at one end of the table and was surrounded by a variety of law enforcement officers. Chief Holt sat at the opposite end of the table flanked by Detective Stanton, Barbara Lowrie, SLED agent Mankey, and Sheriff Whittington.

Skeeter had been through his entire story, but Mankey and Stanton picked it apart, wanting to hear it again. The sticking point was the arrival of two men at Skeeter's home a week ago. The officers had been focusing on one suspect, the man described by Ronnie Dixon as being Harold Cephus. But Skeeter's story introduced an accomplice.

"You're saying he was tall, white, and was wearing a baseball cap?" Mankey asked.

"Yes. Like I said, it was a Braves cap."

"That's all you can remember about him?"

"Look," Skeeter said, "I told you I looked out the window, saw two men getting out of a black Dodge truck, and I turned and ran. I remember it was a Braves hat because I'm a Braves fan."

Frustration was growing around the table. Skeeter's story wasn't exactly shining new light on the case. For the past seventy-two hours, no one had been able to locate, much less apprehend, the individual named Harold Cephus, a.k.a. Deacon, who by now could be five states away.

But no one believed that. There was a strong sense he was still in Preston and still had work to do. Carol Baxley was still under police protection, and when it was offered to Ronnie Dixon, he turned it down. Said he could take care of himself. Barbara Lowrie laughed when she heard about this and didn't doubt the good ol' boy for a minute.

And now Skeeter Ellington had dropped a second suspect in their laps.

"Do you realize we've been looking for you for days?" asked a clearly agitated Detective Stanton. "Why are you just now coming forward?"

Skeeter kept his cool. After all, he had been a shrewd-and-forceful lawyer in his day, and he'd retained his guile and confidence. He could deflect, defuse, or redirect any argument with the best of them.

"Your search for me hasn't been all that rigorous," he said. "I'm sure a few officers worked the phones and others made inquiries at homes out near my house. But I doubt anyone orchestrated a search into the swamp and woods along the Little Pee Dee to find me or my body. Or am I mistaken?"

Barbara smiled. Skeeter was sharp. *Hell, he's probably the smartest person in the room.*

"Where have you been all this time?" Stanton asked, trying to maintain his authority.

"I'm reluctant to say. My port of refuge has worked quite well so far, and I intend to keep it that way. As to why I didn't come forward earlier, I was trying to avoid a fate similar to that of Luther Peacock. Now I suggest you continue to protect Carol Baxley and intensify your search for this screwball and his Braves-cap-wearing sidekick before more bodies start turning up in country shacks. Are we done?"

Silence engulfed the room before Chief Holt finally spoke.

"Mr. Ellington, for the past few days I've dug deeply into your background and also Carol Baxley's, and as I've already told some of the officers as this table, I'm impressed with the efforts you were making to help these women. And I'm a bit ashamed that our law enforcement agencies have fallen somewhat short in addressing the issue of domestic violence. It's a failing that needs to be corrected.

"So I guess I'd like to say thank you, but I'd also add, I don't want you traipsing around Preston like you've been deputized and getting in our way." He paused and closed the laptop in front of him. "Do you understand?"

Skeeter nodded.

"Sergeant Lowrie will return the phone and wallet we confiscated and you're free to go. But I'd suggest you keep your phone charged. I'm sure we'll need to talk to you again."

Barbara's heart swelled in admiration for her boss. He had always been a tough, by-the-book copper, and they'd not always seen eye to eye. But she had long suspected that at the end of the day his heart would be in the right place.

There was a lot of shuffling and throat clearing around the table as everyone rose to leave. Skeeter wasted no time making his way out the door and into the squad room. Barbara Lowrie motioned him over to her desk where she fetched his phone and wallet and handed them over. Skeeter mumbled his thanks and kept going until he was outside and on the street.

Barbara followed and called, "Mr. Ellington."

Skeeter turned.

"I'd just like to second what my chief said. I've gotten to know a friend of yours, Mervin Hayes, and I know you all are trying to do the right thing."

"I don't want my friends dragged into this," Skeeter said.

"They already are, Mr. Ellington. You need to trust us. Trust me."

"I might trust you and I might trust your boss, but I'm sorry. That's as far as it goes."

Skeeter turned and climbed into his Tundra. He cranked it up, backed out of the parking spot, and was gone, leaving Barbara standing on the sidewalk wondering why Skeeter's trust in the local police didn't extend to everyone on the force.

CHAPTER TWENTY-SEVEN

THE SALESMAN AT THE DODGE DEALERSHIP in Fayetteville had been an eager beaver. He was focused on the resale of the shiny black truck and had visions of being salesman of the month. Deacon picked up on it right away.

"I'm just tired of the truck," he said. "Don't get me wrong, it's a beautiful vehicle and all, but I'm looking for something sportier, more compact, easier to park."

The salesman, Butch, was dressed in khaki slacks and a deep-red knit polo. "I've got just the thing," he said.

He showed Deacon a Dodge Challenger that was only a year old. It had been repossessed from a young Marine at Fort Bragg who got behind on the payments.

"All-wheel-drive, a real muscle car," Butch said.

Deacon made a show of being unsure, said he wasn't crazy about the price and thought he should get more for his truck. Butch came down on the price of the Challenger and the clincher dropped when Deacon said he'd pay the difference in cash.

So now Deacon was cruising back to Preston on I-95 in a dark green Dodge Challenger with two wide black racing stripes from front to back. He put his foot down. *Damn, this thing is fast,* he thought as he blew past cars in the right-hand lane. He wasn't crazy about the racing stripes, but at least no one would be searching for him in this model Dodge back in Preston.

The power of the vehicle and the expanse of the interstate gave Deacon a sense of invincibility and a chance to clear his head. He needed to think, formulate a new plan. Things had not gone well. He should have been on the road back to Florida days ago.

The lawyer's escape a week ago was just bad luck, but Deacon knew he had made mistakes, too. He should have never trusted the abilities of Ronnie Dixon and Luther Peacock. Shame about Luther. He hadn't been such a bad guy, but he'd had to go. Maybe the Dixon kid, too, but that could wait. Right now, Deacon needed to focus on the original goal. Eliminate the root cause of the problem, the ones who had broken holy codes, the ones responsible for this chaos.

Deacon snuggled down in the leather bucket seat. The Challenger hummed beneath him. A plan began to materialize. If you need to lure a target into the open, you need bait. And what better bait than someone your target cares about?

Deacon was excited but he didn't need to get pulled over by a state trooper. He slowed and flashed by a sign that read *Preston, Next Four Exits.* *It's time to get to work,* he thought. *Time to do God's work.*

Mervin watched through the front window as the mailman stopped at the mailbox, stuffed a handful of envelopes inside, then motored off to the next house down the street. He went outside to collect the mail and noticed his hangover was beginning to fade.

"Hot damn," Mervin said as he flipped through the mail. He'd found a small package and knew what was inside—the new CD from the Drive-By Truckers. He ordered all his music from online sites these days, seeing how there hadn't been a record store in Preston for years. There was probably one in Charlotte or Columbia, surely down in Charleston, but those cities were two hours away.

Mervin remembered when he was a kid and there were two competing record stores on Main Street in Preston. It was the time of transistor radios, the British Invasion, and sweet soul music. He'd ride his spider bike downtown after school and ask the lady in the record shop for the latest single by The Beatles, Dave Clark Five, The Association, or Tommy James & The Shondells. *Crimson and Clover*, what a great song.

People liked to say that everything stayed the same in Preston, but Mervin knew that was far from the truth, especially in light of events from the past week. His perspective had changed, and he realized that living in a small, rural town could lull you into complacency. Every day was like the previous one. Granted, there were cable news channels and the internet, but it did seem like living in a cocoon. Preston was isolated. The problems of the outside world were far away— until they weren't.

The town had joined the big leagues. It had its own serial killer and a cast of domestic abusers. You could sense the change. People in the checkout lines at grocery stores, Dollar Tree, and the Walmart were shaking their heads and talking about that poor girl who'd been found at the Urgent Care. "And did you hear about Luther Peacock? Why would someone want to kill him?"

People were scared and worried. The killings would surely be a hot topic at church on Sunday and Mervin didn't doubt that preachers would use them to make points in their sermons. He hoped they would also make the point that Jesus wouldn't be happy with men who beat their wives.

Mervin hoped these men of God would tell people to face up to the facts. Tell their congregations that Preston was not immune from the evils of the big cities. Shout it from the pulpits, we must deal with it now or watch as it takes root and blossoms into more hate and tragedy.

But he wasn't optimistic. Such a clear moral direction wouldn't be springing suddenly from local churches. However, all the thoughts of Sunday's go-to-meeting reminded him to call Benny Martin and make a tee time.

He ripped open the package as he walked back to the house and pulled out the CD. It was called *The Unraveling* and Mervin laughed out loud. There couldn't be a better description of what was happening in his hometown. He couldn't wait to crank it up and see what the band had to say this time.

It was still early, only a little after three, so he had time to go for a ride. He'd recently installed a new stereo in his truck, which was where he most enjoyed listening to music.

He'd cruise up 301 toward North Carolina, then circle back on the interstate. Plug in the Truckers and clear the last of the cobwebs from his hangover. Mervin had talked to Skeeter who'd told him all about his meeting at the police station. Skeeter said he'd managed to keep Bill's Corner out of the conversation, so he thought it best he didn't join the fellows for happy hour later that evening. Mervin agreed. They couldn't afford to have Skeeter spotted sitting at the bar in the joint he was using as a hideout.

Skeeter also said he'd called Carol Baxley at the Urgent Care, and she'd almost started crying into the phone. She probably would have, Skeeter said, but she was at work. The craziest thing, amid all this chaos and confusion—another woman had contacted Carol for help. She lived in a trailer park not two miles from where Luther Peacock had lived. Carol told the woman she would meet with her later and see if they could work something out. Mervin told Skeeter to be careful and they signed off.

Then Boot called. He'd sounded subdued, a bit worried. He said he'd be at Bill's around five but didn't want to stay long. He added that he had a suggestion he wanted to pass along and hoped Mervin would be there to listen. Mervin said he would.

Back inside, Mervin called Becca and left her a message saying he was going to happy hour but wouldn't be late. She could call if she wanted some takeout from Bill's.

There was nothing left to do but lock up the house, climb in the Silverado, and pop the new DBT into the stereo. Actually, there was one other thing Mervin decided to do at the last minute. He went into the master bedroom, opened the drawer in Becca's bedside table, and extracted a small wooden cigar box. He took it to the bathroom, lifted the lighter and small pipe from inside, and fired up. Just a couple hits, a mellow buzz for the afternoon cruise.

He replaced the cigar box and headed for his truck, remembering to lock the backdoor on his way out of the house. *Damn*, he thought, as he cranked the truck. *Boot might need to back off on all the grafting and splicing of his cannabis concoctions.* Mervin sat for a minute to let his buzz settle before he backed out of the carport. He turned left out of the driveway, drove through the neighborhood, and honked the horn at a neighbor who was digging in a flowerbed. *That man's always working in the yard,* Mervin thought.

Mervin turned onto 301 and realized he was high as a kite. It was a good feeling. He needed it. He turned up the Truckers CD and when the second track hit, a tune called *Armageddon's Back in Town,* he put his foot down, blew past the city-limits sign, and rocketed toward North Carolina. *Armageddon comes to Preston. Perfect.* He knew the Truckers wouldn't let him down.

The music and steady hum of the truck's V8 lulled Mervin into a mellow fog, and before he knew it, he had driven into North Carolina and was almost all the way to Lumberton before he hopped on I-95 for the return trip. The Silverado was heavy and powerful, the 2500HD model, and Mervin loved the air intake on the hood and the fact that the engine would turn 400 horses at 5,000 RPMs. He put his foot down and was approaching Preston in no time, as the last tune on the Truckers' CD reverberated in the cab.

"Is there an evil in the world?" Patterson Hood sang. "Yes, there's an evil in the world. It creeps up from behind you when you are least suspecting."

Mervin grinned, turned off at the Highway 34 exit, and headed for town. He checked the time and saw he would be at Bill's just after five. Friday happy hour would be crowded. Mervin rolled down Main Street looking for a parking spot and, luckily, saw someone backing out of a spot only a block from the bar.

Mervin put on his turn signal, waited until the other car was clear, then pulled into the spot next to a dark-green Dodge Challenger.

Nice ride, Mervin thought as he climbed out of his truck. *I bet that thing has some juice under the hood.* He punched the lock button on his key ring, heard the *"chirp,"* and started down the sidewalk.

He realized that it was exactly one week ago when he, Boot, and Perch were sitting at the bar wondering where Skeeter was. Only one week and so many lives had been turned upside down. Not to mention the two that had been violently snuffed out.

The thought made Mervin shiver as he stepped into Bill's and saw that the place was busy as expected. It was a big college football weekend, the Carolina-Clemson rivalry game was tomorrow. Thanksgiving was just a few days away. The locals were ready to cut loose.

Mervin saw Boot at the far end of the bar and a stool was conspicuously empty next to him. Mervin slid onto it.

"About time," Boot said.

"Dude, what kind of wacky-backy are you growing out there on that farm?"

Boot smiled. "Nice, ain't it? You need to be careful though. It can pack a wallop."

Bill set a Miller High Life and a shot of Jameson in front of Mervin and hurried down the bar to serve another customer.

"Perch was here for a little while, but he went home," Boot said.

"Worried about the game tomorrow?" Mervin asked.

"That's the least of his worries."

"Yeah, I know. Sorry. College football kind of pales in comparison to what we've been going through."

"I don't know," Boot mused. "It's Carolina-Clemson after all."

Mervin's phone dinged with a text from Becca saying she was fixing spaghetti for supper. She wondered if Mervin could bring Skeeter to the house. He loved her spaghetti sauce. Mervin thought it was a great idea and texted back that he would see what he could do.

"I can see you got other things on your mind," Boot said. "But just hear me out for a minute."

Mervin apologized and stuffed his phone in his pocket.

"I want you and Perch and Skeeter, if we can convince him, to meet me down here behind Bill's tomorrow morning."

"What for?" Mervin asked.

"Y'all just meet me down here at ten o'clock and it will all become clear." Boot tossed a credit card on the bar. "I gotta go," he said.

"Can I at least buy you a shot?"

"Yeah, go ahead."

Mervin signaled to Bill and an Irish whiskey and tequila shot appeared.

"Watch your back, Boot," Mervin said as they clinked glasses.

"Always," Boot said, and he headed for the door.

Mervin called Skeeter and passed along Becca's invitation. He was delighted and said it was just what he needed. Mervin said he was downstairs in the bar and Skeeter could ride with him. But Skeeter replied, no, he would make his own way to Mervin and Becca's house, and they ended the call.

Probably for the best, Mervin thought. He asked one of the bartenders Bill employed on busy nights, a young man named Matthew, for another Miller High Life and told him he wanted to settle up. He paid his tab, nursed the beer for a few minutes, then slid off the stool.

He nodded at Bill on his way out the door, and Bill waved in return. Times had changed. The easygoing Friday happy hour had become a little more tense, a not-so-happy experience. Mervin sent Becca a text saying he and Skeeter would be arriving shortly. She could put the garlic bread in the oven.

CHAPTER TWENTY-EIGHT

DEACON DIDN'T LIKE BARS. He wasn't much of a drinker, and he never got the hang of social chit-chat with strangers. Whenever he was in a crowded place like Bill's Corner, he became self-conscious and felt like everyone was watching him.

Nevertheless, here he was, sitting at the packed bar a few seats down from the driver of the big Ford truck, the man who was handy with a 12-gauge pump. The man was tall and reasonably fit, a full head of hair graying at the temples. Deacon figured he'd be a tough nut to crack in a one-on-one fight.

But it wouldn't come to that. They would never get that close. But this shotgun shooter who people called Boot was going to pay just the same.

Deacon was nursing his second beer when another man came in and took the seat next to Boot who'd apparently been saving it for him. This must be the sidekick who was out at the shack the other night. Average height, kind of pudgy but looked like he worked out every now and then. *Nothing to worry about,* Deacon thought.

He caught a bartender's eye, ordered French fries, and casually said, "That fellow who sat down next to Boot, I feel like I know him."

"Oh, that's Mervin Hayes," the young man said. "He's in here all the time. He and Boot are tight. Another one?"

Deacon didn't want another beer but said, "Sure, one more." He was careful as he observed the interactions between the two men who were in serious discussion.

His French fries and fresh beer arrived, and Deacon squirted a blob of ketchup in one end of the basket.

"Those smell good," said the man to his right who was all dressed up for Friday night in jeans, Wolverine work boots, and a sport coat. He'd been trying his luck with a woman to his right who'd splashed on too much perfume after work.

"Go ahead, help yourself," Deacon said. "I can't eat all these."

He slid the basket over so the man and the woman, whose girth suggested she might need to avoid fried food, could reach the fries.

"That's kind of you," the man said. The woman gave a tight, grateful smile, reached right over, and dipped a big fry in the ketchup.

Wow, I'm blending in, Deacon thought. All the while he'd cast cautious glances down the bar at his two targets who were wrapping up their conversation. He would have given anything to hear what was being said, but it was much too loud in the bar.

The tall one, Boot, left first. Fifteen minutes later, after sending a text on his phone, the second man slid off his stool and exited.

Deacon ate a couple fries and finished his beer. He waved a credit card at the bartender, told the potential lovebirds they could finish the fries, and headed for the door. He felt good. The beers had given him a mellow buzz and reassured him that he was on a righteous path. He was doing what needed to be done. It was as simple as that.

Skeeter pushed his plate away. He'd shown his admiration for Becca's sauce by devouring two heaping helpings of spaghetti, a thick slice of garlic bread, and a couple glasses of red wine.

"More wine?" Becca asked, holding the bottle aloft. "I've got cheesecake for dessert. It's store bought, but pretty good."

Skeeter looked at her like she was out of her mind.

"No way," said Mervin who'd done his bit by packing away a mountain of spaghetti. "You keep going with the wine and me and Skeeter will have a small Scotch."

Skeeter sighed with relief and smiled a thank you at Mervin. It had been a wonderful dinner. Becca was overjoyed that Skeeter was once again at their table.

They'd talked about everything. Skeeter related his story of the past week and Becca told of the anxiety she and her fellow teachers were feeling at the school. Skeeter said he understood and that they had a right to be worried.

Mervin asked about the latest victim who'd turned up at the Urgent Care. He wondered if Skeeter and Carol would help her.

"I don't know," Skeeter said. "It's all a bit chaotic right now. I'm sure Carol will do something to make her feel safe for the time being."

"I'm still a bit in shock about all this," Becca said. "I mean, I'm not naïve. I know that men beat their wives and it's a terrible thing, but this much of it? And in Preston?"

"Well, we're in the Bible belt after all," Skeeter said.

"What's that supposed to mean?" Mervin asked.

Becca laughed. "What? You're going to defend these people just because you got dunked when you were a teenager?"

It was true. Mervin was baptized at the Preston Baptist Church at age thirteen. The preacher had held his nose, put a hand behind his back, and lowered him under the water in a tank behind the choir loft during a Sunday evening service back in 1967.

Mervin thought he'd feel different when he came up for air—but he didn't. As the years passed, he drifted away from the church and felt justified when many so-called Christians started exhibiting tendencies of paranoia and bigotry.

"No," he said. "I'm just not sure I see a connection, that's all. I was thinking earlier today how the preachers in this town could make a difference. This is about morality, isn't it? I mean, I know it's a long shot, but wouldn't it be great if these men of God would denounce this behavior and put us back on the right track?"

"Don't count on it," Skeeter said. "Carol looked into this spousal abuse thing and found that a large number of offenders profess to be evangelical Christians, although they're not regular churchgoers."

"So, what are you saying? They get their heads filled with all this Old Testament male superiority stuff and use that to justify their cruelty?"

"Old Testament, New Testament, whatever," Skeeter said. "But that's pretty much it. They feel they have a divine right to silence a woman who talks back or speaks her mind."

"Sign me up," said Mervin. "I know a wife who needs to learn her place."

"Yeah, you keep that up," Becca said, "and your place tonight will be the backseat of your truck out in the carport."

Mervin and Skeeter howled, and while Mervin was fetching a bottle of Scotch from the cupboard, Becca said, "Y'all can laugh, but I'm serious."

"We're laughing because we know you're serious," Skeeter said.

Mervin poured a nice measure for himself and Skeeter, and Becca topped off her wine. There was a peaceful warmth in the kitchen, a contentment that connects family and friends. It drove their worries away for the moment.

Mervin broke the reverie when he said to Skeeter, "Boot wants to meet with me and you and Perch tomorrow morning out behind Bill's at ten."

"What for?"

"I don't know," Mervin said. "He said it was important, so I called Perch and he said he would be there."

"Okay," Skeeter said. "Who knows what that nut has up his sleeve."

"My money is on that nut making all this right," Becca said. "But

Mervin, if he gets you into another shoot-out with a psychopath, I'll string you both up by your balls."

Skeeter laughed and it got quiet around the table again.

"The Bible belt," Mervin muttered. "More like the divorce belt or the obesity belt."

"The poverty belt," added Skeeter. "The smokers' belt."

"The teen-pregnancy belt," said Becca. "The gay-porn belt."

Mervin and Skeeter looked at each other.

"Becca, is there something you'd like to share with us?" Skeeter asked.

"It's okay, honey," Mervin said. "Nothing will go further than this kitchen."

"That's it," said Becca, sliding her chair back with a screech and getting up from the table. "Get a pillow and a blanket. The backseat of your truck awaits."

CHAPTER TWENTY-NINE

MERVIN, SKEETER, AND PERCH were standing next to Skeeter's truck, talking and drinking coffee out of Styrofoam cups, when Boot turned in the alley, roared toward them in a cloud of dust, and slid to a stop just ten feet away.

He lowered the window. "Y'all get in."

"Where we going?" asked Perch.

"Out to my place," Boot said.

"Out to your place?" Mervin said. "Why couldn't we just meet you out there?"

"No need for Skeeter to be tooling around in his truck in the middle of the morning."

"I could have picked him up and given him a ride," Mervin said.

"Mervin, just get in the truck."

Mervin climbed in the front next to Boot and Skeeter and Perch settled in the back of the king-cab. Boot floored it and they hit the street, took a left, and headed out of town.

"Why all the mystery, Boot?" Skeeter hollered from the backseat over the voice of Lucinda Williams who was singing about all the foolishness in the world.

"Don't worry," Boot said. "Y'all gonna thank me in a little while. Wait and see." He turned up the music in time for the guitar solo.

They took Main Street through town, turned onto the highway that led to I-95, crossed the bridge over the interstate, and ten minutes later were rolling down the long driveway to Boot's two-story farmhouse.

Boot veered onto a dirt road that circled the house and led off toward fields and woods at the back. Jack and Joe bounded off the back porch, and with ears flopping, ran down the road behind the truck. Sheds lined both sides of the road for about one hundred yards, and Mervin wondered if one might contain Boot's thriving cannabis cultivation.

As if he had read Mervin's mind, Perch asked, "You growing pot in one of these barns?"

"No, man, that's a fresh-air enterprise."

They watched silently as Boot pulled over next to a sagging tobacco barn, the last of the structures on the road. He switched off the truck and said gleefully, "Let's go!"

They climbed out of the truck and waited as Boot hopped into the back and unlocked a steel toolbox in the truck bed. He reached in and took out a Colt Python revolver.

"Here you go," he said and handed it to Perch.

He reached back in and took out a Beretta M9.

"Something for you," he said and passed it to Mervin.

"And for my friend who drops guns in the river, try holding on to this one."

Boot handed Skeeter a Glock 17.

"Holy shit, Boot," Skeeter said as he hefted the weight of the pistol. "When did you become an arms dealer?"

Boot pulled an old knapsack out of the toolbox, closed the lid, and hopped out of the truck. Mervin was scratching Jack's head, but when Jack and Joe saw the guns, the two dogs turned and lit off back up the road to the house.

"They don't like the noise," Boot said. "Follow me."

Mervin, Skeeter, and Perch fell in behind Boot and followed him around to the back of the tobacco barn where they saw an assortment of cans and bottles lined up on top of a long board balanced between two cinder-block towers. Behind the bottles, the barn's heavy beams were pockmarked from previous practice sessions.

"It's a shooting range," Mervin said.

"Right on," said Boot and he started pulling boxes of ammunition out of the knapsack. "Perch, go set some bottles and cans on the board in those empty spaces." Boot tossed ammo to Mervin and Skeeter and said, "Load up."

"I'm not crazy about this," Skeeter said.

"What do you mean?" Boot asked. "You bought a gun to protect yourself and Carol Baxley, so what's the problem?"

"I know," Skeeter said. "I regret that. I was never comfortable with it and knew there was just as much chance of me getting shot with it than me shooting somebody else."

"Look, Skeeter, you can petition and fight for gun control all you want, and I got no problem with that," Boot said. "In fact, I agree we need more gun regulation in this country. But for now, I think it would be a good idea if you learned a few basics, because there's someone out there looking to kill you."

They stood silently as Perch returned from completing his task.

"What?" he said. "What'd I miss?"

"Nothing," Skeeter said as he slid a clip into the Glock.

Boot led the would-be marksmen to a spot about twenty feet away, at the verge of a freshly tilled field, reached in the knapsack again, and passed around pairs of foam earplugs. Then he took the Python from Perch and filled the chamber. He raised it with arms outstretched and said, "All you have to do is breathe slowly and squeeze."

There were three loud bangs and two of the bottles shattered. Boot handed the gun back to Perch.

"Y'all just aim and get the feel for it. I'm not expecting you to be crack shots right off. I just want you to know how it feels if there's ever a need."

"More like crack heads," Mervin muttered as he aimed the Beretta, squeezed the trigger, and saw one of the barn's beams splinter a foot above his target.

"You've got to allow for the kick," Boot said.

Perch fired a couple rounds but didn't hit anything. Skeeter aimed the Glock and Boot told him to use two hands. When Skeeter squeezed the trigger, a Pepsi bottle exploded.

Skeeter suppressed a smile.

"Lucky shot," Perch said.

Another half hour was spent shooting, and the more they practiced, the more often a tin can went flying. They exchanged weapons to experience the difference. Mervin had to admit it was exhilarating and he saw how an attraction to firearms might overwhelm common sense. But a morning of target practice hadn't changed his mind about guns. He was glad when they were once again locked safely away in Boot's toolbox.

They climbed back into the truck but before Boot cranked it, he turned and said, "Look, I don't want y'all to think I'm some kind of gun nut. The Colt has been in the family, I have a Glock 20 up at the house that I've had for years, and the Baretta and the other Glock, I bought those at a gun shop in Florence a few days ago after my background check cleared. I've been thinking about this. I want y'all to take one home. Just choose the one you want and be careful."

"I'm fine with the Glock," said Skeeter.

"Yeah, I'm okay with the one I used," Perch said.

"What about you, Mervin?" Boot asked.

Mervin stared out the windshield. "I'm good," he said.

"You're good? What do you mean you're good? You got a gun at home?"

"No, Boot, you know I don't have a gun at home," Mervin said, making eye contact with Boot. "When I got home the other night after we were out at that shack, I promised Becca I would never get in such a situation again. And I meant it. She was hysterical, Boot, and I understood why she felt that way. I never want her to feel that way again."

Silence stretched for an uncomfortably long time. Boot eventually reached down and turned the key in the ignition. The truck roared to life.

"I understand," he said. "It's cool. Don't worry about it."

"Besides," Mervin said. "I always thought you would be there to protect me."

Boot looked at Mervin, smiled, and threw the truck into a U-turn. He punched the gas, and they headed back up the dirt road to the house.

"*I need protection*," Lucinda sang from the stereo, "*I need protection from the enemy of love.*"

Saturdays in Clarke Studios were usually fully booked, but this one had been session free. All the same, it had been a busy day. Hazel had done some final mastering on the Suburbs of Hysteria project, balanced the studio's books, and arranged her schedule for the coming week.

She'd also gotten a call from the Suburbs' lead singer who told her once again how much they'd enjoyed working with her and that they'd recommended her studio to another Charlotte band, a trio called Thunder Pulse.

"They're somewhere between Cream and Nirvana," the Suburb said. "But they're not too bad."

Hazel thanked him for the endorsement and said she looked forward to hearing from Thunder Pulse. Less than an hour later, the phone rang again, and it was a sweet lady from an A.M.E. church near Darlington. She said she managed a gospel quartet and was wondering about the studio's rates. Hazel said she'd be willing to work within the quartet's budget because there was nothing like recording Black gospel music. It was the one thing that gave Hazel the feeling that there might actually be a God.

So, all in all, it was an outstanding day of solitary accomplishment in the studio. Hazel leaned back in the captain's chair in the control room and marveled at all the musical instruments and recording technology at her fingertips. Once again, she was dumbfounded at how this place had endured, a recording studio in a small Southern town well off the beaten track.

But it had, and it was all down to the vision of the late Douglas Jonathan Clarke and, she had to admit, the devotion she'd poured into it over the years. She smiled at the thought of DJ and hoped he was mixing some killer tracks up in rock 'n' roll heaven.

I guess music does make the world go round, she thought. No matter where people might live or what their station in life, some folks are compelled to be creative.

And the talent! There had been so many times when Hazel had been pinned to her chair by the amazing sounds created by everyday folks. Such as old Jerome and his devil blues. And the twelve-year-old girl who came in with her daddy to record some fiddle tunes. Her daddy accompanied her on guitar, and the little girl, her tongue poking out the corner of her mouth, launched into some deep mountain fiddle magic that gave Hazel goose bumps.

Hazel sighed at the memory and started switching everything off in the control room. She slung the bag with her laptop over her shoulder, turned off the lights as she walked down the hall to the front door, stepped outside, and locked the door behind her.

"Excuse me."

The voice startled Hazel so much she dropped her keys. Turning, she saw a thin man, her height, dressed in black and with three days of black-and-gray stubble on his face. She instinctively knew who he was.

"You're Hazel, right?"

"Yes," she said, a hoarse whisper.

"I didn't mean to startle you," he said. "I've been looking for a friend of yours and was hoping you could help me."

"I'll never help—"

Hazel never got the words out. With lightning speed, the man punched Hazel in the stomach. When she doubled over, he followed with a vicious uppercut that landed on her chin and snapped her head back.

"I hope you'll reconsider," he said and hit her again, a savage closed-fist blow to the face. Hazel's knees buckled and everything went black.

CHAPTER THIRTY

SERGEANT BARBARA LOWRIE told the driver of the black Dodge truck that he was free to go. It was the second black Dodge she'd pulled over in the past eight hours. Neither had Florida plates nor any connection to the case, but Barbara had done her duty just the same.

The driver was named Danny Boan. His friends called him Duck, and he'd had several run-ins with the Preston police. Nothing serious, drunkenness and a couple bar fights. Barbara had gone to school with his sister.

"I'll tell Jenny Lynn you said hey," Boan said, his elbow resting on the open window. "I'd heard you were with the police. You look good in that uniform."

Barbara flashed a big smile. "Well, I appreciate that Danny, but just make sure I don't have to see you again in an official capacity. Take care now and stay out of trouble."

How she said it and the way her smile dissolved into a serious stare told Boan that the police sergeant meant business.

"Yes, ma'am," he said. "I hope you catch the bad guy."

Barbara watched the truck's taillights as he roared away. It was getting dark. She should head into town and clock out at the station.

God dang it, she thought as she climbed back into the Explorer. *How could this Cephus character still be eluding us?* She picked up her phone and called mentor Pete Shumpert.

"Where are you?" he asked after one ring.

"Out on the beach highway, a little ways down from the VFW hut. I just pulled a guy in a black Dodge truck. Name of Danny Boan. I went to school with his sister, Jenny Lynn."

"I know ol' Duck," Pete said. "He's been in trouble a few times, but basically he's a good boy. That sister's a piece of work, though."

"You'll have to tell me about her sometime," Barbara said. "I'm heading to the station just to see if anybody's heard anything, then I'm going home. Dang it, Pete, why can't we find this asshole? We know what he's driving. We know it has Florida plates. Preston's not that big. Where can he be hiding?"

"You mean if he's still here?"

"He's still here. You know it. I know it. He's still got business to tend to."

"Yeah, I think you're right," Pete said. "But that doesn't mean he's still driving a black Dodge pickup or he's even staying in Preston."

"Well, what do you suggest we do?"

"Keep working. Keep looking for him. Go back and talk to Skeeter Ellington again. Talk to Ronnie Dixon again. Get a better description. Maybe SLED could bring in a sketch artist, put it out there on social media."

"The Chief has talked to them about that, and they might try it. But they know we don't have the manpower to respond to all the cranks and false sightings that would come flooding in." Barbara sighed. "But something's got to be better than what we're doing. If he hurts somebody else, I don't know what I'll do."

After a moment of silence, Barbara said, "There's something else I've been meaning to talk to you about. The other night out at that shack when we discovered Luther's body, did you see Jake Rainey's reaction?"

"I did," Pete said. "He was shocked."

"I saw that, too. Made me think he's probably not involved after all."

"Maybe not, but I had a different impression. I think he knows more than he's letting on. It's kind of like he's aware of what was going on leading up to Luther's death but had no idea things would go that far."

Barbara smiled inwardly. *Got to admire Pete's insight.*

"So, you still think there might be someone in the police helping this guy?"

"I do."

Hazel groaned, tried to lift her head. She looked down and saw that she had drooled on her Blondie T-shirt. *Where's my jacket? Where am I?* She was sitting on a concrete floor and her butt felt numb. Plastic ties bound her wrists in front of her, and a strong plastic rope secured her tightly to a square, timber post in some kind of warehouse.

She looked around and saw a bed, a lamp turned low, a laptop, and an open Bible on a makeshift table. When she turned her head, everything started spinning. She closed her eyes and waited, opened them, and saw a shiny, two-door muscle car sitting thirty feet away.

A voice behind her said, "I'm glad you're awake. I was worried I'd hit you too hard and maybe killed you. Are you feeling okay?"

Hazel tried to speak, mumbled something resembling "Where am I?" She felt like she might throw up.

"You're safe for now," the voice said. "And you don't have to worry. If you help me gain access to your, shall I say, *bunkmate* for lack of a better term, I'll forgive you for your perverted lifestyle and you can go about your business."

The voice became a face as Deacon appeared out of the shadows and knelt in front of Hazel, his body odor pungent and his breath sour. He lifted Hazel's chin and looked her in the eye.

"I want you to call Carol and ask her to meet you," he said. "It really is the most humane and sensible course of action. You see that, don't you? Otherwise, I'll have to broaden my activities as it were."

Hazel was still groggy, but she'd got the gist of what he was saying. She managed to shake her head and mutter a barely audible, "Fuck you."

Deacon smiled and nodded in sympathy.

"Okay, Hazel," he said. "I understand."

He hit her hard with something in his fist and Hazel's head fell forward, her chin on her chest. She was out cold.

CHAPTER THIRTY-ONE

SKEETER LIFTED THE NOISE-CANCELLING HEADPHONES away from his ears and marveled at the roar from downstairs. Clemson must have scored again.

He smiled. *Poor, long-suffering Gamecock fans*, he thought. Skeeter could care less who won the game, but he did have a soft spot for USC's teams. It was most likely due to the time he spent in law school at the University of North Carolina at Chapel Hill where he encountered a surprising disdain among Tar Heels for their academic neighbors to the south. Skeeter would always smile and nod in deference when someone put South Carolina down, but he knew all along there was little difference in the quality or accomplishments of folks from either side of the Carolina state line. *Just more needless prejudice*, he thought.

It was always noisy in Bill's on a Saturday night, but others were nothing compared to this one. Skeeter knew Bill employed a couple beefy bouncers on the weekend of the big rivalry game, and they would step in whenever a disagreement between a Tiger and Gamecock fan became too heated. Cooler heads usually prevailed, but there was always a fistfight or two. Blind allegiance was the motive, alcohol the lubricant, and the sidewalk was the landing strip when the jerks were tossed out on their ear.

Skeeter had been holed up at Bill's for only a week, but it seemed a lot longer. He settled the headphones back onto his ears and returned to the Shetland Islands where a band of Scottish coppers were trying to unravel a convoluted crime. Skeeter longed for the peace and quiet of his home on the river, but he had to admit, he'd learned a lot during his time in his cramped upstairs quarters and he felt he'd actually caught up with the future.

Bill had loaned him the headphones and given him the Wi-Fi code for the bar. He showed Skeeter how to log in and stream movies and television shows on his laptop. It was like discovering another world. A busboy from downstairs named Jalen brought up a thumb drive for Skeeter to help him expand his streaming options.

Skeeter was astounded by it all, but he wasn't sure if all this easy access to various media and pop culture was a good thing. He wasn't convinced it made for a better life, and most likely, when he returned home, he'd forego this newfound ability. He was perfectly happy with his cable channels and didn't need another universe of TV options to consume his time. After all, time was the most precious commodity of all and Skeeter needed to make the most of it, especially at his age. Television and movies were great, but so were reading, writing, and listening to music.

Time, Skeeter thought, *we have so little*. He thought of Louise Dixon and Luther Peacock and how their time had been so tragically stolen. Their futures snuffed out. It was senseless.

It was something he'd thought about a lot, the sudden loss of young lives due to wars, accidents, or natural disasters. Skeeter had missed the Vietnam War by a whisker and to this day he felt deep sadness for the more than 50,000 young Americans who died in that misguided conflict.

Skeeter often read war histories and he'd come across an account of the Battle of the Somme in World War I that described how almost 20,000 British troops were killed in one day. Twenty-thousand lives lost in one day! How could that much life be rendered insignificant in the blink of an eye? What would those young men have become? Doctors, teachers, scientists, firemen, farmers? Would one have found a cure for a dreadful disease? Would another have composed timeless music? He couldn't get his head around it.

As he'd gotten older, Skeeter had felt more fortunate, blessed, lucky, or whatever you wanted to call it, that he had not succumbed to such a fate. The closest he'd come to death, not counting the night he rode shotgun with Mervin on a racing trip to North Carolina, was an afternoon in the summer of 1970 when he and Perch were working for cotton farmers.

Their job was to walk the fields and check for aphid or boll weevil infestations. It was a summer job that paid pretty well, but one day, they were halfway down a long row in a particularly large field when they heard the buzzing of an approaching crop duster. The pilot saw the two teenagers and figured, for a laugh, he'd give them a buzz.

When Skeeter and Perch saw the biplane banking to make its run right toward them, they turned and ran as fast as they could for Perch's car at the end of the row.

"Run, Skeeter, run!" Perch shouted, and Skeeter did his best to keep up. But the plane was too fast, and just as Perch and Skeeter reached the car, it roared just inches over their heads and drenched them with insecticide. The pilot circled around, and they could see his grin as he banked for another run at the field.

Perch and Skeeter sat in the car, breathing hard and amazed they were still alive. They tried to towel off the chemical smell, and Skeeter remembered Perch saying he didn't care if boll weevils ate every cotton ball in the county, he wasn't setting foot into another field.

Being buzzed by a crop duster wasn't nearly the same as going over the top in World War I, Skeeter thought, and maybe sometimes war could be morally justified. But cold-blooded murder was a different animal, a different kind of evil.

Who'd want to kill Louise and Luther? What's their motive? What threat did Louise and Luther pose? To be honest, Skeeter dreaded the answers to these questions. He knew this person wished him harm, too, and he was scared. He looked around his room, listened to the hum of activity downstairs, and felt safe and secure for the time being. But he worried about Carol and her girlfriend Hazel. He was ready for this drama to be over. More than ready.

Skeeter had lost the plot of the Scottish inspector's investigation, so he clicked over to YouTube and found a concert by the Dave Brubeck Quartet in Paris from the early 1960s. He took off the headphones for a quick adjustment and thought he heard someone on the stairs outside his door. He sat perfectly still and listened. Footsteps in the hall, he was sure of it. He placed the laptop gently on the bed, and as he started to get up, the door handle rattled from someone trying it outside.

Skeeter looked around for something to use as a weapon. There was nothing. Maybe the ceramic coffee mug or a ballpoint pen. He wished the handgun Boot had loaned him wasn't locked in the glove box of his truck.

The doorknob rattled again, louder, then Skeeter heard a voice outside from further down the hall.

"Anything I can help you with, officer?" It was Bill.

"No, sorry, I was just checking doors. Busy night in your bar and all."

Skeeter could hear surprise and guilt in the second voice. Officer? He wondered who it could be and what was going on.

"Nothing up here to worry about," Bill said. "These rooms are filled with kitchen supplies and fixtures from the old department store."

"Okay, great. That's good to know. I'll just head back downstairs and get back on patrol."

"Good idea," Bill said.

Skeeter could tell Bill was pissed. He listened as two people descended the stairs, and the door at the bottom was closed with authority.

Skeeter looked down and saw his hands trembling. His mouth was dry, and perspiration had made his glasses slide down his nose. He sat down heavily on the bed just as a small cheer filtered up from downstairs. Carolina must have kicked a field goal.

"Go Gamecocks," he muttered.

The squad room was quiet. A few officers were at their desks, some on the computer, others hunched over in quiet phone conversations, probably trying to get the latest updates on the Carolina-Clemson game. There was no sign of Chief Holt, Stanton, or any SLED agents.

Well, it was Saturday night after all, Barbara thought. *Even in such urgent times, people had other things to do. At least most of them did.*

Barbara sank into her chair and felt like she might keep sinking forever. She flipped her laptop open, read emails, checked the duty roster, and opened a few news sites to see what the press was saying about events in Preston.

Not much. *The Charlotte Observer* had another story under the regional news tab, but it was just an update of an earlier piece. A few TV news sites had abbreviated updates as well, stories that ran along the lines of *"investigations are ongoing in Preston, but authorities report little progress."*

Barbara couldn't argue with that. She took a deep breath, shook her head, literally trying to shake herself out of such a dark mood. Might as well go home, make some popcorn, and watch a movie, anything to take her mind off the case.

She closed the laptop, gathered her notes, and started for the door where she almost ran headlong into Tyeisha Brooks coming into the squad room.

"Brooks, what are you doing here on a Saturday night?"

"Just stopping in for a second to grab my iPad," she said. "It gives me something to do while I'm sitting outside Carol and Hazel's house."

Barbara gave her a hard look.

"But I still keep an eye on things," she hastily told her sergeant.

"Right. I forgot you had that detail. How's it going?"

"Okay. This sort of thing is always exhausting, but I don't mind."

"Have you seen anything suspicious?"

"Vehicles have rolled by the house kind of slow a few times, but once they see me, they take off. I make a note of the make and model but don't always get the tag number."

"I know it makes for a long night, but I'm glad you're the one doing this."

Tyeisha straightened with pride at knowing her sergeant had her back.

Barbara was telling Tyeisha goodbye and to stay alert when her phone buzzed in her pocket. It was Carol.

"Hey, Carol. What's up?"

Tyeisha watched Barbara frown as she listened.

A few moments passed, then Barbara said, "But she would have let you know, right?"

Another pause, then, "I think she would, given the circumstances. Listen, you stay put. Officer Brooks and I will be there in a few minutes."

Barbara ended the call and saw Tyeisha's look of alarm.

"That was Carol Baxley. She was expecting Hazel to be home by now, but she hasn't showed. She rode over to the studio and Hazel's car isn't there and her phone is going straight to voicemail. Carol thinks she might have gone to have a drink with a client or someone."

"That doesn't sound likely," Tyeisha said. "And she wouldn't turn off her phone."

"No, she wouldn't. We're going over there. I'll drive."

Tyeisha forgot all about her iPad as she hustled to keep up with Barbara who was already out the door.

CHAPTER THIRTY-TWO

HAZEL TRIED TO OPEN HER EYES but only one of them responded. She could see a blurry image of her hands in her lap. Her head pounded with such pain that it made her nauseous. She heard someone talking, a familiar voice. She tried to lift her head but when the pain spiked, her stomach lurched, and everything started spinning. She moaned and let her chin drop back to her chest.

"Miss Hazel," the voice said. "Miss Hazel, here, try to drink some water."

Hazel felt a hand lift her chin and the mouth of a plastic bottle touched her lips. She sipped slowly.

"There you go," the voice said, "take it slow."

After a couple minutes of slow breaths between small sips of water, Hazel tried to lift her head again. It was easier this time, her vision clearer but still from only one eye. She looked up into a worried, time-worn face.

"Jerome? What are you—? Where am I?"

"Miss Hazel, you been hurt bad. We in some old tobacco warehouse way over on the south side of town. We need to be gettin' up and gettin' out of here."

Standing sounded impossible to Hazel. No way she could muster the strength to walk. Nevertheless, Jerome put his hands under her arms and lifted her to her feet. She cried feebly but managed to put an arm around Jerome who felt like a mighty oak. He smelled of a cedar chest and wood fire, and she leaned against him. Together they made their way across the concrete floor to a small rectangle of gray light coming from an open door on the far side of the warehouse.

Outside it was dark, but a full moon made it seem bright in comparison to the gloom inside the warehouse. There were a few trees, tall grass, and Jerome's bicycle leaning against the warehouse next to the door.

"If we go this way, we'll come to a street that'll lead to the highway," Jerome said. "It's only a few blocks and there's a Quik Stop on the corner where we can call somebody."

"I can't make it," Hazel said in a tortured whisper.

"Yes, you can. Now come on."

It was slow going, but they made it through the tall grass down the side of the warehouse to the street, Jerome rolling his bike along with his left hand while he supported Hazel with his right arm. Their progress was excruciatingly slow and after half a block, Hazel said she couldn't go on.

Jerome had an idea.

"Miss Hazel, get up on the bike."

"What?"

"Just get up on the seat and hold the handlebars. Don't try to pedal."

Hazel did as she was told, almost toppling over, but Jerome steadied her. Then he put his left arm around Hazel, told her to lean forward, and put his right hand next to hers on the handlebars. With Jerome walking alongside, they rolled down the dark street in a deserted part of town.

Jerome began talking to take Hazel's mind off the pain. He told her how he had been riding on the sidewalk out by the highway when he saw Hazel come out of the studio.

"This man come up behind you and I guess he knocked you out cause then he stuffed you in his car, one of those new hot rods. Then he took your keys and drove your car around to the back where nobody could see it. I ducked behind a truck and watched him turn out on 301 and come this way. I pedaled hard trying to follow y'all. He was driving slow not to attract attention, I suppose, and thank the Lord he caught a couple red lights that let me catch up."

Hazel's head lolled forward like she was about to pass out, but she was listening. "Thank the Lord," she mumbled.

"Yes, ma'am," Jerome said. "But I almost lost y'all over here then way ahead I seen his taillights turn and I come down this street. When I got here, he'd just disappeared, but I knew he couldn't be too far. So I waited, and sho nuff, about an hour later, I seen that car come out that old warehouse and drive off."

Jerome said the garage-sized door from which the car emerged was locked up tight and he was afraid he wouldn't be able to get inside. Then he found an old, rusted door on the backside of the warehouse that he managed to pry open. It was so dark inside, he walked with his arms outstretched so he wouldn't run into anything. Even when his eyes adjusted, he couldn't see much. He found Hazel by tripping over her outstretched legs.

She was unconscious, tied to one of the building's support beams, and her hands and feet bound. Jerome untied her and found the water bottle on the floor next to her.

"That's when you started to wake up, Miss Hazel."

"Why didn't you call the police when you saw me being taken?" Hazel asked.

Jerome didn't say anything, just kept pushing the bike. Finally, he said in a subdued voice, "Miss Hazel, me and the police don't get along that well. Let's just say they wouldn't believe a word I say and probably think I was trying to cause trouble."

He left it at that. Hazel didn't say anything. She understood.

Jerome huffed and puffed as he pushed Hazel down the street, and after a while, they could see cars coming and going three blocks away at the intersection with 301. Bright lights on the corner confirmed that a Quik Stop store was there, and, buoyed by the sight, Jerome picked up the pace. Ten minutes later, he was helping Hazel off the bike and leaning it against a big metal bin that contained bags of ice. There was one car parked in front of the store and a pickup truck was at the gas pumps, its owner watching this strange arrival as he filled the tank.

Jerome and Hazel shuffled inside and a man behind the register took one look at Hazel and said, "I don't want no trouble!"

"Ain't no trouble here, boss," Jerome said. "We just need some help. My friend's been hurt, and she needs to call somebody to come get her, that's all."

The man was still unsure, but he pointed at a phone mounted next to the cigarette rack behind the counter.

"Thanks, man," Jerome said. "Thank you."

He guided Hazel around the counter, took down the receiver, put it in her hand, and said soothingly in her ear, "Call somebody to come and get you."

Hazel took the phone and tried to remember Carol's number. She wobbled on her feet for a second, lowered the receiver, and looked around. She trained her one good eye on the man who looked like Omar Sharif without the mustache and asked, "Where am I?"

———————⌇———————

Carol was watching from the living-room window when Barbara and Tyeisha pulled up in front of the house. She ushered them inside and before either officer could say a word, Carol started talking.

"I've called everyone I can think of," she said. "Her musician friends, people who've recently been in the studio, even Manuela from the Mexican restaurant, and no one has seen or talked to Hazel today. I don't know what else to do. She should be home by now."

Rufus was watching intently from his perch on the couch, and he could sense Carol's anxiety. His tail thumped the cushions a couple times when he saw Barbara.

"Hey, Rufus," Barbara said, and the Lab hopped down and trotted over to her. "Hey, fella," she cooed as she scratched him behind the ear. Barbara wasn't going to insult Carol by telling her to calm down or that Hazel could come waltzing in at any minute. Carol was smart and her concern was legitimate.

"Let's go to the kitchen," Barbara said. "I could use a cup of tea or coffee. It's been a long day."

"I'm so sorry, I'm just not thinking. And hi, Tyeisha," Carol said as if only just now seeing the young officer in the room. She hugged Tyeisha. "We've felt so safe knowing you've been outside these past few nights."

"No problem," Tyeisha said, returning the hug. "Glad to do it."

"Y'all come on," Carol said and led them down the hall to the kitchen. Rufus padded along behind them and curled up in his usual spot under the table. Barbara and Tyeisha pulled out chairs to sit.

Carol placed her phone on the counter and started making coffee. She knew it would be a long night.

"Are you sure there's no one else Hazel could be with, you know, work related or just hanging out?" Barbara asked.

"I can't be completely sure," Carol said as she slid a paper filter into the coffee machine, "but like I said before, she would have let me know if she was going anywhere. She knew that I'd worry about her just like she was worrying about me."

"You're right. I'm just asking the questions I'm supposed to ask."

"I know," Carol said, and she suddenly started crying. "I can't take much more of this," she hiccupped through the tears.

"Here, let me help with that," Tyeisha said, and she got up and gently took the bag of coffee out of Carol's hands.

"Thanks," Carol said, but before she could sit down in the chair vacated by Tyeisha, her phone buzzed on the counter. She looked at the screen.

"It's her!" she shouted. "Hazel, where are you? I've been worried sick."

The voice wasn't Hazel's.

"Well now, don't get sick, child. You're going to have to get moving if you want to see your husband again. Or is it wife? I can't keep your sordid lifestyle straight." He laughed, "Pardon the pun."

"Who is this?" Carol said. "How did you get this phone?"

Barbara and Tyeisha stood watching Carol. Rufus scooted out from under the table.

The harsh, craggy voice told Carol not to worry about how he got the phone. She should be "gettin' on her horse" and getting over to Rowland, specifically a truck stop on Highway 501 north of town. That's where she could retrieve her precious Hazel. He would be waiting at the back of the parking lot, and she should come alone. If she called the police, Hazel would die.

"What then?" Carol asked. "Are you just going to hand her over and let us go?"

"Well, not exactly," the voice said. "She can go if she's able. But you and I have to discuss your transgressions, and of course, decide what retribution you need to pay."

"What transgressions?"

The voice laughed again. "You've got one hour," he said, and the line went dead.

Carol collapsed into the chair and looked at Barbara.

"He's got Hazel."

"What exactly did he say?"

Carol repeated the conversation.

"Damn, he's smart," Barbara said. "Rowland is in North Carolina, out of our jurisdiction. But I know a couple cops up there, and one of them is a good old Lumbee boy. We can get them to help. He said you had one hour?"

"That's right," Carol said, her eyes pleading with Barbara.

"He might have made a mistake there. You can get to Rowland in twenty minutes, half hour tops. We've got a little time."

"Time to do what?" Tyeisha asked.

Barbara took out her phone to call Chief Holt. She said Tyeisha should stay with Carol while she and Chief Holt liaised with the Rowland police. She was about to say they should enlist the help of the sheriff's department when Carol's phone buzzed again.

They all jumped. Carol looked at the screen. This time it read, "Quik Stop No. 3."

CHAPTER THIRTY-THREE

BARBARA HIT THE BRAKES and the Ford Explorer, its blue lights flashing, screeched to a halt in front of the Quik Stop. Carol was out of the vehicle and into the store before Barbara and Tyeisha could unfasten their seatbelts.

Hazel was sitting in a chair provided by the cashier who was standing quietly behind the register, his eyes wide. She was fighting to stay awake when Carol cupped her face in her hands.

"Oh, Hazel," she said, "honey, you're really hurt bad."

"I'm okay," Hazel mumbled.

Carol the doctor took over. "You're severely concussed and you could have a fracture. I'm calling Wanda Bethea and telling her to meet us at the office. We need to get you checked out."

"Here's my phone," Barbara said. "Call her. I'll make room in the Explorer."

At that moment, another Preston police vehicle roared to a stop in front of the store, its blue lights flashing with equal intensity. Chief Holt and Pete Shumpert climbed out, both dressed in jeans, T-shirts, and jackets that were obviously thrown on in haste.

Holt strode into the store, looked around, and asked Barbara quietly, "How is she?"

"I'm right here," Hazel said, hurting but annoyed.

Holt stepped around Tyeisha and Carol and knelt in front of Hazel.

"Hazel, we're going to take care of you," he said, "but you need to tell us what happened. The quicker we move, the better chance we have of catching this bastard."

Carol tensed and started to say something, but Barbara touched her arm and shook her head to wait a second.

"Jerome," Hazel said.

Everyone glanced around quizzically.

"Jerome saved me."

"Who's Jerome?" Holt asked.

"Jerome. Jerome Sumlin," Hazel said. "He plays guitar. Blues. You gotta hear him."

Holt, Pete, and Barbara looked at Carol. They wondered if the blow to Hazel's head had scrambled her memory, but Tyeisha said, "I know Jerome. Crazy ol' coot lives over on The Hill. Rides a bike everywhere."

"She came in with a Black man," the cashier said.

They all turned.

"But he left. Got on his bike and went away."

Hazel rose from the chair and looked around searching for Jerome. Sure enough, he was gone and so was his bicycle.

"Careful, honey," Carol said, stepping in when Hazel wavered on her feet. "We're going now to get you patched up. You're going to be all right."

She put her arm around Hazel to lead her outside, but Hazel stopped and said, "No, we need to go back. Find the son of a bitch."

Carol protested, but Hazel looked in her eyes and said, "I mean it."

Pete came forward. "Hazel, I'm going to help you to the front seat of the chief's truck. Barbara, Carol, and Tyeisha will follow us. You can show us where you were being held."

"Okay," Hazel said.

Pete smiled. "I've never met you before, but I always heard you used to be some kind of rock star," he said. "From what I can see, you still are."

Hazel's battered face crinkled into a grin, Carol's eyes filled with tears, and they all paraded out of the Quik Stop. At the door, Barbara stopped and turned back to the cashier who was still in a mild state of shock.

"What's your name?" she asked.

"Ara," he said. "Ara Haddad."

"Thanks, Ara. You did good."

With that, they were gone, the two Preston police Explorers roaring away into the night, their lights leaving a trail of blue halogen beams that reflected on buildings, signs, and trees.

Deacon watched from the shadows of a dilapidated warehouse across the street as two men in plain clothes and a uniformed officer, the Indian woman, it appeared, climbed out of police cruisers and made their way toward his former hideout. They waded through the tall grass along the side of the warehouse and disappeared from view.

"Goddammit," he snarled. "There must have been another door. But how did that dyke bitch get loose?"

She was tied up tighter than a camel's ass in a sandstorm, in an abandoned warehouse, on a dark-and-deserted side of town, and he had been gone less than an hour.

This damn town, he thought. *All these misfires.* Deacon had worked hard over the past few years to control his rage and not let it dictate his actions. He had been lucky to escape past episodes without paying the consequences, but he knew that couldn't last and this might be the breaking point.

He felt the red veil of anger starting to cloud his vision and urging him to finish this thing, no matter the cost. After all, what's the worst that could happen? He would just reap the great reward he was promised.

It would be a shame, really. Deacon had concocted such a simple and fool-proof plan, or so he'd thought. He would ingratiate himself with a few of the locals, identify August Ellington and Carol Baxley, learn their movements and habits, determine the best opportunity, and eliminate them quickly and quietly, thus making the world a better place and achieving a measure of revenge. It would be "Good Night, Irene" and he would hightail it back to Florida.

It had been going so smoothly. He'd fallen in with a group of men with whom he was somewhat like-minded, although he had no use for their racism and cultural-war rhetoric. He'd even bonded with a couple allies. Sadly, he'd had to eliminate one, poor Luther Peacock, but the other was still a good soldier who most likely could still be counted on.

He was tired. He wanted to go home. He assessed the situation and boiled it down to the essentials. Eliminate everyone. He had the firepower and the know-how. And he had a vehicle that could lead a merry chase down I-95 if anyone was left to come after him.

He felt his phone vibrate in his pocket with a text from the good soldier. *I think I know where the lawyer is hiding.*

Finally, some good news. And a confirmation that it was time to end this.

Deacon texted back. *Great. I'm coming to your place. Thirty minutes. We have work to do.*

CHAPTER THIRTY-FOUR

SUNDAY MORNING BROKE with bright sunshine and a breeze from the northeast that nudged big white clouds slowly across the sky. It was one of those perfect South Carolina fall days, chilly enough for long sleeves and maybe a jacket, and bright enough to require sunscreen on your face.

Mervin was in the carport going through his golf bag and making sure he had all the essentials: balls, tees, Advil, clean towel, chewable Pepto tablets (you can't be too careful), and sunscreen. Everything was checked off and he was about to toss the bag into his truck when Becca poked her head out the backdoor to tell him his phone was buzzing on the kitchen table.

"Well answer it," he said.

She shook her head, ducked back inside, and a couple seconds later emerged waving the phone at Mervin.

"It's Skeeter," she said. "He says he has some news."

Mervin took the phone and said, "Hey, man. What's up?" He listened a while, aware that Becca was leaning against the truck and watching him.

"Whoa. Damn. Is she okay?" He listened a little more then said, "So they didn't find him?"

Mervin turned slightly to avoid Becca's stare. "No, I agree. You stay there. Tell Lowrie to send someone to watch your back." Another pause, then, "No, man, I'm just saying. Well, do what you want, but I think you need some backup."

Mervin almost asked Skeeter if he had the gun Boot had promised him, but he caught himself just in time. Becca would not want to hear anything about Boot and guns.

"Yeah, we decided to go ahead and play. Benny actually called me to make sure we still wanted our eleven. It's a gorgeous day. Gonna be crowded on the course with all us sinners out there."

Mervin laughed. "I know, we'll miss you . . . or Boot will miss you. I've convinced him he plays better when he's riding with you. Yeah, don't worry, we will. You be careful, too."

Mervin ended the call and stuffed the phone in his golf bag.

"Well?" Becca scowled.

Mervin knew he had to tell her everything, so he started right in with Skeeter getting a call this morning from Carol Baxley who told him about Hazel being abducted, then being rescued in the middle of the night, and how the police searched an old warehouse but didn't find anyone or anything. Mervin told Becca that Carol and Hazel were home now under police protection, and other cops were looking for an old guy named Jerome who apparently was the hero who sprung Hazel.

"Oh my god," Becca said. "That poor woman. She must have been terrified."

"From what Skeeter said, she was pretty tough. They took her for x-rays and thankfully there were no fractures, so looks like she'll be fine."

The way Mervin said it made Becca grin.

"Sounds like you might be a little hot for this Hazel woman," she said.

"No, I'm not," Mervin said a little too defensively. "She's just, you know, kind of cool, that's all. And you should see that studio where she works. The music they record there is amazing."

"Calm down, Dickie Betts, I'm just teasing. I know she plays for the other team, and I also know she is not cooler than me."

"You got that right," Mervin said and pulled Becca in for a kiss.

She pushed him away.

"You know I'm not crazy about y'all playing golf today. What if that nut comes out there looking for you?"

"Baby, he doesn't even know who we are. He's after Carol and Skeeter. Besides, nothing's going to happen out on the golf course."

"Oh yeah?" Becca said. "Those sound like famous last words to me."

Becca went inside and Mervin loaded his golf clubs in the truck. He shivered and zipped his wind jacket tighter, but it wasn't a nor'easter that gave him a chill.

Damn, girl, he thought. *Why you gotta say something like that?*

Boot checked to make sure the safety was on then stuffed the Glock into a zippered pocket on his golf bag. He'd loaded a couple extra ten-round clips the night before and slid one of those into the bag as well. *Better safe than sorry.*

After stashing his clubs securely in the back, he climbed in the big F-250, fired it up, and headed for the driveway. He saw Jack and Joe in the rearview sitting on the front porch watching him leave. It gave him a strange sense of comfort. He knew Jack and Joe would look after the place.

Boot decided to go through town on his way to the golf course. It was such a clear-and-crisp morning with huge white clouds drifting across the sky at a snail's pace, it filled him with a dash of optimism. *Slower than the passage of time*, Boot thought as he watched the clouds. He grinned when he imagined what Mervin's reaction would be to his attempt at profundity.

Out of the blue, Boot thought of James Junior and how they'd always made the most of mornings like this. Whether it was hiking, fishing, or just playing catch in the driveway, they managed to have a good time. Although, to be honest, Boot hadn't been the greatest dad in the world. He'd never been neglectful, but he'd sometimes been indifferent when James Junior needed guidance. Boot hadn't been crazy about his son's decision to join the Marines, but he had to admit, his heart swelled with pride when James Junior marched by in his dress blues during graduation at Parris Island.

He hadn't seen his son in more than twenty years, but a Christmas card two years ago revealed that James Junior was living in Atlanta and tending bar in some swanky joint in Buckhead. It sounded like he was doing all right. Boot sighed with a touch of regret, but he was determined not to let wandering thoughts spoil the day.

He passed a few cars on his way into town, but Main Street was mostly empty. He tooted the horn when he passed Bill's just in case Skeeter needed a wake-up call. The roads to the golf course were just as quiet, and Boot figured 70 percent of Preston's townsfolk were in church, 25 percent were too hungover to attend, and the remaining 5 percent were heathen non-believers who had gone hunting or were playing golf.

The heathen hackers, that's us, Boot thought as he turned into the country club's parking lot. He could see Mervin and Perch unloading clubs from their trucks in their usual spots at the back of the lot under a big Magnolia tree. Boot pulled in beside them and noticed they were strapping their clubs onto separate golf carts.

"What's up?" he called as he climbed out of his truck.

"Perch wants to ride on his own today," Mervin said. "You're with me."

"What's the deal, Perch? You always ride with Mervin."

"I just want to ride by myself today," Perch said, not looking up from the task of getting his gear sorted on the cart. The way he said it left no room for debate. Boot shrugged and started loading his clubs onto Mervin's cart.

"He'll be alright," Mervin said under his breath. "It was around this time of year when Janice died. Anyway, this means you and me can get high."

"Now you're talking," Boot said.

As they waited on the first tee, Mervin told Boot and Perch about the abduction of Hazel Owens and her eventual rescue. They listened, nodded solemnly but didn't say much. Perch wondered if Skeeter should have police protection at Bill's, but Mervin told him Skeeter didn't want it. He said he didn't want to bring negative attention to Bill's place.

"They've got to catch this bastard," Boot said as he pulled the head cover off his driver. There was anger in his voice. He took a couple practice swings, addressed the ball, and with a ferocious swing, drove it long and straight down the fairway.

"Damn, Boot," Perch said.

The course was crowded as expected, and they played at a slower pace than usual. But they all played well. There was little chit-chat, just the frequent "good shot" and "nice putt."

Mervin tried once to give Boot swing advice but the look he received told him it wasn't welcome.

"Skeeter can help me with my game, but not you, okay?"

Mervin held up his hands to say he got it. Boot wanted to beat Mervin. He didn't need his nemesis telling him how to play.

It was almost four o'clock when they finally finished the round and rolled up next to their trucks. Boot and Perch busied themselves unloading clubs and changing out of their golf shoes. Mervin sat behind the wheel of his cart and tallied the final scores.

"Well?" Perch asked as he watched Mervin ciphering with his pencil.

"We all played pretty good," Mervin said. "I shot eighty-four. Perch, you shot an eighty-eight. Good job. And Boot, let me see, you bogeyed eighteen, right?"

"Yeah."

"Well, that means you shot eighty-nine. You broke ninety."

"What?"

Perch laughed at the dumbfounded look on Boot's face. Then he threw his arms around the tall ol' string bean and gave him a hug.

"Congratulations, man," Mervin said. "You know what this means. We gotta celebrate."

Breaking ninety was a monumental milestone for everyone who took up the game. It would change Boot's life. He would be even more diligent now in his quest to beat Mervin.

"I've got an idea," said Perch. "Let's buy a twelve-pack and take the party to Skeeter. He needs to be in on this. I know Bill's isn't open on Sunday, but we can hoist a few in the alley out back and toast Mr. Eighty-Nine here."

"Outstanding notion, El Percho," Mervin said. "I'll call Skeeter. Perch, you pick up the beer. The IGA is on the way and it's open on Sunday. And Boot, if you can hold it together, meet us behind Bill's."

Boot smiled. There might have been the hint of a tear in his eye. "Thanks, y'all," he said. "See you there."

CHAPTER THIRTY-FIVE

SOMETHING WASN'T RIGHT. Carol could feel it. She pushed aside the curtain and looked out the front window. Tyeisha Brooks' police cruiser was parked in its usual spot on the street, but it was too dark to tell if she was inside.

What worried Carol was the second police vehicle parked behind Tyeisha's car. *Whose is it? Why are they here?* Surely someone would have told her if another officer was being sent to watch the house.

Hazel was asleep on the sofa. She had dozed off and on all day. Carol told her that it was not surprising given the nasty blow to her head.

Rufus was curled up at Hazel's feet and when Carol started to leave the room, he raised his head and gave a low growl. She stopped and looked back.

"What is it, boy?"

Rufus gazed toward the back of the house, his ears alert and nostrils working. *That's it*, Carol thought. She found her phone on the kitchen table and punched the number for Barbara Lowrie who answered after one ring.

"Hey Carol. Is everything okay?"

"Barbara, I know you must be exhausted, and I apologize for calling you on a Sunday evening, especially after all we went through last night."

"It's okay, Carol. Honestly. I'm dog tired but guess I'm running on adrenaline. I haven't really been able to sleep. Is Tyeisha there?"

"Well, that's the thing. I can see her car outside but can't tell if she's in it. And there's another police car parked behind hers. Did y'all send someone else over?"

"The chief or maybe Pete Shumpert could have sent someone to relieve Tyeisha, but I didn't hear anything about it," Barbara said. "Not that they would necessarily tell me but let me make a couple calls and get back to you."

"Thanks," Carol said and ended the call. She held the phone under her chin with both hands and wondered what she should do. Go outside and check on Tyeisha? Make sure the doors were locked and hide in a closet?

She and Skeeter had talked about the fear of going to the police a few of the battered women felt. They sensed some paranoia in the women, but also detected more than a kernel's worth of validity in their stories. That's why the second police car outside the house worried Carol.

Hazel appeared in the kitchen door, flannel PJs rumpled and her hair pointing out in multiple directions.

"I think I heard someone," she said groggily. "Outside."

Carol stood still for a moment and heard it, too. First one voice, female, followed by a man's voice.

"That sounded like Vickie," she said. "I don't know who the man is."

"What should we do?" Hazel asked. "Where's Tyeisha?"

At that moment, there was a shout and a thud, and Carol grabbed Hazel by the arm and said, "Let's go!"

They ran for the front door. Rufus was barking to beat the band. As they started across the front yard toward Tyeisha's car, an authoritative voice said, "Stop right there, ladies."

A uniformed policeman, broad shouldered and lean, appeared from around the corner of the house. Rufus barked viciously, determined to protect his family, but Hazel dropped to her knees, put her arms around his neck. "Shush, boy, it'll be alright."

At the sight of the dog, the policeman drew his weapon.

"Let's all be calm," he said. "No one needs to get hurt, not even that good-looking Lab." He stepped closer. "Carol Baxley, I'm here to take you to the station so you can talk to Detective Stanton and help us fill in some blanks from last night."

Carol didn't believe that for a second.

"Where's Tyeisha?" she said.

"Don't worry about Officer Brooks. She knows you need to go with me."

Hazel could feel Rufus trembling. She knew if she turned him loose, he would charge the policeman and probably get shot. "Don't go with him, Carol," she said quietly. "Please. Just stay here."

At that moment, headlights swung down the street and another police vehicle came to a stop in front of the house. Barbara Lowrie stepped out slowly and walked around the front of the Ford Explorer. She was wearing jeans and a Kevlar bulletproof vest over an old sweatshirt. Her long black hair was pulled back loosely into a ponytail and a sidearm in its holster was clipped at her waist.

"Officer Rogers, is there a problem here?"

The policeman was clearly rattled. He jerked his gun back and forth between Carol, Rufus, and Barbara. "I have orders to take Miss Baxley to the station to talk to Detective Stanton."

"I haven't heard anything about that," Barbara said, her voice calm and even. "But if that's what you have to do, let's do it. Why don't you holster that weapon and we'll take Carol downtown?"

Mark Rogers was cornered. He had no plan B; Barbara could see it in his eyes. She also saw how tense he was when he stepped toward Carol. She drew her weapon and flicked off the safety.

"Come on, Sarge, don't try that," Rogers said. "I can blow these two away quicker than you can shoot me, so just toss that pistol on the ground."

Barbara didn't flinch. She'd drawn her weapon several times before in the line of duty but had only fired it once, a warning shot over the head of a couple car thieves who were threatening to run. She had never shot another person, much less a fellow police officer.

Her mind raced. How could she defuse this? Rogers was scared and that wasn't good. He probably didn't want to shoot Hazel and Carol, but he would if someone made a wrong move.

"I can't do that, Mark," Barbara said. "You know that. We've had the same training. You even know what I'm about to say. I'm going to ask you not to make things worse by hurting someone. I'm going to tell you that if you put your weapon down and come along peacefully, things will go much better for you. And it's true. You know it."

"I don't know it," Rogers said, angry now, spitting out the words. "A man has all the cards stacked against him. Look at y'all, the three of you. You'll make up some story about harassment, molestation, or rape and some liberal judge will put me away for twenty-five years. That ain't gonna happen."

He shifted to his left, putting Carol in Barbara's line of fire, but Barbara moved just enough to keep Rogers in her sight. It was a nerve-wracking dance. Barbara and Rogers held their firearms at arm's length, pointing them at each other. Rogers glanced quickly around to see if there was a means of escape. His hands twitched. Perspiration rolled into his eyes, but he couldn't wipe it away.

"Mark, listen to me," Barbara said. "You've got nothing against these women, and they've got nothing against you. Let's stop this thing. Work it out. I'm not sure how much you're involved but if you put down the gun and talk, you could help us. That will be huge in your favor."

Rogers tried to blink away the sweat. His face softened a bit.

"I didn't know he was going to kill Louise Dixon and Luther Peacock," Rogers said. "I had nothing to do with that."

"Okay, that's good. I believe you," Barbara said. "Here, hand me the gun."

Holding her pistol in her right hand, she extended her left hand to Rogers, and took a small step forward. Rogers shrank back then moved to grab Carol who had been standing frozen on the spot the entire time.

At that instant, Rufus broke free from Hazel's grip and launched at Rogers, sinking his teeth into the policeman's leg. Rogers howled, aimed his gun down at the dog, and Barbara didn't hesitate. She fired two quick rounds, both hitting Rogers square in the chest and knocking him to the ground. Rufus whimpered as Hazel gathered him into her arms and lifted him away from Rogers.

"Take him inside," Barbara said, and Hazel led Rufus to the house by his collar.

Carol rushed forward and knelt next to Rogers. He was still breathing but wouldn't be for long. Barbara kicked Rogers' gun aside and stood over him, watching as his chest rose and fell, pain etched on his face. His eyes found Barbara's and all they revealed was coldness and hate.

"You bitch," he said.

It was what Barbara needed to hear. There wouldn't be any late nights of guilt and self-recrimination now. She holstered her weapon and watched as he made a gurgling, choking sound and his head lolled to one side.

"Stay here with him," she told Carol. "I need to call it in."

She turned and walked toward her Explorer, not once looking back.

CHAPTER THIRTY-SIX

THEY PULLED INTO THE ALLEY like a convoy. First, Mervin, next came Boot, then Perch rolled in bringing up the rear. Skeeter was sitting on the concrete steps that led to Bill's backdoor. He grinned as the three trucks came to a stop.

Mervin revved the Silverado's motor, stuck his arm out the window, and waved it in a circular motion. Boot and Perch obliged by revving their trucks, too. Mervin dropped his arm straight down and the trucks went quiet.

"Woooo!" Boot hollered as he leaped out of his big, jacked-up Ford.

Skeeter stood and started toward Boot but only made it a step or two before Boot embraced him in a bear hug that almost lifted him off the ground. This time, Skeeter remembered to turn his head sideways so his glasses wouldn't get crushed.

"An eighty-nine!" Skeeter said. "Good for you, Boot. You deserve it."

"It's because of all those pointers you've been giving me over the years. They finally paid off."

"Yeah, but don't stop there. You're only sixty-five, Boot. You can go lower."

"I will, Skeeter. I will."

During Boot and Skeeter's love fest, Perch had plopped a twelve-pack of cold Miller High Life on the open tailgate of Mervin's truck. He cracked it open and passed around cans of beer. Tops were popped; Mervin held his aloft and motioned for the others to do the same.

"To Boot," Mervin said. "Crack shot with a 12-gauge pump and a Ping putter. Congratulations on breaking ninety. May you continue to break it time and time again."

"Hear, hear," the other three said, and they all took hefty slugs from the cans.

"That was a nice toast, Mervin," Perch said. "You got a way with words."

"It's all that book learning," Boot said, "and having a schoolteacher for a wife."

They laughed, and Skeeter said he wanted to hear all about Boot's round. Boot described it in detail, with Mervin and Perch chiming in to embellish his better shots.

When they ran out of golf stories, Mervin asked Skeeter if he'd heard about what happened to Hazel Owens. He said he had. After a long phone conversation that morning with Carol Baxley, Skeeter had been on edge all day.

"But in a way, it kind of makes me optimistic," he said. "This guy is getting desperate. He's going to make a mistake and get caught."

"Or get killed," Boot said.

Daylight was fading fast, and they were down to the last round of Millers. Mervin said he needed to be getting home and Perch agreed, saying he was "wore out."

"Before you go," Skeeter said, "another toast." He reached in his jacket and pulled out a half-pint of Jameson.

"To the three friends I can't wait to play golf with again," he said and took a hit off the bottle. Before he could pass it to Boot, a car turned into the far end of the alley, half a block behind Perch's truck.

"I wonder who that could be?" Perch said.

"I've seen that car before," Mervin said. "It was parked on Main across from Bill's the other night. I remember because I parked next to it."

They all watched the car idling at the end of the alley, Skeeter still holding the bottle of Irish whiskey, the others with their beers. The driver's door opened and a man in full-camouflage gear climbed out, raised an AR-15 to his shoulder, and started walking down the alley.

"Holy shit!" Boot yelled and tossed his beer to the ground. He pushed Skeeter and said, "Get behind something," just as the first burst from the automatic weapon peppered Perch's truck and sizzled over their heads.

"Get in the truck," Mervin shouted as he climbed behind the wheel and fired up the Silverado. Skeeter and Perch scrambled into the truck bed, but Boot dashed around to his truck, keeping low and away from the approaching attacker. He knew right where the Glock was in his golf bag, and he had it in his hand and the safety off in seconds.

He scooted down to the tailgate of Perch's truck, then with both hands on the Glock, he stepped out and squeezed off most of the ten-round clip.

Startled, the camo man dove behind a dumpster.

"Boot!" Skeeter yelled. Boot ran for Mervin's truck, stopping for half a second to grab the second clip from his golf bag. He climbed in the passenger's seat and hollered, "Kick it!"

Mervin floored the gas, took a hard left at the end of the alley, and heard the tires squeal as they gained traction.

"I think I hit him," Boot said. "I think I got the bastard."

Mervin's head was spinning, his hands were sweaty, and all he could think of was getting away from this madman. He was flying down Fourth Street, one of Preston's broader thoroughfares, and he knew he could weave into the backstreets and buy some time.

Mervin turned to Boot and said, "I'm going to stop at the next corner so Skeeter and Perch can get inside. Holler out the window and tell them."

Boot did as he was told, and when Mervin screeched to a stop, Skeeter and Perch leapt from the truck and into the backseat of the king cab.

Mervin turned to see if they were all right and couldn't believe his eyes. Two blocks behind them a dark green Dodge Challenger powered around a corner and headed straight their way.

"Damn," Mervin said and hit the gas so hard everyone was pinned to their seats. "Somebody call the police. Tell them where we are."

"My phone is in my truck," Boot said.

"Mine's in my golf bag," said Perch.

Skeeter just shrugged to say his was probably in the room above Bill's.

"Are you kidding me?" Mervin yelled. "Are you saying we don't have a phone?"

"Where's yours?" Boot asked.

Mervin was concentrating on the road and the rapidly gaining Dodge Challenger. "Back there. In my bag."

"Well, you better do your thing, Mervin, and out run this sucker. Maybe we'll come up on a police car."

"Fat chance of that," Skeeter said. "It's Sunday. They're all home watching football."

Mervin knew that was probably true. His knuckles white on the wheel, he careened through various neighborhoods to the outskirts of town and found himself on a long stretch of county highway. The Challenger had been maintaining distance, but now it started to creep closer.

"I can't lose him," Mervin said. "That thing's a muscle car. My truck is fast but not that fast."

Just then, he passed a road that seemed familiar.

"Boot, get ready. I'm going to hit a U-turn at the next crossroads. When he goes by, let him have it."

Boot nodded and held the Glock in front of him. Skeeter and Perch ducked low in the backseat.

Mervin came to a crossing where a flashing overhead light signaled it was a major intersection. He hit the brakes, skidded to the right, then spun the wheel hard to the left and accelerated back in the opposite direction.

The Challenger careened onto the shoulder but stabilized quickly and started to turn, too. That's when Boot leaned out the window and opened fire.

Four rounds were all he had, one hit the driver's side door, one shattered a side window, and the other two must have missed.

"I did my best," Boot said as they sped back in the direction from which they'd come. He fished out the second clip and slammed it into the Glock.

"You did great," Mervin muttered, but he could see the Challenger swerving around to follow them. He came to the intersection he'd recognized and hit a hard right onto a hard-packed, red-clay road lined on both sides by scrub bushes and small fir trees.

"Where are you taking us?" Skeeter asked.

Mervin didn't answer. He just kept the pedal to the floorboard. The Challenger was behind them again, its headlights having trouble penetrating the dust kicked up by Mervin's Silverado.

Mervin's headlights revealed that the dirt road was running out fast and he knew he should start slowing. There were only small trees and bushes ahead but then Mervin spotted a break to the left that was nothing but two tire tracks disappearing between a batch of blackberry bushes.

"Hold on!" he shouted.

Mervin aimed for the opening, hit the brakes, and the Silverado began to skid. It went airborne for a moment, its hood outstretched in space before dipping gracefully down as the truck made its landing fifteen feet below, bouncing hard off the ground and coming to a stop next to some scrub pines.

"What the hell, Mervin?" Boot said, rubbing his head where it'd bounced off the ceiling of the truck.

"I'll be damn," Skeeter said. "We're in the clay pit."

"I'm going to grab my phone," Mervin said. "You guys run. Run!"

With that, they were all out of the truck. Skeeter, Boot, and Perch took off in different directions while Mervin rummaged around in a pocket on his golf bag for his phone. He found it, turned it on, and looked up just as the Dodge Challenger slid to a stop at the edge of the clay pit, its headlights sending out dusty beams of light overhead.

Mervin turned on his phone as he ran, but using it was impossible in the fading light and all the jostling up and down. He spotted a thick patch of scrub brush, knelt next to it, and dialed 9-1-1. His call was answered after two rings.

"This is Preston police. What's your emergency?"

Mervin recognized Jimmy Glover's voice.

"Jimmy, this is Mervin Hayes. We're in the clay pit. We're in trouble. We need help."

"Mr. Hayes, could you speak up? I can barely hear you."

"I can't," Mervin said. "That guy, the one who's after Skeeter and Carol Baxley, he's here and he's armed. He's trying to kill us."

Right then a deafening burst of automatic fire erupted off to Mervin's left, followed by the *pop, pop, pop* of Boot's reply.

Jimmy Glover heard the gunfire and was now all business.

"Where are you?" he asked. "Where is this clay pit?"

"Outside of town. The north side, past the Needle Acres subdivision." Mervin realized this wasn't helping Jimmy. "Call Pete Shumpert, he'll know."

Mervin heard huffing and puffing and heavy footfalls off to his right. Then he saw Perch lumbering across the clay pit floor, heading for a bracket of fir trees on the far side. Another burst of automatic fire, this time from farther away, and Perch grunted and fell face first into the dirt.

"Perch!" Mervin yelled, and he stood and started to run. Almost to Perch, he slammed on the brakes and looked to his left. Stepping into the open was the camo-man. He was raising the AR-15 to his shoulder.

"Oh, Becca," Mervin said. "I'm so sorry."

Two loud bangs made Mervin jump and the camo-man staggered backwards then crumbled to the ground. Mervin looked down and saw Perch on his side, his right arm outstretched, and the Colt Python revolver in his hand.

"I hit him, Mervin. I think I hit him."

Mervin rushed over and knelt.

"You had your gun the whole time. Why didn't you say?"

"I was scared," Perch said, grimacing, his voice barely a whisper.

Mervin saw blood pulsing from a wound in Perch's thigh and another, bloodier hole in Perch's right side. Boot ran up and knelt, too.

"I got him, Boot," Perch wheezed.

"Yeah, you got him," Boot said, choking on the words. "The best shot I've ever seen."

Mervin couldn't speak. He just knelt there on both knees then realized he was still holding his phone. He'd never ended the call.

He raised the phone to his ear and heard Jimmy Glover.

"Mr. Hayes! Mr. Hayes!"

"Jimmy, I'm here."

"Just stay put. Help is on the way."

"I'm not going anywhere," Mervin said. "And tell them to send an ambulance, too."

"Too late for that," Boot said, and he and Mervin watched as the light disappeared from Perch's eyes.

Mervin's chin sagged to his chest and Boot moved away to give him space. He walked over to where their attacker lay sprawled on the ground. One of Perch's bullets was lodged in the camo-man's vest and the other had struck him in the neck and exited the back of his head.

Boot stood over him and was tempted to add a couple rounds of his own but suddenly felt completely deflated, incapable of even the smallest exertion. He walked back to where Mervin was now standing after placing his jacket over Perch's head.

"Where's Skeeter?" Boot asked.

"I don't know," Mervin said and yelled, "Skeeter! "Hey Skeeter, where are you?"

"Here," came a reply from not far away, and then they saw Skeeter making his way toward them. "I found a hole in the wall some kids must have dug and crawled in there."

Then he saw Perch.

"Oh, dear god," he said and sank to one knee. Mervin walked over and put a hand on his shoulder. "This is my fault, Mervin," Skeeter said. "This is all my fault."

"No, hell, it ain't," Boot said. They could hear sirens, and more headlights started bouncing to a stop where the Dodge Challenger sat, its lights still on. "Ya'll go meet them and tell them what happened. I'll stay here with Perch." He walked over and grabbed a handful of Skeeter's jacket at the neck and lifted him to his feet. "Now go on!"

Mervin took Skeeter's arm and turned him away. "Follow me," he said, and Skeeter did so, trundling along behind Mervin, his shoulders sagging and head low.

Boot watched them go. Alone now, he let the tears flow.

CHAPTER THIRTY-SEVEN

AFTER STATEMENTS WERE GIVEN, stories told, and a timeline was constructed, it became evident that both dramas, the one in Hazel and Carol's front yard and the shootout at the clay pit, happened almost simultaneously.

Tyeisha Brooks had gotten out of her car to stretch her legs when Mark Rogers accosted her behind the house and tased her so powerfully she passed out. It was her boots Vickie Vanderhall had seen, and when Vickie started to run, Rogers caught her and whacked the back of her head with his pistol, knocking her out.

Both women had recovered, although they were sore and shaken. After a long night of answering questions and telling her story over and over, Barbara Lowrie was told she could go home, although there would be further review of her use of a firearm. She knew it was purely protocol, but she was too tired to worry about it. Chief Holt told her she could take a couple days off, and Barbara said maybe she would.

In a rare display of emotion, Pete Shumpert gave her a brief hug and told her everything would be all right. It was the first time Barbara almost broke down, but she didn't. She thanked Pete and walked out of the police station.

Since the clay pit was outside city limits, both Preston County sheriff deputies and Preston police responded to Mervin's call for help. After assuring the paramedic that they were all right, Mervin, Boot and Skeeter were bundled away to the sheriff's department where they were ushered into a conference room, given cups of coffee, and gently interrogated by Detective Stanton and Sheriff Whittington.

They did their best to tell the officers what had happened despite the shock and fatigue they were feeling. When Mervin came to the part about Perch running past him, hearing the gunfire, and watching Perch fall, Skeeter buried his face in his hands. Boot stood and paced behind the chairs, choking back rage instead of tears.

Whittington and Stanton didn't say anything, just allowed the emotions to run their course. When they'd subsided, Mervin finished his story, telling them how Perch had saved his life.

Whittington nodded and told them they'd been through a lot and it would take time to process it all. He said he would be as supportive as he could. Even the usually ill-tempered Stanton showed empathy by telling them he would keep them informed as the investigation progressed and even offered to give them a lift home.

"Thanks," Mervin said, "but I've called my wife to come get us. She should be here soon."

"She's already here," Whittington said. "Waiting for y'all in the lobby."

They all stood and shook hands. Mervin put an arm around Skeeter's shoulders and guided him out of the room. As soon as Becca saw them, she rushed forward and threw her arms around Mervin and Skeeter who were still standing close. Then she reached out and grabbed Boot by the sleeve and pulled him in.

"Oh, Mervin," she said. "Perch."

They stood, wrapped together, heads bowed, Becca quietly crying. Whittington, Stanton, and a couple other deputies watched respectfully from a distance. They knew bonds were tight in this small town, and while they might not have known Perch Gordon personally, they felt the loss, too.

"Let's go," Boot said, and he broke off and headed for the door. The others gathered themselves and followed.

Mervin remembered something, stopped, and turned to Whittington. "What about my truck?" he asked.

"We'll get it towed out," the sheriff said. "But from what I heard, it took quite a beating. I'll let you know when you can come get it."

Mervin thanked him and went outside. It was dark. He had no idea how late it was. Becca was behind the wheel of her idling Acura, and Boot and Skeeter were crammed in the back seat. Mervin climbed in beside her and she backed out of the parking spot and pointed the car toward town and Bill's Corner.

They rode in silence, heartbroken but hoping this nightmare had finally come to an end.

Monday morning arrived with gusty winds and ominous gray skies. Word spread quickly around town about events from the night before. From the Waffle House to Main Street shops, people were all abuzz, astounded by the news that Henry Gordon, that fellow who used to own the insurance agency, and a policeman named Mark Rogers had been shot and killed.

It all had to do with the killings of Louise Dixon and Luther Peacock, they said, and the stories grew wilder with each telling.

Multiple gunmen had squared off with police in a gun battle outside of town.

The ringleader had been shot so many times he couldn't be identified.

Rogers had died in the line of duty, trying to protect that female doctor from the Urgent Care.

And on and on it went, the jungle telegraph beating out various versions of a story that would be talked about for years.

By midday, representatives from every regional media outlet had descended upon Preston and were hungry for any morsel of information they could get. They were interviewing people on the street, filming the comings and goings at the police station, and hounding every official for a comment.

Chief Holt hunkered down with a patrol officer who doubled as the force's ombudsman, and they cobbled together a press release that was heavy on big-picture facts but short on detail. Basically, it said that after a short pursuit on Sunday evening, the suspect in the killings of Louise Dixon and Luther Peacock was cornered on the outskirts of Preston where he was shot to death in an exchange of gunfire. The death of Mark Rogers was being treated as a police internal matter, and more information would be forthcoming.

"This concludes a case that has caused much distress in Preston, and we want to assure everyone that the threat to public safety has been eliminated."

Of course, this didn't come close to satisfying the newshounds who waited outside the station and peppered every officer who came and went with questions about the killings.

Barbara Lowrie had hardly slept but she arrived at work at 8 a.m. in polished boots and a freshly dry-cleaned navy-blue uniform. She sat up straight at her desk and scrolled through emails, although the lines around her eyes betrayed her show of confidence.

"What are you doing here?" Holt asked after he'd watched Barbara come in and take a seat at her desk. "I told you to take a couple days. You need to step back, decompress."

Barbara wasn't sure what that meant.

"I couldn't just sit at home, sir," she said. "I just need to get on with it. Take my mind off things."

"Okay," Holt said, eyeing her closely. After a beat, he walked back to his office.

Barbara sighed. Maybe she should call Carol Baxley and see how they were holding up. Maybe she should check on Tyeisha. She didn't know what to do.

She looked around and made eye contact with Pete Shumpert who was at his desk on the far side of the squad room. He smiled and she smiled back.

Barbara watched as Pete stood up and walked her way.

"You okay?" he asked, taking a seat in a chair next to her desk.

"I'm fine. I need to stay busy."

"Mark Rogers was an asshole," Pete said.

Barbara laughed despite herself.

"I mean it. He was not only an asshole, he was a mean, hateful bully. And a misogynist, too."

"Well, maybe so," Barbara said. "Nevertheless."

"Nevertheless nothing. You did what any smart, veteran police officer would do. It makes me proud to work with you."

Barbara sat back in her chair and rubbed her face with her hands.

"Thanks, Pete. That means a lot. If I'm honest, I'm not feeling that great. When I got home last night, it hit me, what I'd done, taken another person's life. I don't know. I'm scared, sad . . . and angry."

"Look, I'm not going to sit here and tell you it will get better with time, and I don't know what Holt told you either, but all I will say is you'll need to deal with it in your own way. It might be a good idea to talk to a counselor, or maybe not. For now, just take a deep breath. When thoughts of last night come to you, take a deep breath, deal with them, and let them go. I'm not saying it's easy."

Barbara smiled. "I'll try, Pete."

He quickly changed the subject.

"Why do you think Rogers went after Carol Baxley last night? He could have grabbed her anytime during the past few days."

"I've been thinking about that," Barbara said. "I figure he'd been in touch with this Harold Cephus fellow and they decided to put an end to this thing. Most likely, he was intimidated by Cephus and just followed his orders."

"That's possible," Pete said. "Another thing that's puzzled me, why wasn't he wearing his vest?"

Barbara shuddered at the memory of her two rounds landing squarely in Mark Rogers' chest and knocking him to the ground.

"Oh, I imagine he didn't expect any opposition from a couple lesbian women on a Sunday afternoon. Thankfully one of those lesbians is smarter than most of us, sensed something was wrong and called me."

"True that," Pete said with a grin. "Plus, he should never have underestimated the warrior squaw."

Barbara couldn't help herself. She laughed out loud and said, "Pete, you do talk some crazy shit sometimes."

"You just call me if you need anything," he said, getting up and walking back to his desk.

———〜———

Mervin and Becca didn't talk much when they got home Sunday night. They were both exhausted and Mervin was still in shock.

When he got up Monday morning, he found a pot of coffee waiting for him and a note on the kitchen table.

I love you. There's some vegetable soup in the fridge for your lunch. I'll see you this evening. B.

Mervin gulped and thought once again about how lucky one man could be. He poured a cup and sat down at the table. He hurt all over. His arms and shoulders throbbed from gripping the steering wheel during the chase. His hips and back were tight and painful from trying to run across the floor of the clay pit.

Oh well, he thought, *I've got no truck and no plans for the day.* He thought of Perch, the look in his eyes as he died, and he vowed right then to never take another day for granted.

He checked his phone for messages and saw a text from Boot asking if he was okay. One from Bill said that he'd heard what happened and was on his way to the bar to check on Skeeter. He said he would call later. There was even a text from Benny Martin who sent condolences about Perch and said they could play as a threesome on Sundays whenever they liked.

Mervin grunted in pain as he rose to refill his coffee mug and while standing at the kitchen window, then he responded to the texts. On the off chance, he punched the number for Skeeter's landline, and not surprisingly, Skeeter answered after the third ring.

"So, you've already gone back to your house."

"Yeah. I talked to Bill this morning, gathered up my stuff, and came home. I don't know how I'll ever be able to thank him."

"Drink a lot in his bar might do it."

"Well, that goes without saying."

There was a moment of silence then Mervin said, "Skeeter, you do know you're not responsible for what happened to Perch. All of us, Boot, Perch, and me, we got involved on our own. You and Carol Baxley were just trying to do what was right."

"It's okay, Mervin," Skeeter said. "I appreciate it, I really do, but I can't talk about it right now."

"No worries. We're here for you, Skeeter. Just know that." Mervin paused. "How's your house? Everything okay?"

"It's fine. A little musty but I'm doing some cleaning. It's good to be home."

"I bet. Hey, listen, I'm going to call you later today. Be by your phone, okay? Or at least check your messages."

"Will do. And Mervin, thanks."

CHAPTER THIRTY-EIGHT

STEADY RAIN BEGAN TO FALL at midday and continued at various intensities throughout the afternoon. It forced the TV crews outside the Preston police station to seek shelter, but it didn't dampen their determination to get the story. Most hunkered down in their vans or nearby coffee shops to await news from the squad room.

Inside was a beehive of activity as officers working the case made phone calls and mined databases in an effort to learn more about the late Harold Cephus, his connection to the late Mark Rogers, and more importantly, to make sure there were no more cohorts out there who might be involved in the plot to kill Carol Baxley and August Ellington.

By late afternoon, pieces began falling into place and the puzzle was almost complete. Chief Holt called Barbara Lowrie and Pete Shumpert into the conference room where Detective Stanton, SLED officer Mankey, and Sheriff Whittington were waiting at the table.

"Everyone has been doing tremendous work," Holt began, "and now we have a positive ID for the suspect. His name was not Harold Cephus. It was Travis Conn. He was the older brother of Silas Conn."

Barbara and Pete sat back, visibly shaken.

"Wow," Stanton said. "So, was he here trying to get some sort of revenge for his brother?"

"We don't know for sure but that's a definite possibility. Phone records show that the two brothers were in frequent contact over the past two years. Text messages we managed to unearth from Travis Conn's phone reveal that the younger brother was angry and devastated by his wife's departure. They also show how much he hated Ellington and Baxley and how he held them responsible for destroying his marriage. And we already know from previous statements that he was a violent, dangerous man."

"Delusional, too," Mankey added. "And suicidal. If you closely review the file on Silas Conn's death in Myrtle Beach, it becomes more obvious that he stepped in front of that truck on purpose and took his own life."

"And that's what we think drove Travis Conn over the edge and sent him here on a mission to avenge his brother's death," Holt said.

"How'd you identify him so fast?" Barbara asked.

"Turned out, it wasn't that hard," Stanton said. "There was a temporary tag from Fayetteville on that Challenger he was driving and when we called the salesman at the dealership up there, he gave us the info on the title from the black truck that was traded.

"Registered owner was Travis Conn who listed the town of Luraville, Florida, as his residence. The truck was purchased from a Dodge dealership off I-75 near Lake City, Florida."

"We made some calls to police down there and he was known to them," Holt said. "Fingerprints were emailed, and sure enough, it was Travis Conn. Apparently, he was a bit of a loner. Couldn't hold a job, had been kicked out of the National Guard, lived for a while in an old

Airstream camper. And he was on their books for one charge of assault and battery, and another of domestic abuse, but he was never convicted."

"So, he was married then?" Pete asked.

"There were no legal documents to that effect," Holt said. "Apparently, he lived with a woman who filed the charges, later dropped them, and she hasn't been seen or heard from since."

"In the bottom of a swamp," Barbara muttered. Holt shot her a *not-now* look.

"He didn't do much to cover his tracks," Pete said.

"I think at first he hoped to come to Preston, scout around and try to formulate a plan to kill Ellington and Baxley without being caught," Stanton said. "Maybe he wanted to do it in a way so the blame would be placed on someone else. Who knows?"

"That would kind of explain why he started hanging out with those fellows who gather out at Earl Tyler's place," Pete said. "He was probably trying to set up a fall guy."

"Someone like Luther," Barbara said.

"But why the whole Harold Cephus thing, and calling himself the Deacon? What was that all about?" Pete asked.

"Well, you might remember when we were searching for people named Harold Cephus, one that popped up was a preacher from Florida who'd recently died in a boating accident," Holt said. "Guess where he was from? Lake City, Florida."

"Damn," Whittington said. "So I take it he and Travis Conn had crossed paths."

"More than that. It turns out Conn not only met this Cephus, but apparently fell completely under his spell. We got some background from others who attended the church down there, the Holy Redeemer Tabernacle of Divine Truth . . . or something like that."

"Sounds Pentecostal," Barbara said.

"Maybe, but most likely unaffiliated with any denomination," Holt said. "Anyway, Cephus was in his seventies, one of those fire-and-brimstone types who preached that man was king of his castle and had every right to keep his woman in line."

"Bottom of a swamp," Barbara mumbled again, and the men sitting around the table couldn't suppress their laughter this time.

"Okay, enough of that," Holt said, grinning. "Folks down there told us Travis Conn was a devoted attendee at the church and eventually became . . . drum roll, please . . . a deacon. It might have been the first time he ever felt like he had a purpose in life."

"So Cephus and Silas Conn die around the same time, it throws Travis Conn for a loop, he assumes the name of his late mentor and comes north to Preston to plot revenge for his brother while carrying out the doctrine of his spiritual guide at the same time," Whittington said. "Amazing."

"But tragic, too, especially in the case of Mark Rogers," Holt said. He looked at Barbara. "You okay?"

"Yeah, I'm fine. Go ahead."

"There's not much to tell, really. Rogers' history with women consisted of one failed relationship after another. A woman he'd hoped to marry walked out on him just weeks before Travis Conn arrived on the scene. A previous girlfriend confided in friends that Rogers had struck her, but she never pressed charges. We learned all this from Jake Rainey, his closest friend on the force. Rainey said Rogers was 'primed and ready' to follow someone like Harold Cephus, who undoubtedly told him that the women were at fault for his misery."

"The look in his eyes," Barbara said. "I could see that he was tortured, but he was scared, too. And angry."

No one at the table said a word. There was no "You did the right thing," or "He brought it upon himself." The other officers were wondering if they would have shown the courage Barbara did when she pulled the trigger.

Jimmy Glover stuck his head into the room. "Sorry, boss. Those TV folks are getting restless. I think they're coming up on their deadlines for the evening news."

"Tell them I'll speak to them in half an hour, forty-five minutes tops."

Jimmy disappeared and Holt turned to his colleagues.

"So, any questions? Have we got most of it covered?"

"Great work, Chief," Whittington said. "I for one want to see this thing wrapped up and put to bed."

"Sounds good to me," Stanton said.

"But what about Perch Gordon?" Barbara asked. "What about his friends who did as much as we did to put an end to it?"

"Don't worry. We're going to tell the whole story. Those fellows have lost a close friend. They'll need some privacy and time to grieve, but at the same time, their actions need to be acknowledged."

"I agree," Pete said. "It would be good for the town. It would help us heal. Give us a local hero to mourn and remember. Besides, people are already talking about Perch and Mark Rogers."

"Absolutely," Barbara said. "Let's put it all out there and move on."

Holt pushed back his chair and stood. "You all need to get out of here. We've got work to do to get our statements ready for the press. Get out of here. Go home. Watch an old movie. Go to a bar. Have a drink. Just try to forget about all this for a little while."

He looked around the table. "And thank you, each of you. This has been a tough one," he sighed. "See you in the morning."

Mervin waited until he was pretty sure the lunchtime rush had ended, then he gave Jessie Mae a call.

"Mr. Mervin, you all just come on over whenever you want. I'll pull a couple tables together and make sure we got some fresh cornbread."

"Now don't go to any extra trouble, Jessie Mae," Mervin said. "I know y'all like to be out of there by eight, so I promise we won't hang around."

"Y'all just come on and if it starts gettin' late, I'll run you out," she said. "And I'm sorry about your friend, Mr. Gordon. He used to come in every now and then. Tears me up. People been talking about it all day. Lord, what's this world coming to? The things been going on in this town. I hope it's all over."

"Me, too," Mervin said. "I appreciate it. We'll see you around six-thirty."

He ended the call then pushed the numbers for Boot and Skeeter who both said they'd love to meet for supper at Jessie Mae's and thanked him for making the arrangements.

Mervin took a breath and dialed Hazel Owens' phone. He wasn't exactly sure what to say. She answered on the second ring, didn't recognize the number, her voice suspicious.

"Hazel, this is Mervin Hayes. I came by the studio a few days ago."

"Oh, hey Mervin," she said, relieved. "Are you okay?"

"I'm fine. More importantly, how are you? I heard about your ordeal in that warehouse."

"I'm better," Hazel said, "or at least I'm getting better. It was awful. I wouldn't want anyone to have to go through something like that. But I heard you had a bit of an ordeal yourself yesterday."

"Yes, it was an interesting day," Mervin said. "I'm feeling better, too, and I'm glad you're on the mend. Listen, the reason I'm calling, and I don't know if you and Carol have already made plans for supper, but I was hoping y'all might like to join us at Jessie Mae's Diner. It's just going to be me, my wife Becca, and our friends Boot and Skeeter."

Hazel was quiet for a moment. "You know that sounds kind of nice. Carol's at work right now but I'm sure she'd like to see Skeeter. After all, it was those two who brought all this craziness down on us."

Mervin laughed. "You've got a point. We're thinking around six-thirty. Does that sound okay?"

"Perfect," Hazel said. "And Mervin, thanks for thinking of us."

"No worries," he said. "I look forward to seeing y'all this evening."

Becca walked through the backdoor two hours later looking exhausted and still stressed from the night before. Mervin told her about the arrangements he'd made for supper and hoped Becca would be fine it. Her face lightened and she visibly relaxed.

"That sounds great," she said. "Any word on your truck?"

"Not yet. We'll have to take your rice-burner."

She gave him a playful punch in the gut then took his face in her hands and kissed him.

"I've been thinking about you all day," she said.

"If I didn't know better, I'd think you loved me."

"Don't push it, pal," Becca said. "I need to go freshen up." She pushed him away.

"You seem pretty fresh already."

She took a swing and Mervin ducked.

CHAPTER THIRTY-NINE

MERVIN WAS HAPPY to let Becca drive them over to Jessie Mae's and they spotted Boot and Skeeter's trucks as they pulled into the dirt parking lot. Boot and Skeeter were chatting with Jessie Mae when they came through the door, and only a few tables were occupied by evening diners.

"Mr. Mervin," Jessie Mae exclaimed, breaking away. "Y'all come on in. I got y'all set up back here."

She led them to a far side of the dining area where two wooden tables were pushed together and covered by red-and-white checkerboard tablecloths. Six chairs had been placed at the ready.

Becca gave Skeeter a hug and asked how he was doing.

"I'm fine," he said. "Just glad to be back out at the house."

"I guess I don't deserve a hug," Boot said, standing there in jeans, a flannel shirt, and his Tiger Paw cap. "Even though I'm pretty sure I helped save your sorry husband's life."

"Shut up, Boot," Becca said. "You're an ornery old cuss." She wrapped her arms around his waist and gave him a squeeze.

"That's what I'm talking about," Boot said, and Mervin just rolled his eyes.

Just then, Carol and Hazel came through the front door and Jessie Mae led them over to the table. Carol and Skeeter looked at each other then stepped into a deep embrace. Carol started crying. Skeeter held her tight, his hand on the back of her head. The others stood quietly, watching.

"I'm so sorry about your friend," Carol said. "I never thought anything like this would happen. I just wanted to help those women. I'm so, so sorry."

"Shhh," Skeeter said. "This isn't your fault or my fault. You did help them. And we're going to keep on helping them."

After a few seconds, Boot broke the ice.

"I don't think I know y'all," he said. "My name's Boot Pearson. I understand y'all are roommates or something."

Becca couldn't contain it. She burst out laughing so hard everybody joined in.

"Boot, you truly amaze me sometimes," she said.

"I'm just trying to get to know these lovely ladies," he said with exaggerated innocence.

More laughter, then Jessie Mae said, "Y'all need to sit down. We ain't got all night."

Everyone did as they were told. Mervin and Becca sat at one side of the table, Carol and Hazel took the seats opposite, and Skeeter and Boot slid into the chairs at either end.

Jessie Mae took out a notepad. "We're out of a few things, but we'll get y'all fed. Mr. Mervin, I made up some salmon patties just in case."

"Dang, Jessie Mae, you know me too well," he said. "That's what I'll have with whatever vegetables you got left, maybe fried okra and butter beans."

Jessie Mae jotted it down. Becca ordered the salmon patty, too. Boot went with beef stew, and Skeeter, Hazel, and Carol ordered vegetable plates.

"I'll get it out in a few minutes," Jessie Mae said and headed off to the kitchen.

There was an awkward silence as everyone fidgeted and took sips of water and sweet tea. Then Boot turned to Hazel and said, "I heard you used to be a rock star back in the '80s. You ever meet Stevie Ray Vaughan?"

Hazel gave him a quizzical look then smiled. "No, I never did," she said. "But I wish I had. He was badass."

"No shit," Boot gushed. "He was the man!"

And they were off and running.

They talked about music, Hazel's studio, and Boot said he remembered DJ Clarke. He related a story about how DJ got him hooked on the Jimi Hendrix album *Axis: Bold as Love* and it changed the way he listened to music. Hazel smiled and said that sounded like something DJ would do.

The food arrived and they all tucked in. It was delicious—the country-cooking aromas and hot cornbread lifted their moods and nourished their souls. The conversation drifted to Perch, and Mervin, Skeeter, and Boot sat quietly while Becca told Carol and Hazel about their late friend.

She told them he was a gentle soul who had loved his wife Janice deeply. She told them how he'd taken over the family insurance business and used it to help folks around town. He was an avid reader and loved to talk about events happening around the world.

"From what I've been told, Perch saved my husband's life last night," Becca said. "What can I add to that? I'll remember him always."

Mervin's eyes welled with tears.

"I was looking straight down the barrel of that gun," he said. "It was a matter of seconds. I mean, Boot, when we were out at your place, Perch could barely hit the barn."

"Don't try to explain it, Mervin," Boot said. "He was dying. He pulled the trigger twice. One of those bullets found the mark and you and me and Skeeter are sitting here eating fried okra and mashed potatoes. That's all there is to it."

Before anyone could comment, Jessie Mae's granddaughter Helen arrived with a pitcher of tea in one hand and a pitcher of ice water in the other.

"Hey, Helen," Becca said. "It's so good to see you. How are things at school?"

"They're fine, Mrs. Hayes. My grades are good."

"They better be. You were one of my shining stars."

Helen gave a shy smile and moved on to another table.

"I forgot you were a schoolteacher," Hazel said. "That's cool. It must be so gratifying."

"Sometimes," Becca said. "Other times I could skin those little rug rats."

Carol's phone buzzed.

"Oh, no," Hazel said. "I hope you don't have to go back to work."

"No. It's Barbara Lowrie." She answered the call. "Hey, what's up?"

Carol listened and everyone watched her.

"I'm not at home right now," she said. "We're at Jessie Mae's Diner having supper with Skeeter and his friends." She listened some more then said, "Another half hour maybe?"

Carol looked at Mervin who nodded.

"Great. We'll be looking for you."

She ended the call and turned to the others. "Barbara Lowrie said she was on her way home and wants to stop by and talk to us. She said she has some news. I hope that's all right."

"Sure," Mervin said. "It will be good to see her. I understand she was a hero, too."

Carol and Hazel looked at each other.

"Yes, she was," Hazel said. "If anyone's a badass, it's Barbara Lowrie."

Hazel told the story of what happened in her front yard the day before, emphasizing how Rufus and Barbara combined to save the day. Ten minutes later, Barbara came through the door and Carol waved her over.

"I think I know everyone here except you," she said and extended her hand across the table to Becca.

"Hi, I'm Mervin's wife, Becca. It's really good to meet you."

"Bless your heart," Barbara said. "You and me need to have a talk about this outfit." She nodded at Mervin, Boot, and Skeeter.

Becca liked her immediately.

"Hazel just finished telling us about yesterday. That was a brave thing you did."

"I don't know about that. Just what I was trained to do."

Hazel and Carol made room, and Barbara slid a chair up to the table.

"How you doin', Sergeant Lowrie?" said Jessie Mae, who seemed to appear at the table. "Can I get you something to eat?"

"No thank you, ma'am, but a glass of tea would be nice."

Jessie Mae walked off and Barbara turned to look around the table.

"From the look of those empty plates, I can tell y'all must be ready to go home, so I'll get right to it," she said. "We've identified the man who was shot and killed in the clay pit, and we've established a connection between him and Mark Rogers. His name was Travis Conn, and he was the older brother of Silas Conn. His wife was the first woman you two helped, am I right?"

Carol and Skeeter just nodded, stunned at the news. Barbara told them all about the death of Silas Conn in Myrtle Beach, the late Florida preacher Harold Cephus, how Travis Conn became enamored with the old man's sermons, and how the deaths of the two men triggered Conn's crusade to Preston to kill Carol Baxley and Skeeter Ellington.

"How'd he know about us?" Carol asked.

"He'd been in contact with his brother. We found text messages from Silas saying how he'd discovered what y'all had done and blamed you for destroying his marriage. He was delusional and his older brother had a history of violence, a dangerous combination. It'll all be on the news tonight."

They sat there in silence taking it in. Then Boot spoke.

"I hear you saved these two ladies' lives. More importantly, you saved the real hero, Rufus."

Barbara laughed. "Yeah, Rufus saved all of us. I'm going to make sure he gets a commendation for bravery."

"Y'all need to bring Rufus out to my place to meet Joe and Jack," Boot told Carol and Hazel. "They're just a couple of old blue-tick hounds but they'll take Rufus on a nice run through the country."

"I'm gonna take you up on that," Hazel said. "Rufus needs to get out of the house and stretch his legs."

Skeeter had hardly said a word all evening. When he gave a slight cough, everyone turned his way.

"Do you know the status of our friend Perch? Henry Gordon?" he asked, looking at Barbara whose face softened.

"I'm really sorry about Perch," she said. "What he did was amazing. I know he meant a lot to y'all. I imagine the medical examiner has finished any examinations he needed to make. His body should be released tomorrow if y'all need to make arrangements."

"Thank you," Skeeter said. "I'll call you in the morning if that's okay, and we can start making plans."

"Absolutely," Barbara said.

"Well, I can see Jessie Mae is itching to close up and go home," Mervin said, "but before we go, let's lift a glass to Perch."

They all clinked glasses above the table, then Boot said, "Let's do one more to Rufus and Preston police Sergeant Barbara Lowrie, who was described just a few minutes ago as a *badass*."

Everyone laughed and clinked glasses again. Chairs were scraped back on the linoleum floor as everyone stood to leave.

"You know, sergeant, if you're on your way home, I don't know of a better way to end the day than with a take-out from Jessie Mae's kitchen," Mervin said. "You should ask her what she's got left."

"Mr. Hayes, that's the best advice I've gotten in a long time."

Mervin walked over to the register, paid Helen for everyone's meal "and whatever the sergeant is having." There were a couple feeble objections, but everybody knew it meant a lot to Mervin to treat his friends.

In the parking lot, Skeeter motioned for Mervin to walk with him to his truck while Becca made small talk with Hazel and Carol.

"I need you to come out to the house tomorrow," Skeeter said.

"That might be tough."

"Why's that?"

"Because I don't have any wheels, Skeeter. For all I know, my truck is still sitting on the floor of the clay pit."

"I forgot about that. Well then, can I come to your place?"

"I'm not going anywhere. What's going on?"

"I've got Perch's will. I drew it up for him years ago. I need a witness when I open it."

It hadn't been what Mervin was expecting.

"Okay," he said. "How about late morning, around eleven?"

"That's perfect. See you then."

Skeeter climbed into his big Toyota and fired it up. Mervin slapped the hood and walked back across the lot to where Becca was telling Hazel and Carol goodbye. He turned in time to see Barbara Lowrie coming out of Jessie Mae's with two take-out bags, one in each hand.

Jessie Mae was right behind her.

"Y'all know that I'll have turkey and dressing on Thursday," she hollered.

Mervin gave her a thumbs up. "We'll see you around lunchtime," he said.

CHAPTER FORTY

SKEETER SAT AND TOSSED a ten-by-eight-inch envelope onto the middle of the kitchen table. Mervin sat across from him and saw a label on the envelope—*Last Will and Testament of Henry Allen Gordon.*

"I take it you know what it says," Mervin said.

"Pretty much, from what I can remember."

Skeeter opened the envelope, took out the will, and handed it to Mervin who took a sip of coffee and began to read. After a couple of minutes, he looked up at Skeeter.

"Am I reading this right? Perch left everything to you and me and Boot?"

"That's right," Skeeter said. "His entire estate, for what it's worth."

"How much is it worth?"

"There's his house and its contents, his truck, and a couple of investment accounts that have done pretty well. Probably comes to around two million."

"Damn," Mervin said. "What should we do? Shouldn't Boot be here?"

"I'll talk to Boot."

Mervin handed the will back to Skeeter who slid it into the envelope and closed the clasp.

"We talked about it a lot," Skeeter said. "Perch didn't have anybody. He said we were his family. He just wanted his money to be spent on a good cause. He knew we would do that. Hell, Mervin, we're all going on seventy. We don't need much at this stage."

"I might need a new truck."

Skeeter tossed him a set of keys.

"I know it's a Ford, but you can drive Perch's truck while we sort this out. It's still parked behind Bill's with a few bullet holes in the tailgate. I'll run you down there when we're done."

"What else we got to do?"

Skeeter fidgeted with the envelope and asked if he could have some more coffee.

"Spit it out," Mervin said as he filled both their mugs.

"I had a long talk with Carol this morning and we've come up with a plan. But it all depends on how you and Boot feel about it."

"Go on," Mervin said.

"Well, this past year has really opened my eyes. What Carol and I tried to do to help those women was hard. And it seemed every time we had one safe and settled, another one called for help. It showed us there was a real need here, not only in Preston but in this whole region. We need a sanctuary, a shelter where women can go when their lives are in danger. Some of them have kids, and they need protection, too."

"Y'all are thinking that Perch's house fits the bill."

"It's perfect, Mervin. All those bedrooms. It's downtown, not too far from the police station but on a quiet street. It's got that great secluded backdoor. These places can't be advertised, you know. In fact, they need to be operated in as much secrecy as possible."

"So, what are you proposing?"

"That we turn Perch's house into a women's shelter and use the balance of his estate to set up a foundation to fund it. We'll name the foundation after Perch and Janice."

Mervin didn't need to think about it.

"Sign me up," he said. "Now let's go get Perch's truck. I'm tired of being stuck at home. Makes me nervous."

Skeeter and Mervin rose from the table but before they could get out the door, Mervin said, "I just thought of something. Do you think we could donate some of Perch's money to some kind of organization for Syrian refugee relief?"

Skeeter gave him a curious look.

"It's a long story," Mervin said. "Trust me."

Mervin's Silverado was delivered from the clay pit late in the afternoon, hooked to the back of a wrecker driven by a good ol' boy who said he thought the frame might be bent.

"There was a bunch of golf clubs scattered on the ground and we just threw them in the back," he said. "Hope they're okay."

Mervin had forgotten all about his golf clubs. He peered into the truck bed and saw his precious Taylor Made irons scratched and bent and looking like so much scrap metal. The head had snapped off his driver and his putter was nowhere to be seen.

This meant only one thing. *New clubs!* Mervin started practicing in his mind how he would explain it to Becca. "Honey, I can't really play with them in that condition and I don't think they can be fixed. Besides, it will probably be covered by the insurance on my truck."

His thoughts were interrupted by the wrecker driver who wanted to know where he should take the truck. Mervin gave him the name of a body shop he'd used in the past and watched as the Silverado was towed down the street. It was like watching an old friend being carted off to the hospital.

Mervin walked back inside, passing Perch's truck parked in the carport. Skeeter had called earlier to tell him Boot was on board with the plan for Perch's estate. Boot was glad Perch's money would be going to a good cause and implied that he sure didn't need it. This led Mervin and Skeeter to speculate about the breadth of Boot's cannabis business.

Skeeter also told Mervin that he'd talked to Barbara Lowrie who said Perch's body had been released and was at the Franklin Funeral Home. Skeeter and Mervin discussed it and decided a Saturday funeral would be best. Perch had paid for two plots in the Evergreen Cemetery, so he'd be laid to rest next to Janice.

"Something kind of weird though," Skeeter had said. "When I called Carol and Hazel to tell them about the funeral, Hazel said she hoped it would be early in the day because she had a really important session booked at the studio that afternoon."

"Probably no big deal," Mervin said. "I'm sure she operates that place on a shoestring. She's got to grab all the business she can."

"I suppose," Skeeter said.

So the funeral was arranged for 11 a.m. on Saturday at the Preston Methodist Church, which was where Perch and Janice attended when they felt like it. There would be a brief graveside service afterwards.

Before they'd ended the call, Mervin asked if they should go to Bill's and have a drink.

"I don't see why not," Skeeter replied. "I'll call Boot."

"It's going to feel strange."

"Come on, Mervin, best foot forward. Get your backside in Perch's truck and drive it downtown. And park it right in front of Bill's."

For some reason, this made Mervin feel a lot better.

Bill paid even more attention to them than usual. They were like a wagon with a wheel missing, the three of them sitting there nursing beers and watching a college football talk show on the TV above the bar.

"Did you play golf today?" Boot asked Mervin.

"No, Boot, I've been on the phone with Skeeter and the church and the funeral home getting Perch's funeral arranged. And then I had to talk to insurance adjusters and the fellows at the body shop."

There was a bit of irritation in Mervin's voice and he immediately regretted it. "Good news, though," he said. "My truck is basically okay, and my golf clubs will be covered by my insurance."

"You're getting a new set?" Skeeter asked.

"Yep, and there ain't nothing Becca can do about it. They're already paid for."

They clinked their beer bottles in a toast to Mervin's good fortune, then Boot said, "It ain't fair. Just when I'm closing in, you go and get new clubs."

Skeeter laughed. "Relax, Boot. You're going to get him."

Bill was still hovering, and he raised a bottle of Jameson in Mervin's direction. Mervin nodded and pointed at the others so it would be shots all around.

"And one for yourself, Bill," he said. "You've been an amazing ally. All of us, Perch included, appreciate how you looked after Skeeter."

Bill nodded his thanks and said it was no big deal. They drank, and in a delicate fashion, Bill asked about what happened in the clay pit. Boot gave him all the details, and Bill shook his head in disbelief.

"All this craziness in this little town," he said. "People will be talking about it for years."

"Maybe," Mervin said, "or maybe not. People have extremely short attention spans nowadays. Three months from now, most folks won't even remember Perch Gordon or the Conn brothers. They'll be Googling this and Tweeting that and posing like pop stars for Instagram. We've devolved into a self-centered mess."

"Damn, Mervin," Boot said. "You've been reading magazine articles again, haven't you?"

They laughed and Bill placed fresh beers on the bar. "These are on me," he said. They showed their thanks by taking hefty slugs.

"I talked to Carol a little while ago," Skeeter said. "She said she met with the woman who'd contacted the Urgent Care a few days ago looking for help. Her husband's been beating her. She's only nineteen."

"Damn. How are we going to stop this?" Mervin asked.

"Well, Carol actually got some good news. In light of recent events, Preston police are going to assign a special team to address domestic violence. They hope it will give abused women the confidence to call them. She heard all this from Barbara Lowrie."

"That woman is the bomb," Boot said. "She'll make it work."

"Calm down, Boot," Mervin said. "We know you got the hots for Lowrie."

"Shut up, Mervin. I'm just saying she's tough enough to get it done."

Skeeter and Bill grinned at each other over the ongoing pissing match between Mervin and Boot.

"Anyway," Skeeter said, "Barbara also told Carol that Mark Rogers will be buried Friday. He has some family, a sister who's coming down from Richmond and his mother is making the trip up from Charleston. His father's dead apparently. It's a sad story, really."

"I've been meaning to tell you," Bill said, looking at Skeeter. "I saw Rogers go up the stairs Saturday night and he tried to get into your room. He was in uniform and everything. I politely asked him to leave."

"I heard him rattle the doorknob and I heard you talking to him. I was scared as shit. I hate it that he's dead, but he must have had some serious issues."

"I wonder how the police are going to treat his death?" Bill asked.

"Barbara said the entire force is required to be present, but he's not being given the full honorary send-off, whatever that means."

"It means it's a sad thing," Boot said. "Just think, that dude's gonna be buried in Preston and probably ain't nobody ever gonna come visit his grave."

With that sobering thought, they all sat there staring into their beers.

"Not to mention we've got the funerals of Louise Dixon and Luther Peacock to go to," Mervin eventually said.

"Damn," Boot said. He motioned for Bill to refill the shot glasses. "What a mess."

CHAPTER FORTY-ONE

THE FUNERAL FOR PERCH GORDON had been really nice, Hazel thought as she arranged microphones and set up sound baffling partitions. She'd never known him but from what people said, he must have been a fine fellow.

She had been surprised when the one called Boot got up to say a few words at the graveside service. His elegy was heartfelt and funny. The story about Perch catching the big fish as a teenager and earning a nickname for life was a hoot. It was destined for Preston mythology and had brought tears to a lot of eyes amidst the laughter.

Dressed in a long-sleeve black T-shirt, black jeans, and Doc Martens, Hazel was happy to be back in the studio. She stepped into the control room where Stephon Vanderhall was sitting in the captain's chair, his eyes scanning all the knobs and switches.

"What do you think?" Hazel said. "Are you ready to help me record some music?"

He looked up at her with an anxious expression of both fear and excitement.

Hazel laughed. "Don't worry. It's going to be fun."

Just then, someone knocked on the front door and Hazel told Stephon to go let them in. A few seconds later, Daniel Sims, the drummer from WeirdoCat, came down the hall with a kick drum and a cymbal. He was followed by Stephon who was carrying a snare drum.

"Hey!" Hazel shouted as they passed the control room door. "Thanks for agreeing to do this."

"No problem," Daniel said. "I've been looking forward to it. Not to mention, it gave me a great reason to get out of Lumberton for a day."

A few minutes later, there was more knocking on the front door, quieter than the rapping made by Daniel. Hazel went down the hall and held the door open wide while Jerome shuffled inside holding one of those soft guitar cases that can be worn like a backpack.

He'd tried to smarten himself up a bit, but his faded jeans were still worn and several layers of T-shirts under his jacket indicated he might have been sleeping rough.

"You might have been able to hide from the police, but you can't avoid me," Hazel said and she threw her arms around the old man. "I'll never be able to thank you enough."

"Hush, Miss Hazel, you ain't gotta thank me. I'm just glad you okay."

She led him down the hall and introduced him to Daniel who was setting up his kit behind one of the partitions. They greeted each other warmly and Hazel said, "That young man in the control room is Stephon Vanderhall. He's going to be my chief engineer on this session."

Jerome grinned at the sight of the teenager sitting at the control panel and gave him a wave through the big glass window. He placed his guitar case on the floor, opened it, and took out an old red Gibson ES-335. Despite a few scratches and signs of age, it looked well loved and cared for. Hazel helped him plug it into a vintage Fender amp that was part of the studio's arsenal.

"That's a sweet guitar," Daniel said, eyeing the old Gibson.

"Had this thing about forty years," Jerome said, strumming a chord and tuning a couple strings. "We've seen a lot."

Hazel gave Jerome a stool to sit on, slid a microphone up close for him to sing into, and handed headphones to both Jerome and Daniel. She was visibly excited. A Black man in his early seventies and a White dude in his late twenties were about to make music together for the first time. She knew it could go either way, but nevertheless, these were the moments she lived for.

"Let's have a good time," Hazel said. "Jerome, I suggest you just take off, and Daniel, you'll have to find the groove. How does that sound?"

Jerome nodded and Daniel said it sounded great to him. Hazel lowered the lights in the studio, retreated to the control room, and closed the door behind her. She shooed Stephon out of the captain's chair and said through the control room's mic, "Okay, let's get some levels."

They settled on a nice, slightly overdriven tone for Jerome's guitar and workable volumes for his vocals and Daniel's drums.

"Whenever y'all are ready," Hazel said.

No one counted it off. Jerome just started playing a minor-key melody that droned through the studio and filled the room with a dark, vibrant energy. He didn't use a pick, just his thumb on the low E and his fingers taking care of the rest.

A minute later, Jerome started to sing.

"Ain't nobody gonna drop a deal on me. Ain't nobody gonna tell me what I need." He shifted to a middle part around a B7 chord and sang, *"I just need you, girl. I just need you. You better believe."*

Daniel was transfixed by the sound of Jerome's voice in his headphones, and he dropped in perfectly with a steady beat and perfect fills on the high hat when Jerome returned to the melody.

Hazel let it percolate and marveled as the two musicians began to sense each other's moves. Their tempo and timing became second nature, and the song took a more cohesive shape as it thundered along.

At one point, Jerome took off on a scorching solo, grimacing in concentration, his eyes closed. It was frighteningly intense, and Daniel rose to the moment with deft drumming that gave the song even more vigor.

Hazel turned to look at Stephon on the couch. His hands were laced together on top of his head and his eyes were big as saucers. She was forty-five years older than the kid, but Hazel felt it, too.

The music was hypnotic, beautiful, and as magical as she hoped it would be. The song continued for almost ten minutes, and then Jerome made eye contact with Daniel and they wove into a loosely knitted crescendo before slamming to a close.

"Hot damn!" Daniel said, unable to contain his excitement. "That's more fun than people should be allowed to have."

Jerome laughed and asked, "How was that one?"

Hazel stood in the control room to make sure Jerome and Daniel could see her.

"It was okay," she said. "What else you got?"

Jerome flashed a huge grin through his gray whiskers. "Miss Hazel, I got everything you need. You just keep that tape rolling or whatever it is you're doing in there."

For the next three hours, Jerome sang songs of lust, lost love, being mistreated, being misunderstood, and struggling to survive. Hazel sat behind the control panel and concentrated on capturing every note. She was astounded at the emotion on display just a few feet away and she shivered at Jerome's words about being misunderstood.

They made her think of DJ Clarke and his dreams of starting this studio. She thought of the struggles she'd had with identity and sexuality and her decision to come home from New York. She thought of Carol who went out of her way to help women abused by husbands and boyfriends.

And Hazel thought about Preston and how Jerome's words so perfectly described the whole damn town.

"Where were you when the whip came down? You were looking for love on the wrong side of town."

She sat back and let the blues wash over her. They were down-and-dirty blues, the small-town blues. And to Hazel, they'd never sounded better.

ACKNOWLEDGMENTS

FIRST, I'D LIKE TO THANK Tim Conroy, Trisha Barge, Carla Damron, and Debbie Bloom who all read early drafts of this book and gave me tremendous feedback, insights, and suggestions. Their encouragement propelled me forward and gave me confidence when I really needed it.

A big thanks to the people at Koehler Books. Publisher John Koehler, editor Joe Coccaro, and acquisitions editor Greg Fields have offered amazing support and guidance all along the way, and for that I am truly grateful. It was Greg's praise of the book and enthusiasm for the story that sent me on this journey of publishing a debut novel, and a mere thank you to him seems woefully inadequate.

Last but certainly not least, I'd like to thank the happy-hour regulars at Bar None in Columbia, South Carolina, and the members of the Bar

None Golf Association. Their friendship, banter, and brotherhood in the bar and on the course served in no small part as inspiration for this book. To paraphrase the old saying, you're only as strong as the bar you dance on and the friends who hold you together.